FINISHED BUSINESS

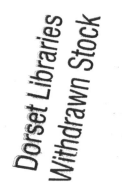

FINISHED BUSINESS

David Wishart

CRÈME de la CRIME

This first world edition published 2014
in Great Britain and the USA by
Crème de la Crime, an imprint of
SEVERN HOUSE PUBLISHERS LTD of
19 Cedar Road, Sutton, Surrey, England, SM2 5DA.
Trade paperback edition first published
in Great Britain and the USA 2015 by
SEVERN HOUSE PUBLISHERS LTD.

British Library Cataloguing in Publication Data

Wishart, David, 1952- author.
  Finished business.
  1. Corvinus, Marcus (Fictitious character)–Fiction.
  2. Murder–Investigation–Fiction. 3. Rome–History–
  Empire, 30 B.C.-476 A.D.–Fiction. 4. Detective and
  mystery stories.
  I. Title
  823.9'2-dc23

ISBN-13: 978-1-78029-063-8 (cased)
ISBN-13: 978-1-78029-547-3 (trade paper)

Except where actual historical events and characters are being
described for the storyline of this novel, all situations in this
publication are fictitious and any resemblance to living persons
is purely coincidental.

Typeset by Palimpsest B   k Production Ltd.,
Falkirk, Stirlingshire, Sc   and.

To the grandchildren: Jade, Joshua, Matthew and Leo

DRAMATIS PERSONAE

The names of historical characters are given in upper case. Only those who appear, or are referred to, in more than one part of the text are included.

Corvinus's household
Bathyllus: the major-domo
Meton: the chef
Perilla, Rufia: Corvinus's wife

Imperials, senators, civil servants and the military
ASIATICUS, D Valerius: Gaius's former brother-in-law; a wealthy senatorial recluse
BASSUS, T Herennius: a junior finance officer (quaestor), friend of Sextus Papinius
CAESONIA: Gaius's wife
CALLISTUS, Julius: Gaius's freedman-secretary, de facto head of the imperial fiscal department
CAPITO, C Herennius: Bassus's father, an imperial fiscal officer (procurator)
CERIALIS, Anicius: a backbench senator
CLAUDIUS, Tiberius: Gaius's uncle
CLEMENS, M Arrecinus: co-commander of the Praetorian Guard
GAIUS CAESAR: the emperor (Caligula)
GRAECINUS, Julius: senator and philosopher, currently a city judge (praetor)
LONGINUS, Cassius: Surdinus's erstwhile colleague in the consulship. Currently governor of Asia, but recalled to Rome by Gaius
MESSALINA, Valeria: Claudius's wife
PAPINIUS, Sextus: a tribune (officer) in the Praetorian Guard
PAPINIUS, Lucius: his brother; also a Praetorian tribune
Surdinus, L Naevius: the victim
Surdinus, L Naevius Junior: his elder son
VINICIANUS, L Annius: a respected and influential senator, friend of Gaius, and Marcus Vinicius's nephew

VINICIUS, Marcus: a literary friend of Perilla's, married to Gaius's sister Livilla

Others

Cilix: a garden slave on Surdinus's estate

Crispus, Caelius: Corvinus's acquaintance in the foreign judges' office; an expert in scandal

Felix, Julius: Gaius's freedman-spymaster

Gallio, Naevius: Surdinus's bailiff

Hellenus (Marcus Naevius Surdinus): Surdinus's estranged younger son

Leonidas: Surdinus's estate manager

Otillius, Titus: Tarquitia's husband

Postuma, Naevia: Surdinus's niece

Secundus, C Vibullius: Corvinus's friend in army admin

SOSIBIUS, Valerius: a freedman

Sullana, Cornelia: Surdinus's ex-wife

Tarquitia: Surdinus's mistress

Trupho: a heavy

ONE

November in Rome sucks.

Oh, sure, the temperature's still OK, and in any case, me, I'd far rather have to put on an extra tunic than be broiled alive as happens in the summer months, when most of the Great and Good head for the Alban Hills or further afield. But November is wet, wet, wet; things can get pretty miserable after the fifth consecutive morning of trudging through the rain-soaked streets for your Market Square shave-and-gossip, and until you get to the end of the month, the Winter Festival seems a lifetime away. So, barring the days when the sun does consent to shine – and they can be glorious – I generally stick pretty close to home.

Which was what I was doing, with the usual half-jug to keep me company, when our major-domo, Bathyllus, buttled in to say I had a visitor.

'The Lady Naevia Postuma, sir,' he said. Smarmed. Yeah, well, I knew the reason for that as soon as he mentioned the name: Bathyllus is the snob's snob, and it wasn't often we got a visit from the wife of the senior serving consul. Particularly when she was a total stranger.

I sat up straight on the couch just as the lady herself sailed in. *Sailed* being the operative word, or maybe *barged* would be more apt. Something suitably nautical, anyway, not to say aggressive, because Naevia Postuma had a nose like a trireme's beak and the armoured superstructure to match. Plus an overall weigh-in tonnage that would've been enough and to spare for two consuls' wives. Luckily for him, our little bald-head had stepped aside pretty smartly to let her past, or he would've been scuttled.

'Valerius Corvinus! It is *so* nice to meet you!' She hove to and glanced behind her. Bathyllus quickly pulled up a chair and she docked, smoothing her voluminous but impeccable mantle around thighs as thick as tree trunks. 'I was, though, also hoping to see your wife?' There was the faintest tinge of a question at the end.

Mid-morning's not exactly the time a visitor from the top social bracket expects to see the visitee sinking the booze. As surreptitiously as I could, I replaced the wine cup on the table beside me and tried to look as if I'd only been taking the occasional sip, possibly for medicinal reasons. Not that it worked, mind: the cup got a look that had ice forming on the inlay.

'Ah . . . Perilla's out, I'm afraid,' I said.

'So it would appear.' The Look turned to me, just long enough to register but stay within the boundaries of politeness. 'A pity, but no great matter. I did have my reasons, which I will come to in due course, but fortunately my principal business is with you.'

Fortunately. Yeah, right. Still, I was the host here, and the duties of a host are sacrosanct. 'Could I offer you some refreshment, Naevia Postuma?' I said.

'Very kind. If your kitchen staff could provide a cup of warmed milk? With a spoonful of honey, and just a touch of nutmeg.'

'Sure,' I said. Warm *milk*? 'No problem. Bathyllus, would you—?'

'Buffalo's, or goat's at a pinch. Certainly not sheep's, please, and warm cow's milk is an abomination of nature.' Well, I'd agree with her there. 'I drink nothing else at this time of day, in this weather.' The wine cup got another pointed glance. 'Nor should you.'

'Right. Right. Bathyllus, ah, see what you can do, pal, OK?' Like find a passing goat to mug. Outside bet though that was, you saw even fewer buffaloes than goats on the Caelian, and I doubted if their milk featured to any great extent in our chef Meton's store cupboard. 'Now, Naevia Postuma. About this business of yours . . .'

She sniffed. 'I would have thought that was obvious. If not its precise nature, then at least in general terms.'

'Really?'

'Certainly, with the exercise of some basic nous on your part.' Ouch. 'According to various friends of mine with whom I discussed the matter, you have considerable past experience in handling, ah, problems of this sort – which, although personally I find a little eccentric in someone of your social class, is rather convenient, under the circumstances. It concerns a murder.'

'Uh . . . is that so, now?'

'Of my uncle, Naevius Surdinus. You knew him, of course.'

'No, I can't say that I did.'

She frowned. 'That is extremely odd. He certainly knew you, or at least he knew your family. And he most definitely knew your wife, Rufia Perilla, of that I'm positive, for reasons which, as I said, I will come to.' Then, when I still looked blank: 'Lucius Naevius Surdinus? Suffect consul with Cassius Longinus ten years ago?'

'I'm sorry. No bells. I can't answer for Perilla, mind. She gets about socially more than I do.'

'Well, again it's no matter. Although it is strange.'

I prompted, 'A murder, you said.'

'Yes. At his estate on Vatican Hill. His head was crushed by a lump of masonry.'

Delivered straight out and deadpan, without a smidgeon of expression.

'He was hit from behind?'

'Oh, no. From above. A considerable way above. The block came from the top of a tower at the edge of the property, some distance from the villa itself. Uncle Lucius was having it reno-vated and he liked to see how the work was progressing.'

'Renovated? Then it was in poor condition?'

'Dreadful. Ruinous, in fact. It was centuries old, originally some sort of watchtower, I think, and it had been abandoned for years. He'd taken a fancy to turn it into a philosopher's sanctum. Philosophy was his hobby, you know, or rather more than a hobby, particularly astronomy and astrology. Also, he wanted somewhere quiet to take himself off to on an evening. Away from the villa itself.'

'Oh? Why would he do that, especially?'

'For the usual reason. Uncle Lucius was married, to Cornelia Sullana, and the marriage was not a particularly happy one. These things happen, of course, and when they do it's good for both parties concerned to have some private space. Or don't you agree?'

'Yeah. Yeah, I suppose so.'

'Mind you, I should say that when he died – that was three days ago, by the way – he and Sullana had been divorced for almost a month, so that aspect of things was academic.'

'You, uh, know the reason? For the divorce, I mean?'

'No. He gave none, neither to me nor to anyone else – Sullana, presumably, excepted. And I didn't ask, because it was no business of mine. Besides, as I said, he and Sullana had not been a couple, properly speaking, for many years. That might well be reason enough. Although . . .' She stopped.

'Although?'

'Nothing. Or nothing that I wish to expand on. As I say, it wasn't my business.'

I shelved that for the time being. 'Did they have any family?'

'Two sons, both living. Lucius Junior, the elder, intends to run for praetor this coming year. The younger, Hellenus – Marcus, really, but he prefers the nickname, and the family indulge him – is, well, rather a disappointment.'

'In what way?'

'He's an artist.'

I stared at her. 'He is *what*?'

'Yes, I *know*, Valerius Corvinus. Totally dreadful, and a serious embarrassment to his poor father, but there it is, what can you do? Young people today, I don't know what the world is coming to. He absolutely *refused* to enter on a proper political career – I mean, refused point blank, if you can imagine that. He and his parents are estranged, and although Uncle Lucius never went as far as to disinherit him, there's been, to my knowledge, no contact with either his father or his mother for at least the past two years. He has, I understand' – she sniffed – 'a workshop or a studio or whatever you'd call it somewhere near the Circus, and there he stays.'

Yeah, well, not that I was going to let on to the lady, but I could sympathize with that because I'd done more or less the same myself, barring the art bit. And knowing how my own father had reacted when I told him where he could put his plans for my future, I could appreciate how Hellenus's had felt. Not to mention the guy's mother: anyone with the name Cornelia Sullana belonged to one of the top families in Rome, and those lads and lasses are sticklers for tradition. An artist as a descendant would have the old dictator himself spinning in his urn.

'Getting back to the business of the tower,' I said. 'You say it was in a very bad condition.'

'Oh, yes. Completely ramshackle, particularly the upper storeys. The builders Uncle Lucius hired to do the renovations are charging him a fortune because they say they're taking their lives in their hands working on it.'

'Then your uncle's death could've been an accident? I mean, the weather now being what it is, if he'd simply been in the wrong place at the wrong time—'

'It was quite definitely murder, Valerius Corvinus,' she said firmly. 'The family and everyone else will tell you differently, of course they will, but I know that for a fact. Alexander told me.'

'Who's Alexander?'

'*The* Alexander.' Then, when I looked blank, 'Oh, really, young man! Get a grip, please! King of Macedon? Philip's son?'

I was boggling slightly.

'Ah . . . right,' I said. 'Right.'

'I presume you had *some* education.'

'Yeah, well, it's just that—'

Which, luckily, was when Bathyllus smarmed back in with one of our best silver cups balanced on its matching tray.

'The chef apologizes, madam.' He set the tray on the table beside her. 'We seem unaccountably to be out of buffalo milk, but he hopes goat's will suffice.'

Uh-huh. I smothered a grin. Knowing our Meton, whatever he'd said when Bathyllus had relayed the order, it hadn't been that. What's more, I'd bet he'd qualified the nouns with a few choice adjectives and participles of his own, too.

'I'm sure that will be perfectly adequate.' She sipped, and I winced. 'Yes, indeed. Delicious.'

Bathyllus bowed and buttled out.

'Ah . . . you were talking about Alexander, Naevia Postuma,' I said, and added carefully, just in case I'd got it wrong after all, 'Alexander the Great, that would be, yes?'

That got me a look that should've curdled her milk. 'Naturally it would,' she said. 'I must say, Valerius Corvinus, from what I've heard about you, I'd've expected you to be much quicker on the uptake than that. Alexander is my control.'

'Control?'

'In the spirit world. Regarding my uncle's murder, he was quite definite. As he was, in fact, that I should follow my friends' suggestion and consult you on the matter. I've never known him so insistent.' She sipped again. 'This really is quite delicious.

Hymettus honey, I do believe, and from flowers grown on the southern slopes.'

'Yeah. Yeah, very possibly. So, ah, let's just be absolutely clear about this, shall we? You're saying that your only reason for believing that your uncle was murdered is that Alexander the Great told you so, right?'

'Indeed. But there is no *only* about it. Alexander is never wrong. Never. And he says that it is absolutely vital that you find the murderer.'

'He vouchsafe why?' Or best of all, just give the stupid woman the name of the fucking perp straight out and save us all a lot of time and grief faffing around. But then for some arcane celestial reason, that never happens with chatty spirits, does it?

'I'm afraid not, no. Only that it was of the utmost importance.'

Well, bully for Alexander. This thing needed nipping in the bud before it went any further. 'Now look, lady . . .' I began, just as Perilla breezed in from her honey, wine and poetry klatsch.

'Hello, Marcus,' she said. 'Bathyllus said you had a visitor. How lovely to see you again, Naevia Postuma. And how is your husband, the consul?'

'Gaius is very well, thank you, my dear. He would send you his regards.'

'What a beautiful mantle. Is it new?'

'Actually, yes, as it happens. From a little shop that's just opened in the Saepta. Next to Argyrio's. You know it?'

'Fabatus's? Oh, yes, although I haven't been there yet myself. Calventia Quietina told me about that when I talked to her a few days ago. She said—'

Jupiter on wheels! 'Ah . . . Perilla,' I said. 'Naevia Postuma here thinks her uncle has been murdered. She wants me to—'

'I don't *think* it,' Postuma snapped, turning back to me. 'I *know*. And I have explained why, fully and concisely.'

'Because Alexander the Great told you so,' I said neutrally, with one eye on Perilla. The lady had parked herself on her usual couch. She looked remarkably unfazed at the news, which I thought under the circumstances was pretty odd.

'Quite.' Postuma reached into the fold of her mantle and took out a small book-roll. 'However, I'm glad you're here in person, Rufia Perilla. It makes things *much* simpler. As I told your husband, my visit had two purposes. This is the second.' She handed the roll to Perilla. 'As you can see, there's a letter attached.'

Perilla took the roll and read the tag.

'Hipparchus's commentary on the *Phaenomena* of Eudoxus,' she said. 'I'm sorry. I don't understand.'

Postuma sniffed. 'To tell the truth, my dear, I haven't the faintest idea of the whys and wherefores myself. My uncle left it to you in a codicil to his will which he added only a few days ago, and in this instance I am simply the messenger. Perhaps the letter will explain.' She got to her feet. 'Now, I'm afraid I have a very tiresome committee meeting to attend at Queen Juno's temple this morning, and I must be running along.' The mind boggled: Queen Juno's temple was halfway across town, on the Tiber side of the Aventine, and *running* was something the lady just wasn't built for. '*So* nice to see you both. You will, of course, accept the commission, Valerius Corvinus. I will see to it personally that my uncle's family give you every cooperation.'

And she was gone.

TWO

'Alexander the Great?' I said.

Perilla smiled. 'Oh, yes, dear. Everyone knows about Naevia Postuma's little eccentricity. The wives, anyway. It's a harmless aberration, really, and in every other respect she's absolutely normal.'

'Jupiter!'

'Of course, there was the occasion when she saw a white horse come through the floor at a diplomatic dinner. The king of Commagene was most surprised.'

'Yeah, I'd imagine he would be.'

'He'd thought it was a camel.' I gave her a look, and she laughed. 'I'm joking, Marcus. About the camel, that is. The horse was real enough, if you know what I mean.'

Bathyllus reappeared. 'Can I get you something to drink, madam?' he said.

'Fruit juice, please, Bathyllus.'

'You, sir?'

'No, I'm fine, pal.' Then, as he turned to go: 'Hey, Bathyllus. That goat's milk. Neither of us touches the stuff. So where did it come from?'

'I understand Meton uses it to bathe his feet in, sir. He says it does wonders for softening hard skin.'

'Ah . . . right. Right.' Well, that cleared that one up. I just hoped he'd used fresh, but knowing the evil-minded bastard as I did, I wouldn't take any bets. Southern-slopes-sourced Hymettus honey my, ah, foot. 'Off you go, sunshine.'

He went.

'So,' Perilla said. 'What's this about a murder?'

I told her what little I knew. 'Only six gets you ten it was no such thing. If the man was silly enough to go furkling about at the foot of an old tower when his builders told him it wasn't safe, then it's not surprising he got himself brained. Oh, sure, I'll go through the motions, talk to the family like Naevia Postuma wants, but if everything seems above board then Alexander of Macedon can go and chase himself.'

'What about this?' Perilla held up the book-roll. 'Don't you find that a bit odd?'

I shrugged. 'If you knew the guy, then—'

'But I didn't, Marcus. Or only very slightly, because his interest was philosophy, not poetry. We may have met at the occasional literary get-together and exchanged a few words, but that was all. I certainly haven't seen him recently.'

'So why should he leave you something in his will? Particularly at such short notice?'

'I have no idea. Perhaps the letter will explain.' She broke the seal, opened it and scanned the lines. 'No. No, it doesn't. See for yourself.' She handed it over.

I read it through. It was frustratingly short and to the point.

The day before the Ides of November, Lucius Naevius Surdinus to Rufia Perilla, greetings.

I send you this in the hope that it may prove interesting. My best wishes to your husband, Marcus Valerius Corvinus. I have not seen him since he was a boy, barring that one occasion when we exchanged a few words at his cousin's

daughter's wedding, but I have the fondest memories of his
father. He was a most agreeable gentleman, and the best
of neighbours.

I laid it aside, frowning. 'Dated four days ago, the day before
he died. And it doesn't make any sense,' I said. 'Dad's house
was on the Palatine, not the Vatican, so unless the guy has moved,
they were never neighbours. And if Dad was anything, he certainly
wasn't "agreeable".'

'Come on, Marcus! Just because the two of you didn't get on
together, at least not until latterly, that doesn't mean to say that
everyone shared your opinion. Personally I found him perfectly
charming.'

I grinned. 'Yeah, well. Maybe. But it's still not an adjective
that springs readily to mind. And I can't remember Surdinus
being at the wedding at all, let alone chatting to the guy.'

'There were over three hundred guests, dear, so that's hardly
surprising, is it? And you know what kind of condition you were
in by the end.'

'Even so.'

Messalina's wedding had been the year before, a month after
our adopted daughter Marilla had got hitched to Clarus over in
Castrimoenium. Me, I don't normally go for these big society
bashes, and I've never had much to do with that side of the
family: when he was alive (he'd been dead now for just shy of
twenty years), Cousin Barbatus had been too much like Dad in
many ways, a poker-rectumed pillar of the establishment, and
we'd had absolutely nothing in common. Messalina I'd just kept
clear of, particularly when she'd hit marriageable age, because
that lady was pure mad and bad. This was her second marriage,
and what had come as a surprise to everyone was the identity of
the groom. The emperor's uncle Claudius didn't seem much of
a catch on the face of it – he was more than twice her age, to
begin with, and a twitching, stammering idiot into the bargain
– but no doubt the link with the imperial family made up for
that. I doubted whether it would last, though, at least on his side,
because the phrase *not suited* was putting it mildly: my guess
was that young Messalina would've been looking around for
better entertainment than her new husband could provide
practically as soon as the nuts were thrown. As far as the actual

wedding itself went, Perilla was right: all I could remember of it was being bored out of my skull, downing too much booze, and spending the next two days heaving my guts out after being stupid enough to try the bears' paws braised in wine lees and honey. All in all, not a memory to treasure.

'What about the book?' I said. 'Thingummy's *Commentary*. Anything odd about that?'

Perilla unrolled it and skimmed her way through – it was only a couple of dozen pages long – while I waited.

'No,' she said finally. 'Or at least nothing I can see. It's exactly what it says it is, and rather a cheap copy at that. Certainly not one worth leaving specifically in anyone's will.'

'Annotations? Margin notes?'

'Absolutely none. In fact, judging from its general condition it may never have been opened.'

'Maybe eccentricity runs in the family.'

'Naevius Surdinus wasn't particularly eccentric, dear, at least as far as I could judge from scant acquaintance. Egotistical, self-opinionated, domineering and bad-tempered, yes, but not eccentric.'

Well, nobody's perfect. 'Hmm. A puzzle, then. File and forget, for the present, at least.' Bathyllus had come back in with her fruit juice. 'By the way, sunshine,' I said to him as he set it down, 'you happen to know where old Naevius Surdinus's place is? Exactly, I mean.'

'Of course, sir.' Silly question; any major-domo worth his salt – and Bathyllus rated a good ton of it – carries a list of the top five hundred's addresses around in his head. 'On the Vatican. The hill itself, at the southern end, bordering on Agrippina's Gardens.'

Prime site: Agrippina's Gardens were an imperial estate as of six or seven years back, and consequently any property bordering on them had social cachet in spades, not to mention top-rate resale value. We were talking serious money here.

'So you're going over there, are you, Marcus?' Perilla sipped her juice. At least it wasn't buffalo's milk. Or goat's.

'Yeah. I'll do that tomorrow. Like I said, it's probably a fool's errand, but if it means getting Naevia Postuma off my back, I may as well give it a shot. Besides, I haven't got anything better to do, have I?'

Alexander, wherever he was, would be delighted.

THREE

The next day was one of the good ones, for November – clear sky, hardly a breath of wind, and pleasantly warm. Which was just as well, if I was to hoof it all the way across town, over the river and up to the Vatican. The only really practical alternative would've been to take the litter, and that I don't do unless it's really pissing down and the journey's absolutely vital. Even then, I hesitate: we're a one-litter family, us, and I generally leave it for Perilla, who's the social animal of the partnership and prefers not to turn up wherever she's going soggy, spattered with mud and definitely not *soingée*. If push really comes to shove, there's a public litter-rank on Head of Africa, just up the road, and I can pick one up from there.

Still, like I say, there was no need at present, and once you're over the Sublician and through the more built-up parts of the Janiculan Marsh district, and the ground starts to rise, the city – if you can call it that any more – opens out. Me, I'm a left-bank man myself, with a preference for crowds, narrow twisting streets and proper pavements, and west of the river is just somewhere I don't usually have any reason to go. But if you like greenery, fresh air, relative peace and quiet, and the closest Rome comes to countryside, then Transtiber's the place. Certainly it's the hot end of the property market, with more private estates than you can shake a stick at, and if you've got ten million or so to play with and want to avoid the riff-raff then a little place on the slopes of the Janiculan or the Vatican is just the thing.

The Naevius place was pretty typical: several acres of bosky woodland with a drive leading up through a network of formal gardens to a villa that you could've put our house on the Caelian into a small corner of. I gave my name and business to a gate-guard big enough to have bounced me off the wall without breaking sweat, and carried on towards the villa itself.

I'd got to within a hundred yards or so when a woman came

through the arch of what looked like a walled garden just to the right of the main drag and cut me off.

'Hello,' she said. 'Can I help you?'

Mid-twenties, a looker, well-enough dressed in a smart tunic and cloak, but not OTT. The accent, though, didn't really fit the setting. Certainly not upper-class Roman. I'd've guessed middle of the range, at best, and there was a distinct northern twang. She didn't quite look the part, either: when she got closer I noticed the too-obvious make-up and the reddish hair. Gallic blood; north Italian was right.

No *sir*, mind, and she had a certain assurance about her that didn't fit with, say, a freedwoman attached to the family. I was puzzled.

'Yeah,' I said. 'The name's Valerius Corvinus. Naevia Postuma sent me.'

'Oh.' The friendliness dropped down a distinct notch. 'Yes, she did send a slave yesterday to say you'd be coming. A load of complete nonsense, but that's the Lady Postuma for you. She does get these bees in her bonnet. Well, we'd best get it over with.'

Not a good beginning, although I supposed I couldn't expect much more, under the circumstances. And I had a certain sympathy with the lady's feelings, if she was part of the family after all.

'And, uh, you are?' I said.

'Tarquitia.' I must've looked blank. 'She didn't mention me to you? Not surprising, really. I'm – was, I suppose now – Lucius Surdinus's mistress.' I blinked, and she laughed. 'Don't look so shocked, Valerius Corvinus. It was all perfectly above board, and I've nothing to be ashamed of. Quite the reverse. Now, you'll want to talk to me, no doubt.'

I glanced over at the villa. 'Sure. If you'll just lead the way.'

'No, I think we'll have the conversation out here, if you don't mind. It's a pleasant-enough morning, there are seats in the rose garden, and we'll be perfectly comfortable there for however long it takes. You can go up to the house and pursue your enquiries there later. I'm not, as you can imagine, exactly flavour of the month with Lucius's surviving nearest and dearest, and I'd rather avoid any unpleasantness.'

Said without a trace of expression, except maybe for the slightest tinge of contempt. I was more puzzled than ever.

'Fine with me,' I said. 'Lead on.'

We went back through the arch and into a formal garden planted with rose bushes, with a late bloom or two showing through the greenery.

'We'll sit here, if that's all right,' she said. There was a stone bench against the nearside wall. I sat on one side, and she perched on the other, leaning her back against the wall. 'Now, where would you like to start? I warn you, I don't know anything about the actual circumstances, because I wasn't here at the time. But about anything else, please feel free to ask. I'm not shy.'

Yeah, well, that was putting it mildly: the lady just radiated self-confidence, and apart from that little hiccup over not wanting to go up to the villa, she was perfectly at ease.

'You were Naevius Surdinus's mistress,' I said.

'Yes. For the last year or so. I'm a . . . I suppose the best word is "entertainer". I sing a little, dance a little, play the double-flute, not very well. Juggle. Do acrobatics.' She glanced sideways at me. 'I do the most *amazing* set of cartwheels. I could show you, if I weren't wearing this tunic.'

I grinned; I was beginning to like Tarquitia. 'Yeah, well,' I said. 'We'll take that on trust for the present, shall we?'

'If you like. I work – worked – at the Five Poppies club, mostly. That's near the temple of Juno the Deliverer, off the vegetable market. Do you know it?'

'No. I'm afraid not.'

'Pity. It's a good place, and they give good value. You should go there some time. Tell them I sent you.'

'Yeah,' I said equably. 'Yeah, I might just do that.'

'Anyway, I also did freelance, which is how I met Lucius. I was contracted to one of his friends' dinner parties as part of the after-dinner entertainment; our eyes met across a not-so-crowded room, and that was that. More or less, give or take a month or so of what you might call casual dalliance. He set me up in my own flat and we became a regular item. End of story.'

'Did his wife know?'

She laughed. 'The Lady Sullana?' She stressed the word 'lady', and I could just hear the capitalization fall into place. 'Of course. Practically from the first. Lucius told her himself, and frankly I don't think she could've cared less. Except for the scandal aspect of things, that is. Sullana was always very prim and proper. So long as Lucius didn't flaunt me in public, I didn't exist.'

'What about the rest of the family? Did they know?'

'Oh, yes. Given that by "the rest of the family", you mean Lucius's son, Naevia Postuma and a few other odds and sods. But then the same applies. As long as I didn't get above myself and become a social embarrassment, I could be ignored, and everything was just peaches and cream.'

'So what changed things?'

She frowned. 'How do you mean?'

'Well, you're not exactly tucked away now, are you? Or am I wrong?'

Her face cleared. 'Oh. That's because of the sale.'

'What sale?'

'Of the Old Villa.'

'Old Villa?'

'It was the original building, in Lucius's grandfather's time. He was the one who made the family fortune.' She grinned. 'Not legitimately, I suspect, because the family are very tight-lipped on the subject. Anyway, he decided to build a new villa, much grander, with the original forming one of the wings. Only like Lucius, he and his wife didn't really get on, so he kept it for her as a separate property. The only link between the two is a single corridor, which I'm having bricked up.'

'*You're* having bricked up?'

'Oh, yes. At my end, at least, and as soon as I can, really. I own it, you see. Lucius sold it to me last month, when the divorce came through.'

'*Sold* it to you?'

'Yes.'

'You, ah, mind telling me how much for?'

'Not at all; that's no secret.' Another grin. 'It set me back all of five silver pieces.' Jupiter! 'Oh, it was all done perfectly legally: cash paid over in front of witnesses, proper signed bill of sale and everything. I can show you, if you like. The family – I mean Lucius Junior, of course – was furious, but there you are, he'll just have to put up with it. And my Lucius added a clause guaranteeing access in perpetuity, so that's all right. Naturally, it means that by sitting here I'm currently trespassing on his property, which might technically be actionable, so I'd be glad if you didn't mention that when you do see him.'

'Fine.' It wasn't, altogether, but there you go; at least she'd been upfront, and I could always get the other side of the story from Junior himself. 'Why did he do it, do you know? Sell you the Old Villa for five denarii?'

'Because he wanted to. It's as simple as that.'

'Is it?'

She sighed. 'Look, it wasn't my idea, if that's what you're thinking. You can believe me or not as you like, it's up to you, but that's what Lucius told me himself. If you want my guess – and it's only a guess – he liked me a lot more than he liked his son, let alone his wife, and he wanted to show it. Not just with money, but with part of his life. And this estate was his life – that and his hobbies. That was one reason he and Sullana didn't get on. You know he was consul once? Or suffect consul, at least.' I nodded. 'Well. That was ten years ago, and he hasn't been near politics since. He just gave that side of things up completely. No serving on committees, no speeches in the senate, no angling for inclusion on diplomatic missions, no sucking up to the Movers and Shakers' lobby. Nothing. All he wanted was to live quietly. Sullana's ambitious. She didn't understand it, and it drove her up the wall.'

'What sort of man was he? In himself, I mean. I know about his wife, but how did he get on with his sons? He had two of them, didn't he?'

'That's right. The other one's Marcus. I'm sorry – again I can't tell you anything about him. I know he exists, and that's his name, but absolutely nothing else. We've never met, of course, and Lucius only mentioned him once in passing. I suppose, if Lucius didn't exactly disinherit him, he'll have some claim on the property?' There was the hint of a question in her voice.

'Yeah, I'd assume so, but I'm no lawyer. Perhaps it'll be in the will.' Casually, I added, 'Have you seen that?'

'No. That side of things has nothing to do with me, or I assume not. The property sale was quite separate, and that went through while Lucius was still alive.'

'And how about the elder son? Lucius Junior? What was his father's relationship with him?'

'Oh.' She smiled. 'That's a long, sad story in itself. Junior's one of nature's strivers, not too clever but desperate to get on. You know he's running for a city judge's post this coming year?' I nodded again. 'If he gets it, it won't be because he's fit for the job. The poor sap's never been really fit for any job he's gone for, and it's a miracle that he's got as far as he has. The trouble is that his father has always known it and made sure he knows it too. So. That tell you something about how they viewed each other?'

'Yeah,' I said. 'Yeah, it does.' Like she'd said, it was sad. 'So how was Surdinus with everyone else? Outside the immediate family? With you, for example.'

'Exasperating.' She gave me another straight look, and I was surprised to see the beginning of tears in her eyes. 'Very, very kind, generous, and loving, but exasperating. Stubborn as a mule. Whether he was right or wrong, you couldn't shift him, or stop him doing what he'd decided to do. He had very firm opinions and views on every subject under the sun, whether he knew anything about it or not. And he was always – in his own mind – right.'

'He have any enemies?'

'Absolutely none, or none that I know of, certainly. He never really had an opportunity to make any. He'd lots of friends, though. Or maybe not friends – professional acquaintances, rather. Men who shared his hobbies. You know he was interested in philosophy?'

'Yeah. Naevia Postuma told me that.'

'Not just abstract philosophy, although that was part of it. He was a . . . practical philosopher, if that's not a contradiction. An astrologer. He cast horoscopes, and he was very good at it, too; so good it was frightening.'

'You like to give me an example?'

She was quiet for a long time, staring at a point on the far side of the garden. Then she said, in a small voice: 'Yes.'

I waited. Nothing. Finally, she turned to me, and this time the tears were definitely there.

'Look,' she said, 'I haven't mentioned this to anyone else, and I won't. But I've decided that I like you, right, and I feel someone should know, besides me.' I said nothing. 'Five days ago, Lucius came to me to say he'd just finished casting his own horoscope for what was left of the year. It was quite clear, he said. Before the year was out he'd be dead.'

'*What?*'

'He was quite calm, perfectly reconciled. He said that he'd had a good life, on the whole, and I wasn't to be upset when it happened. That he'd done his best according to his own beliefs and was glad to go. He thanked me and hoped that I'd be happy. Those were his exact words. He wouldn't say any more on the subject, even though I pressed him very hard, begged him, in fact, and it was the last time I saw him alive.' She stood up. 'Now, that's all I can tell you. You'd best be getting up to the house.'

And she walked back through the gate, leaving me staring. Shit!

FOUR

The villa, like I say, was huge: a central block with two flanking wings reaching out to enclose symmetrical hedged walks studded with bronze and marble statues. In front of the main entrance was a big fountain: Centaurs and Lapiths fighting, with the water coming out of their mouths. Impressive as hell. I glanced over at the wing to the left: it was older and just a bit shabbier, and sure enough it wasn't properly integrated with the main building. Also, it had an entrance of its own. No sign of Tarquitia, though, and the place looked deserted.

What the two entrances had in common was that both of them were hung with greenery, the sign of a house in mourning.

There was a bell-pull to the right of the door. I pulled it, and the door was opened immediately by a slave in a mourning tunic.

'Marcus Valerius Corvinus,' I said. 'I'm here at the request of your dead master's niece, Naevia Postuma.'

He didn't answer, but bowed and stepped aside, opening the door wider. I went in. The vestibule was bigger and more expensively fitted out than our atrium.

'The young master is in the library, sir.' The door slave took my cloak and laid it on top of an inlaid chest that could've belonged to one of the Ptolemies. 'If you'd like to follow me?'

The library, it transpired, was on the first floor, and getting there took us a good two minutes' walk. The slave opened the cedar-panelled door, bowed me inside, and said to the guy standing by the window: 'Marcus Valerius Corvinus, sir.'

'That's fine. You can go,' the guy said. Then, as the slave bowed again and went out, closing the door behind him: 'Pleased to meet you, Corvinus.' Yeah, well, he didn't sound it, and the look I'd got when the slave had given him my name would've frozen the balls off a Riphaean mountain goat. 'Sit down, please.'

I did, on one of the reading couches. Perilla would've loved the place, because the walls were lined with book-cubbies, and all of them looked occupied. I hadn't seen anything like it outside the Pollio Library.

Lucius Naevius Surdinus Junior was tall and thin, with a dissatisfied twist to his lips that reminded me of the old emperor. Tiberius. The Wart. The nickname would've suited Junior here, too – all in all, not one of Rome's best lookers, particularly since, being in mourning, he hadn't shaved. Wading birds in moult came to mind.

'I'm . . .' I began, but he held up a hand.

'Yes, I know exactly why you're here,' he said. 'Cousin Postuma sent a messenger yesterday afternoon. She's a very forceful lady, besides, as you know, being the wife of a man to whom the emperor granted the honour of a suffect consul-ship for the latter half of the year, and both of these facts make her difficult to refuse.' The dissatisfied twist became an actual scowl. 'That doesn't mean that you're particularly welcome.'

Shit, I wasn't having this. 'Look, pal,' I said. 'Just remember that coming here wasn't my idea, right? Judging from what Naevia Postuma told me, I'd say she was off with the fairies and your father's death was a complete accident. But, like you said, she's a hard lady to refuse. So if you'd just cut me a bit of slack and let me go through the motions to my own satisfaction, then we can all get on with our fucking lives with a clear conscience. OK?'

He'd blinked and bridled, but the scowl had faded.

'Very well,' he said. 'What do you want to know?'

'Anything you can tell me, basically. And then if you'd let me take a look at the scene of the incident, maybe let me talk to any of the staff who might've been around the place and seen something, that should more or less do it.'

He grunted. 'That seems fair enough. Although as for myself I can't tell you very much.'

'You weren't here at the time?'

'Yes, I was, in fact. But in my own suite, in the east wing.'

'Alone?'

The scowl was back. 'I'm not married, if that's what you mean. I was, but my former wife and I decided to part company.' Jupiter! Marital discord and divorce seemed to be par for the course in this family. 'So, yes, I was alone. We're talking, by the way, about very early morning, halfway through the first hour, four days back. At least, according to the slaves, that's when my father went out. And his body was found an hour or so later, when the workmen arrived.'

'He made a habit of visiting the tower that early? When there was no one around?'

'Not the tower, specifically. He liked to walk around the grounds after he'd breakfasted, if the weather was good. And the tower was on his usual route. He generally stopped off there, just to see how the work was progressing. If he wanted to talk to the workmen about anything in particular, then of course that was a different thing.'

'So where is this tower exactly?'

'In our south-east corner. In fact, it's part of the boundary wall.'

'And he was found exactly where?'

'At the base, next to the entrance. The block of masonry that fell on him was beside the body. It's still there, of course. The workmen have checked, and it came from the parapet directly above.'

'No one was around at the time?'

Junior shrugged. 'None of the workmen, certainly. As I said, they don't come until later, and then only if the weather is good. And none of my outside slaves has reported seeing anything, which is not surprising. The gardens where they all usually work are mostly on either side of the main drive, or around the house itself.'

'Anything else you can tell me?'

'About the accident? No, I think that's all.'

'About your father, then.'

That got me a long, slow stare. 'Nothing that's relevant,' he said at last. He turned away, towards the window. 'Apropos of which, I notice you were talking to the woman Tarquitia before you arrived.'

'Yeah? How did you know that?'

He indicated the window. 'The view from here is superb, which is why it's one of my favourite rooms. You can see right down the drive, almost to the main gate. You can certainly see as far as the rose garden.'

'All right. Yes, I met her and we talked. So?'

'Let me be clear about this, Corvinus. As far as I am concerned, that woman has no connection with our family, and no claims on it. She's a troublemaker and a gold-digger, and my advice to you would be to take anything she says with a very large pinch of salt.'

'Would it, now?' I said. 'So does that mean she's not the owner of your west wing? What she called the Old Villa?'

The scowl was back in spades. 'At present, unfortunately, yes,' he said. 'But I'm contesting her ownership. And *that* is frankly none of your business.'

'Does she feature in your father's will at all?'

'*Valerius Corvinus!*'

I shrugged. 'It's just that, if she is a gold-digger, I thought that she might. And that'd be quite interesting. If, which it won't, of course, the death turned out to be murder after all.'

Again I got the long, slow, considering look. 'As a matter of fact,' Junior said finally, 'she is one of the beneficiaries, and quite a substantial one. My father left her the interest on fifty thousand sesterces, the capital to be hers absolutely on marriage.'

Shit! Fifty thousand sesterces was a hell of a lot of gravy, particularly to an 'entertainer'. And the interest, at the average rate of eight to ten per cent, would come to just shy of five thousand a year. Quite a respectable income, to put it mildly.

'Does she know?' I said.

'I expect so. There's no reason why she shouldn't; he was open enough with her where everything else was concerned. But, of course, you'd have to ask the lady herself. If you can trust her to give an honest answer.'

I let that one pass. Still, it was something that needed serious thinking about. By the gods, it did. I stood up.

'Well, if that's all you can tell me, Naevius Surdinus,' I said, 'I won't take up any more of your time. Thank you for talking to me, and of course my condolences. If I could just have a look at the tower?'

'Certainly.' There was a bell-pull beside the door. He walked past me and pulled it. 'My estate manager, Leonidas, will show you it. I'll have him fetched. Good day, Corvinus.'

FIVE

Despite his Greek name, Leonidas turned out to be a bustling little Sicilian, officious and desperate to be of use, who prattled all the way. Which was absolutely fine with me.

'He was a lovely man, sir. A lovely man, and a lovely master. No one could've asked for a better, I'm sure. And so quiet-living. Give him his books and charts and his astro-what-d'ye-call-'em thingies, or a couple of them clever friends of his to sit with over dinner and a cup or two of wine of an evening, and he was happy as a sandboy.'

'You happen to know any of their names?' I said.

'The friends? Well, now, let's see.' He stopped. 'There was the two Julii, Canus and Graecinus. No relation, although as you'll guess from the family name, they was both Gallic gentlemen originally. Graecinus, he's one of the city judges this year. Then there's Aemilius Rectus. Rectus by name and Rectus by nature, you might say. He's a proper stiff one, that gentleman. Comes of being a . . . what's-its-name, begins with an S. Sort of philosopher.'

'Stoic?'

He beamed. 'The very word, sir, well done! Comes of being a Stoic, like. They all was, the master included, come to that, but he was the real article, right down the line, accept no imitations. Not that he couldn't be affable enough when he was in the mood. A senatorial gentleman, like Graecinus, been a city judge himself in the past. There was plenty of others, on and off, but them three was what you might call the master's regulars.'

We set off again, along a side path off the main drag. 'Your master wasn't political himself?' I said.

'Bless you, sir, no, not these many years. He gave that sort of thing up altogether after he'd done his consulship.'

'You know why?'

'No, sir, I don't. Not for sure. But between you and me I think it had something to do with the troubles after that bastard Sejanus was chopped. Pardon my Greek.'

'Is that so, now?'

'They sickened him. That's my view, anyway, for what it's worth. All those men dead, some of them no more guilty of treason than I am, just because they were too friendly with the man or they were some sort of relative of his. A witch-hunt, my master called it. You heard of a gentleman by the name of Blaesus?'

'Junius Blaesus, sure.' He'd been Sejanus's uncle, and the Wart had forced him into suicide.

'Well, he and the master had been thick together for years, and he said Blaesus hadn't a treasonous bone in his body. Very upset over the death, he was. My belief, it finished him with politics, and after that he hadn't a good word to say about the old emperor, or the whole boiling of them. Here we are, sir. You can see the tower just ahead.'

From this distance, it didn't look too bad: like Postuma had said, it was an old watchtower, thirty or so feet high, at the corner of the boundary wall, pierced with three sets of windows, one above the other. It was only when we got closer that I noticed the poor condition of the masonry, the gaps between the stones where the pointing cement had crumbled away, and the ragged line of the top. The ground in front of the entrance had been cleared, and there were the usual signs of building activity in progress: piles of dressed stone, a stack of wooden props and planks, and a mixing trough with several water buckets beside it. This being November, the bags of cement themselves and the workmen's tools would be inside, under cover.

'The master was lying here.' Leonidas walked over to a spot just in front of the entrance and stopped. His voice had lost its chatty tone and he spoke softly, like he was standing next to a grave. Which, in a way, I supposed he was, or the next thing to it.

I joined him. Two feet or so out from the threshold and slightly to one side there was a large block of dressed stone, with old masonry covering its exposed top and edges. I stood beside it and looked up at the parapet above. Sure enough, I could see a matching gap.

Bugger. Well, it had to be done.

'Can I get up there?' I said.

Leonidas's eyes widened. 'You're not serious, sir!'

'Sure I am. Unfortunate, but there it is.'

'It's dangerous. And I don't think the young master would allow it.'

'Yeah, well, I won't tell him if you won't, pal.' I stuck my head inside and took a look. As I'd expected, the ground floor, if you could call it that, was fully taken up with cement bags and builders' tools, but there was a ladder leading upward through a hatch in the ceiling to what had to be a newly constructed first floor. Presumably when I reached that there would be another to the second storey, and so on.

Right, then. Here we went.

The first bit was easy-peasy: whoever Surdinus had contracted knew their stuff and were making good on each level before moving up to work on the next. The first-storey flooring was solid, and built on top of sturdy beams laid at their ends on stretcher stones tied into freshly cemented masonry. So was the second, when I reached it. And the third.

The fourth, on the other hand, was what had to be the parapet level, right at the top of the tower . . .

Oh, hell. Now we came to the difficult bit.

The ladder was there, sure, plus a couple of bits of scaffolding reaching up from the third storey, but where the parapet level was concerned, the builders had only got as far as putting in the framework that would eventually take the tiles, or whatever

arrangement Surdinus had had in mind for the topmost level of
his hideaway. There was flooring of a kind, but it was no more
than a skeleton of loose planks. Above it was the parapet itself
– waist-high, it would be – and the open air.

Fuck.

Still, it was better than nothing. And at least I'd established
that someone could get all the way up from below. Plus, if I'd
come this far, I couldn't very well give up now.

I climbed the ladder and stepped gingerly sideways on to the
plank laid across the set of rafters that would form the ceiling
of the tower's third storey and the roof of the tower itself. It gave
slightly under my weight, but it felt firm enough, and there were
other planks around the perimeter allowing access to the parapet
on all of its sides. I was in the open air now, of course, and at
this height the wind was a major problem. I rested my palms on
the top of the parapet to steady myself and leaned out, to look
below and get my bearings . . .

The stone I was leaning on shifted, and I let go quickly,
straightened, and stepped back – a bit too far back, because my
heels found the edge of the plank and for a moment I teetered
between falling backwards between the beams and down to the
floor below and forwards over the parapet itself. I got my balance
finally and stood sweating.

Shit. That had been close.

OK. Fine. So we'd do this next bit carefully. Very, very
carefully.

I was on one of the flanking sides of the tower. Its front –
where there was a gap in the stonework – was the stretch to my
left. Keeping my eyes firmly on my feet, and trying to avoid
using the parapet as a handrail, I edged along the plank and
round the corner to the matching one on that side. The gap was
halfway along; only ten feet or so, but it felt like forty. I got to
it at last, and stood for a couple of minutes sweating like a pig
and breathing hard before I felt confident enough to take a proper
look.

There was still a good half-inch of cement covering the top
of what had been the stone below the fallen block. It was old
and crumbling, sure, but there were clear marks along its length
of what must have been the knife or chisel that had been used
to prise the missing block free. And on the plank beneath

the marks, where I was standing, was a scattering of cement granules.

Shit. It had been murder after all.

Score one for Alexander.

Leonidas was waiting for me when I got down, looking anxious as hell, as was quite natural: the life of a slave responsible for one of Rome's social elite falling and breaking his over-privileged neck while he's a guest in the master's household would not've been worth a copper quadrans, even if it were said purple-striper's own stupid fault. Under ordinary circumstances, I wouldn't't've put him at that kind of risk. Only the circumstances weren't ordinary, and the risk had been justified. In spades.

Leonidas wasn't alone. There was a big guy with him, a good head and shoulders taller than him and built to match, dressed in a tunic two sizes too small for him that looked like it'd doubled as a bag for carting earth in. Or more likely (I caught his scent, and wished I hadn't) carting manure. He was looking anxious as hell, too.

'All right, Cilix,' Leonidas said to him. 'Tell the gentleman what you've just told me.' Then, turning to me: 'This is Cilix, sir.'

Twice Leonidas's size or not, the big guy was shooting him worried sideways looks like Leonidas was some sort of ogre that might any minute leap on him and gobble him up. Leonidas, on the other hand, was puffed up like a bantam with self-importance.

'Go ahead, Cilix,' I said. 'You're one of the garden slaves, right?'

Not a difficult guess to make, that one, given the tunic and the smell.

He swallowed. 'Yes, sir. It's about the day the master died, sir.'

Long pause.

'Go on, boy.' Leonidas sounded dangerous. 'Better out than in.'

'I . . . saw someone, sir. A stranger.'

My interest sharpened. 'Here? At the tower?'

He shook his head. 'No, sir. Level with the house, he was, more or less, moving through the bushes close in to the wall. Stealthy, like. There's a bit of the wall collapsed just shy of the north-east corner, that hasn't been fixed yet, and I think he was heading for that. But he was coming from this direction, right enough. And it was about the time when the master . . . when he . . .' He stopped and swallowed again.

Shit! 'Can you describe him at all?'

'Oh, yes, sir. He passed quite close. He was a freedman, sir; at least he was wearing the cap. A bit bigger than Master Leonidas here, but not much, and not so . . . not so . . .' He reddened and glanced down at Leonidas's stomach.

I grinned again. 'Not so fat,' I said. Leonidas gave a soft growl, and the guy winced and nodded. 'Age?'

'Not all that young, sir, but not old, neither.'

'Thirtyish? Forties, maybe?'

'The second, yeah. Yes, sir. Least, that's what I'd guess. An' he had a big mark here.' He touched his finger to his left cheek. 'Black. A sort of blotch, like a stain.'

'Dirt?'

'Could of been, sir. I didn't see it clearly. But it dint look like dirt; it looked like one of them what's-their-names.'

'Birthmarks?'

'Yeah. Or maybe a scab or a scar of some kind from a disease he'd had. I'd a mate of mine, once, sir, he got this manky disease when he was—'

'Stick to the point, boy!' Leonidas snapped.

'Yes, sir. Sorry, sir.'

'And he just walked right past you?' I said. 'Just like that? Close enough for you to see the mark on his cheek? He didn't say anything to you, and you didn't say anything to him? You just ignored each other.'

The guy had reddened again. 'S'right, sir. More or less. He dint see me, you see.'

'Didn't *see* you?'

'No, sir.' If he'd been any redder he could've doubled as a six-foot-six beetroot.

'Tell the gentleman why not,' Leonidas said through gritted teeth.

''Cos I was crouched down in the bushes at the time, sir,' Cilix mumbled. 'Havin' a . . . you know.' He swallowed again. 'Havin' a crap, like.'

Jupiter! 'Ah . . . right. Right.' I glanced at Leonidas, who was quietly fizzing. 'That would explain it.'

'I'd of got up and said something to him, sir, all the same, because I thought he might be a poacher, like, but things'd got a bit messy just then and—'

'Cilix, the gentleman doesn't want to know!' Leonidas snapped.

Spot on the button: the precise details were things, in this case, that I could do without. 'So why haven't you told anyone about this before?' I said.

Cilix glanced anxiously at Leonidas, but said nothing. Leonidas cleared his throat.

'That'd be because the garden slaves aren't allowed to ease themselves in the grounds, sir,' he said stiffly. 'Master's orders.'

Cilix nodded violently. 'Yeah, right,' he said. 'I thought I might get into trouble, sir. Over the crap side of things, like. I'd never of done it, honest, unless I was desperate. Which I was – you know how it is when you're caught short on the job, you've got to go, whatever. Pissing's OK, you're allowed to piss, all right, no problem, so long as there's no one from the house around and you do it well off the paths and out of sight, like, but crapping's—'

'*Cilix!*'

I was grinning. 'That's OK, pal,' I said. 'I get the general idea.'

'Only I thought now you being here, an' the master's death maybe not being an accident after all, I'd best say.'

Joy in the morning! Me, I've given up trying to work out why slaves know everything that goes on practically instantaneously by osmosis, but they do. Even the Cilixes of this world. I took out my purse, reached for his hand, turned it grimy palm up and slapped a half-gold piece into it. He stared down at the coin, then up at me, mouth open in astonishment.

'Thanks for the information, sunshine,' I said. 'Enjoy. It's cheap at the price, believe me.' It was: six got you ten our loose-bowelled friend had just described Naevius Surdinus's killer, and that doesn't happen too often, particularly within what was, in effect, only five minutes of the start of an investigation. We were miles ahead of the game for once, and a half-gold piece in exchange wasn't OTT, by any means.

All we had to do now was find out who the guy was, and why he'd done it. Oh, and of course break the glad news to Surdinus Junior.

SIX

'Well, at least we don't have to worry about chasing alibis,' I said to Perilla at dinner as Bathyllus served the dessert. 'The big question is, who was the guy working for? And if he's a freedman, is he a home-grown one or was he specially hired for the job?'

'Of course, he might also have done it as a favour. For a friend,' Perilla said.

'How do you mean, lady?' I picked up my spoon and looked down at the bowl Bathyllus had put in front of me. In it was a sort of yellowish-grey paste mixed with what looked like thick flower petals. 'Gods, Bathyllus, what the hell's this?'

'Rose hip and calf's brain custard, sir. With a sprinkling of cinnamon.'

'For *dessert*?'

'It would seem so, yes. A new recipe Meton is trying out.'

'Hmm.' I tasted it. Not bad. Not bad at all. Slightly nutty, with a perfumed aftertaste. I could've done without the cinnamon, though. 'How do you mean?' I asked Perilla again.

'I was thinking of his mistress. Tarquinia?'

'Tarquitia.'

'A freedman friend would fit with her social background. And as far as motive goes, she's the only obvious suspect at present.'

'Come on, Perilla!' I spooned up a bit more of the custard. Yeah, definitely one of Meton's winners. 'Tarquitia's no murderess.'

'She now owns what is essentially a substantial part of the Naevius villa, which she can either sell for a large sum to a third party or, far more likely, given the circumstances and the awkwardness that would cause him, do a deal with Surdinus Junior for a similar or probably even larger amount. And on top of that there's the fifty thousand sesterces legacy. Not bad going, in her position, for what was in effect a year's work. I'd say that was an excellent motive.'

'Perilla, she already owned the property when Surdinus died. Plus, she didn't know she was a beneficiary in the will.'

'So she told you. And as far as the Old Villa is concerned, Surdinus's death simplifies things enormously. She's free now to turn it into ready cash, which she couldn't creditably have done while he was alive, and furthermore – again given the circumstances – it would be the natural thing to do. Obviously, she can't live there herself, can she?' She poked at her own plate of custard with her spoon, pushed it aside and reached for an apple. Not a calf's brains person, Perilla.

'You didn't meet her,' I said. 'She was genuinely fond of him, and genuinely upset. And in any case, she was sitting pretty. You don't kill the golden goose.'

'That's the goose that lays the golden eggs, dear.' She began peeling the apple with her knife. 'And we don't know that the eggs *were* currently all that golden. We only have Tarquitia's word that the relationship was all sweetness and light. What if Surdinus were getting tired of her? The property sale, yes, that was over and done with, although again we don't know for certain that the idea originated with him. However, the will's another matter. If Surdinus changed his will once, he could do so again, for any reason or none, but with him dead she could be absolutely sure of being set up for life.'

'*If* she knew of the existing terms. I don't think she did. And what about the business with the horoscope? That was weird, if you like.'

'Again, she could have made the whole thing up. We don't know.'

'It fits with the date of the letter to you, whatever the hell that was about. From the looks of things, leaving all the whys and wherefores aside, Surdinus knew or at least thought he was booked for an urn shortly and was setting his affairs in order before he went.'

Perilla sighed and put the knife down. 'Even if that part of it was genuine, it isn't relevant. In fact, it could have put the idea of murder into Tarquitia's head in the first place. Marcus, you're not being reasonable about this. Just because you're smitten with the girl—'

'Come on, lady!'

'That doesn't mean you can throw common sense out the window. For the present, she's the obvious candidate. Admit it.'

I grinned. 'OK. Fair enough. Admitted. Even so, it's early days yet.'

'Certainly it is.' Perilla picked up the knife and the apple again. 'No argument. But what do you actually *know* about her and her relationship with Surdinus? Apart from what she told you?'

'Not a lot. Before she took up with him she worked at a club called the Five Poppies, near the vegetable market. Or at least so she said, and there was no reason for her to lie because she volunteered the information herself. I was thinking of going over there tomorrow, having a talk with the owner. See if he or she can fill in a bit of the lady's background. Then there's Surdinus's ex, Cornelia Sullana. I got an address for her out of Junior when I gave him the news that his father's death was no accident. Pretty smartly, too, with no griping.' I took another spoonful of the custard. 'In fact, I'd say he was more pleased than not that I might be sniffing around in that direction, just like he was over the significance of Tarquitia being mentioned in the will. Not much love lost there either, I'd imagine, which is interesting.'

'I wouldn't say that Sullana seemed a very likely possibility, dear. I mean, what possible reason would she have for wanting her ex-husband dead? Not a desire for revenge because he'd divorced her and taken a mistress, surely. From what you told me, they'd been virtually estranged for years, and she knew all about Tarquitia long before the divorce happened.'

I shrugged. 'She'd no reason that I know of. But then nobody does have one, not an obvious one, as far as I can see – barring your front-runner, Tarquitia. I'll just have to dig around, see what comes up. There's the other son, too. Marcus. Hellenus, whatever. That's another possible angle. Oh, sure, Postuma said he hadn't had any contact with his father for years, but if he wasn't formally disinherited he'll have a share of the estate. We don't know his circumstances, and maybe he suddenly needed a large amount of cash urgently enough to tempt him to cut corners.'

'That is pure speculation, dear.'

'Sure it is, no arguments. But I have to start somewhere.'

'What about the actual killer? The freedman?'

'Lady, Rome is full of freedmen, and whoever used the guy as the perp isn't exactly going to advertise their relationship, particularly if he owes his cap to them, which would point the finger pretty effectively. Me, if he was one of my dependants and the fact meant I could be traced through him, I'd make damn sure he got himself well and truly lost for the duration. Get him out of the city altogether, for preference, certainly put the bugger in strict quarantine. Oh, I'll ask around for a shortish forty-plus-year-old freedman with a mark on his cheek, sure, but I don't think I'll get any joy.' Sad but true: most of the time, unless of course they come specifically to his attention for some reason, to your average middle- or upper-class Roman another man's (or woman's) freedmen dependants, like their slaves, are non-people, featureless nonentities. They just don't get noticed, because they're of no importance. Ask any three-namer to describe his next-door neighbour's major-domo to you and the chances are you'll just get a blank look. Ask some of the more pukkah-sahib types to describe their own and four times out of five you'll get the same.

'You might be lucky,' Perilla said.

'Yeah, well, just don't hold your breath, that's all.' I finished off the custard. 'You don't want yours?'

She shuddered. 'No. Definitely not.'

I reached over and swapped the plates. Not wholly greed: Meton can take it really personally if the empties tray comes back with an untouched dish on it, and risking Meton's displeasure is not something you do lightly.

'What about Surdinus's relationships outwith the family?' Perilla said. 'I mean, in terms of enemies?'

I shrugged again. 'From the looks of things, there isn't much mileage there. Not if you believe Tarquitia, and if she were the guilty party, the chances are she'd be only too glad to bring out the dirty linen. He wasn't involved with politics, which is the main area for a guy of his class where making enemies is concerned.'

'Business relationships?'

'Possibly. That's one side of things I'll have to check with his ex-wife. But the impression I got was that his mind didn't run that way. He was a stay-at-home, for a start, and an interest in philosophy and astrology doesn't chime too well with hard-headed business sense.'

'You said he was a Stoic, dear. Stoics aren't ivory-tower philosophers by any means, and they're positively expected to involve themselves in business and politics. So if Surdinus kept clear of these areas he's an anomaly rather than otherwise. And personally I think for a businessman a certain facility in making predictions about the future might prove a very useful skill.'

I laughed and ducked my head. 'Yeah. Yeah, fair enough. So when push came to shove, maybe he wasn't a proper card-carrying Stoic after all. But I'm only repeating what I was told by his estate manager and his mistress: he didn't go out much from choice, and he seems to have picked his friends and acquaintances for their ability to talk philosophy rather than business or politics. And they were exclusively that – friends. There were no enemies that anyone's mentioned, either Manager Leonidas or Tarquitia. Oh, sure, again it's something to check – I've got a few names for his regular dinner guests, so talking to them may open up an angle or two – but I'm not too hopeful on that side of things.'

'So where *are* you hopeful?'

'The gods know, lady. Nowhere, at present. Tarquitia . . . well, I take your point, all of your points, but I can't really believe in Tarquitia being behind the murder. Like I said, all I can do is dig around and see what comes up, see what feels promising.'

'Starting tomorrow?'

'As ever.'

SEVEN

I started, though, with Surdinus's ex: mornings aren't the best time to go visiting clubs, so I'd put that off until later in the day.

Cornelia Sullana had a house up on the Pincian, between the Gardens of Pompey and those of Lucullus; prime hillside property, in other words, although not in the Vatican league. From the looks of the place – old, detached, rambling, in its own grounds and with a well-established garden around it – I'd guess it was part of the family estates, going back at least to her ancestor the dictator's time. Which, of course, made complete sense: belonging, as she did, to a long-established patrician family like the Cornelii, she'd have property in her own right spread throughout the city and far beyond. Rome's ultra-pukkah patrician families have always been a hard-headed bunch where making and keeping money's concerned, and being banned from trade they've put all their efforts over the past five hundred years or so into land, stone and mortar. Or rather, in most cases, into the cheap lath, rubble and cement that the city's tenements were built from, that bring a huge return in rents for a very modest outlay, and keep on bringing it year after year. Particularly if the expense of minor concerns like repairs and renovation is kept to a minimum, which it usually is. Even though she was no longer part of the Naevius ménage, Surdinus's widow, or whatever you liked to call her, wouldn't exactly be short of a sesterce or two.

I gave my name to the door slave, and after half an hour or so spent kicking my heels in the vestibule, I was shown into the atrium, where the lady herself was waiting to grant me an audience.

Cornelia Sullana was comfortably into her fifties and dolled up like a woman twenty years younger. Not that it had much effect on her basic appearance, mind: she was bony and angularly ugly, with an expression on her sharp-featured face like she'd just swallowed a pint of neat vinegar. An image of a discontented parrot in moult eyeing up a particularly recalcitrant nut came to mind. I could see, given their avian similarities, where Surdinus Junior had got his looks from.

'Valerius Corvinus,' she said. 'I assume, from the communication I received from Naevia Postuma, that you are here in connection with the death of my former husband.'

'Yeah. Yeah, that's right,' I said. I glanced at the couch opposite her – she was sitting on a chair – but if I was expecting an invitation to use it, I didn't get one.

'Then I'm not sure that I can help you in any way. Nor am I aware of any need or reason to do so, since the death was a complete accident.'

'It was no accident,' I said. 'Naevius Surdinus was murdered.'

'So Postuma claims, of course, but that is complete nonsense. The tower was unsafe. Everyone told him so, I told him myself, but Lucius never did listen to reason. The silly man deserved all he got, and there's an end of it.'

'He was murdered, Cornelia Sullana,' I repeated. 'I checked for myself. The whole thing was deliberate, and it was planned in advance. Someone climbed to the top, pried the stone that killed him loose from the parapet above the entrance, waited until he was directly below and pushed it free.'

She stared at me. 'You're sure about this?'

'Absolutely certain. The tool the killer used left marks in the cement, and there was cement dust on the plank below where the stone had been.'

'But that's . . .' She frowned. 'Who on earth would want to kill Lucius?'

'Yeah, well,' I said, 'that's the question I was hoping you might help me with.'

'Frankly, I can't see anyone bothering.'

Ouch. She meant it, too. How many years had they been married? It had to be thirty-five, at least, given her age and the age of Surdinus Junior. 'As far as the actual killer is concerned,' I said, 'one of the garden slaves saw a freedman moving through the grounds at about the time when your husband—'

'Ex-husband.'

'When your ex-husband died. Shortish, probably in his forties, with a distinctive mark on his cheek. A large scar or a birthmark. Any bells?'

'No. Certainly he's not anyone I recognize. Oh, you might as well sit down, Valerius Corvinus. I suspect this is going to take rather longer than I anticipated.'

I sat. 'Did your . . . Did Naevius Surdinus have any enemies?' I asked. 'Anyone who'd want him dead?'

'Of course not,' she snapped. 'I told you. Lucius wasn't effective enough to make enemies, as any decent man would in the normal course of events. All he cared about was his silly philosophical studies.'

'I know he wasn't involved in politics, but . . .'

'Certainly he was not.' Clearly, from her tone, this was a sore point, which was understandable: not to be involved in politics, for a woman with the background of Cornelia Sullana, was unthinkable. 'Not since his suffect consulship ten years ago. And the trouble I went to, the strings I pulled, to get him that and properly on the ladder you would not *believe*! Wasted, completely wasted, all because that fool Bassus was forced to kill himself.' So, Leonidas had been right about that. 'Bassus may have been guilty of treason, Corvinus, and so justly condemned, or he may not; the truth of the matter is immaterial. These things happen, one shrugs them off and forgets. I told Lucius as much at the time, but as I said, he never did listen to reason. A most exasperating man.'

Exasperating. The same adjective Tarquitia had used. Well, they had that much in common, anyway. 'How about his business interests?' I asked.

'What business interests? Lucius didn't have a single businesslike bone in his body. Where his investments were concerned – and he had a considerable number, over a very wide range, mostly inherited from his father and grandfather, who *were* proper businessmen – his bailiff had complete charge of these. I, of course, made any necessary major policy decisions and kept a very close watching brief on the man himself. Gallio has been the family's bailiff for over thirty years, as his father and grandfather were before him, and I have no doubt he is perfectly honest, at least as honest as that class of men usually are. Nonetheless, you cannot be too careful, and I' – she sniffed – 'most certainly am. Or was, I should say, until Lucius and I parted company. Gallio, now, can do as he likes.'

'You don't have any connection with the rest of the family, then?'

'With my elder son, you mean? Only as much as I have to. He may be my son, Valerius Corvinus, but Lucius has always been a grave disappointment to me. In a different way, naturally, to his father, but there you are. As a boy he was sullen, secretive and spectacularly unintelligent. As a man, he has retained and developed these traits. Oh, I admit he's tried to make something of himself in life, but if he's succeeded to some small degree it has not been on his own merits but by the doing of others, not least of myself, and without my guiding hand he will no doubt sink to his natural level. My elder son is nothing but one long talentless scowl.'

Gods! So much for the son and heir. *No love lost* had been right. 'How about your younger one?' I said.

'Marcus?' She sniffed again. 'Or Hellenus, rather, as he prefers to be called. That says it all. Marcus, I could indeed have made something of. He was intelligent, personable, an excellent talker. Unlike his brother, prime material in every way. But it was not to be, unfortunately, and the choice was his. No, I have no connection whatsoever now with Marcus. I have no idea, even, where he lives.'

'What about your husband's bailiff? Where would I find him?'

'*Gallio?*' She looked at me in surprise. 'Why should you want to talk to him?'

'No reason.' There wasn't: that aspect of things seemed well above board. But at this point in the investigation I couldn't be too picky, and it was always best to get more than one viewpoint.

'Very well, then. He has an office on Iugarius, near the Carminal Gate. I call him Lucius's bailiff, as indeed he is, but not exclusively so. These days, the firm is quite large, and it has other clients besides the Naevius family.' A third sniff. 'A sign of the times, Corvinus, and not a change for the better. His grandfather was Lucius's grandfather's freedman and knew his place, but these days it seems that where preserving or ignoring class distinction is concerned, anything goes. We'll have freedmen running the empire very soon and the old families letting them do it, encouraging them, even. You mark my words.'

'Uh . . . moving on,' I said. 'The divorce and, ah, related aspects.' We were on delicate ground here, I knew, but I couldn't go without broaching the subject of Tarquitia. 'Maybe I could ask you about them.'

That got me a long, cool stare. 'You mean my husband's mistress, I suppose?' Sullana said. 'The nightclub girl.'

'Yeah. More or less.'

'You think she had a hand in Lucius's death? It wouldn't surprise me, of course; she had him wound round her little finger, and if she features in his will . . .' She stopped. 'Does she?'

'Ah . . . yeah. Yes, so I believe, anyway.'

'Substantially?' I said nothing, which I suppose was an answer in itself, because she went on: 'There you are, then. You don't have to look any further.'

'Maybe not, but—'

'She's a gold-digger, first to last. Not that that aspect of things concerns me, apart from rousing the natural anger that anyone would feel in those circumstances; as I said, I no longer have any interest in the family whatsoever. In fact, I was quite pleased when I heard that Lucius had more or less handed her the Old Villa as a gift, because our dear son will be absolutely livid.' A twisting of the sour lips into what was almost a smile. 'How dreadfully embarrassing for him. But although I had very little time for my husband, that does *not* mean that I can sympathize with his killer.'

'She was his first? Mistress, I mean.'

'As far as I'm aware, yes, although it's much more likely than not. Lucius had many failings, but philandering was not one of them. In fact, I was quite surprised when he took up with the girl, and frankly I believe – despite the obvious untruth of the belief – that his interest in her was fatherly rather than sexual. He certainly talked of her more as a favourite daughter than a mistress.'

'He talked to you about her, then?'

'Oh, yes. Right from the start of their relationship, which was – as you probably know – just over a year ago. He was quite open about it.'

'And you didn't mind?'

'Valerius Corvinus, my husband could have slept with half of Rome and I would not have minded one bit, so long as he did not advertise the fact and observed the proprieties. Knowing he did so with a nightclub slut far less than half his age meant nothing to me. Absolutely nothing. If we were still married after thirty-seven years it was by no doing of mine. Had he told me any time these thirty-odd years that he wanted a divorce, I would have agreed without a thought.'

'But he didn't. Not until a month ago.' I hesitated. 'Ah . . . forgive me for asking this, Cornelia Sullana, but why did he do it then? Not so he could marry Tarquitia, if that were possible, because he didn't marry her when he could. And she didn't claim that marriage in future was on the cards. So why the divorce?'

She was quiet so long that I didn't think she would answer. Finally, though, she said: 'Because I goaded him into it.'

'Goaded?'

'Made him angry. By telling him about my own affair.'

'Uh . . .' This I just didn't believe: the lady, as I said, was well past fifty and looked like the back end of a cart into the bargain. Yet there she sat, like a dowager-matron who could've posed for the mother of the two Gracchi, confessing to screwing around behind her husband's back. 'Come again?'

She must've noticed my expression, because that sour smile was back, fleetingly. 'Oh, not recently. It was twenty . . . no, twenty-five years ago. With a man called Cassius Longinus.'

That name rang a faint bell: I remembered Naevia Postuma mentioning it. 'Surdinus's colleague in the consulship?'

'Yes. Although of course that was much later, and pure

coincidence, when the affair was well and truly over. Longinus was everything that Lucius wasn't, and still is. He's governor of Asia at present, so I hear.'

'Surdinus never knew?'

'He never even suspected. We were very careful, and in any case I doubt if someone like Lucius would have noticed anyway.'

'But he would've minded.'

'Of course he would. And did, even twenty years after the event. That was the whole point of telling him.' She stood up. 'And now, Valerius Corvinus, that is about all I can tell *you*. I've answered your questions as frankly as I can.' Jupiter, she'd done that right enough, latterly! 'And I wish you every success. I may never have got on with Lucius – despised him, in fact, if the truth be told – but I bore and bear him no animosity, certainly not now he is dead. You can find your own way out, I think.'

I did.

EIGHT

S o. Onwards and upwards. Or in this case, downwards, both physically and socially, all the way from the dizzy heights of the Pincian to the vegetable market, between the western slopes of the Capitol and the river, and Tarquitia's Five Poppies Club. This, by a happy chance, would take me down Iugarius, where according to Sullana her ex-husband's upwardly mobile not-quite-a-bailiff had his office. I could call in there on the way. Besides, it was an excuse to drop in at Renatius's wine shop, also on Iugarius, for a quick restorative cup of wine and – hopefully – more detailed directions.

As it happened, the quick cup of wine turned into two slower ones plus a plate of cheese, olives and pickles, but I got the directions OK. Like Sullana had said, Gallio's office was near the Carminal Gate at the south end of the street, on the ground floor of a newish tenement block which was owned by the family. According to my informant, one of the regular bar-flies, it was a pretty thriving business, and Gallio himself was now the senior partner of three, the other two being his sons. Certainly, when I

pushed open the door and went in, the place had a busy feel to
it, with half-a-dozen clerks working full out. I gave my name
and business to the nearest one, and he led me through the back
to a small inner office where the man himself was sitting behind
a desk.

The senior partner was right: you didn't get much more senior
than Naevius Gallio and still be on the right side of an urn. He
had to be eighty at least, and what he was doing still working
the gods alone knew, because mobile – upwardly or in any other
direction – was something the old guy, by the evidence of the
crutches behind his chair, wasn't any longer to any great degree.
Even so, he seemed bright enough when he waved me to a
stool.

'Now, Valerius Corvinus, what can I do for you?' he said. 'I
know, of course, of Naevius Surdinus's death – a terrible business,
that, simply terrible – but not what your connection with him
might be.'

I told him, and he sat back.

'Murdered?' he said. 'Surely not! Who would want to murder
Master Surdinus? You're certain?'

Same question as Sullana's, and I gave him the same answer.
'Absolutely. The stone that killed him was loosened and dropped
on him deliberately.'

'But this is – excuse me a moment, please.' There was a cup
of water on the desk. He picked it up with both hands and drank,
so shakily that some of it was spilled. I waited until he'd put the
cup down again. 'It's unbelievable. Why would anyone do something like that?'

'His ex-wife, Cornelia Sullana, said that you managed his
business affairs.'

'That's quite correct. Or administered, rather, under instruction.
My family, as you'll have guessed from our name, have had
charge of the Naevius estate for three generations. My grandfather
was the first Naevius Surdinus's freedman-bailiff.'

'So Sullana told me.' This next bit was going to be tricky. 'Uh
. . . I understand that shortly after they were divorced, about a
month ago, Surdinus made over part of the property on the Vatican
Hill to his mistress, Tarquitia.'

The old lips pursed. 'That is correct. Through a duly-witnessed
process of sale, for the sum of five denarii.'

'And that when Sullana ceased to be his wife she had no more to do with his financial affairs.'

'Naturally not.'

'Ah . . . have there been any other major changes since, do you know?'

'I do.' You could've used Gallio's tone to sand wood. 'Of course I do, since he gave the task of carrying them out to me. Four, to be precise, all in favour of the lady you named. The transfer of a tenement building in the Subura, for a similar amount to what she paid for the Old Villa. Ditto an oil-pressing concern in Veii. Ditto, a blacksmith's and saddler's business near the Capenan Gate, back here in Rome. Ditto, an ironmonger's shop in the Velabrum.'

Jupiter! 'All this was in a *month*?'

'Yes. Total value in the region of three hundred thousand sesterces. And he was planning on more.'

Gods alive! The guy had been haemorrhaging money like there was no tomorrow.

And, of course, for him there hadn't been . . .

'You didn't try to stop him?' I said.

Gallio just looked at me. 'Of course I tried,' he said. 'What do you think? But in the last analysis the property was his, to do with as he thought fit, and Master Surdinus was a very stubborn man. There was very little I could do.'

'You didn't tell anyone? Like his son, perhaps?'

'Naturally I did. However, in the younger Surdinus's case, the same strictures applied. There was nothing he could do about it either. His father was perfectly sane, so there was no question of diminished responsibility. Not legally, anyway. He had a perfect – and absolute – right to do as he pleased.'

And Tarquitia hadn't told me. Nor, for that matter, had his son.

Shit.

I carried on down Iugarius to its end, by the Tiber. We were definitely downmarket here: the ground between the blunt end of Capitol Hill and the river, like that whole stretch of riverside south to Cattlemarket Square and beyond, is low-lying, and even nowadays after all the improvements to the drainage system and the riverbanks themselves, it's prone to flooding. Added to which, in summer the stink from the Tiber and the thriving insect population are definitely two of the area's most notable features, meaning that anyone of a sensitive disposition who can afford to own or rent elsewhere on higher ground, or at least somewhere that doesn't smell so obviously of Tiber mud and sewage, generally does just that, for reasons of simple self-preservation. Mind you, there're plenty who can't or don't, and the area round the vegetable market is seriously full of tenements that make up a micro-community of their own. Well-off it isn't: the Poppies' clientele would be low-spending regulars, porters and stallholders from the market, with a sprinkling of local tradesmen with actual shops to their names to add a bit of class and raise the tone.

I found the place with a bit of help from a passing bag-lady trudging home with her string bag loaded down with assorted root vegetables, and tried the front door. Locked, of course – it was far too early for customers – and knocking on it didn't produce an answer, either.

Bugger.

Well, I hadn't come all this way to give up that easily. There was an alleyway at the side, and investigating it revealed a small courtyard full of empty wine jars and a back door to the place through which a guy was carrying a couple of fresh jars to add to the pile.

'Hi.' I waited until he'd dumped them and straightened up. 'Could I have a word, do you think?'

'Sorry, mate,' he said. 'I'm busy and we're closed. Open an hour before sunset. Come back then, OK?' He turned to go back inside.

'It's about Tarquitia.'

He stopped and turned back, and I saw his eye catch the purple stripe on my tunic beneath the cloak.

Rapid reassessment. Yeah, well, rank does have its privileges.

'Ah . . . right, sir,' he said. 'What about her?'

'She used to work here, yes?'

He was still looking at me suspiciously, which was understandable: you wouldn't get many purple-stripers hanging around area like this, and even fewer would be interested in the staff of a third-rate nightclub like the Five Poppies. Not interested enough to have a name to hand, certainly.

'Yeah, she did,' he said at last. Then he shrugged. 'What the hell? You'd best come inside.'

I followed him in. The place – it was just one room, and not a big one, at that – was pretty basic, with a few plain wooden tables and stools, a bar counter with its wine rack behind and a low stage at one end. Someone had decorated the walls, though, with murals, and they were surprisingly good: Silenus on his donkey, hung with grapes and holding up a wine cup; what looked like a rout of Bacchanals; and a woodland scene with a satyr sitting beneath a tree playing the double-flute while a couple of deer and a set of birds in the lower branches listened.

'You the owner?' I said.

'Nah. Barman and general dogsbody, me.' He pulled up a stool at one of the tables and indicated another. I sat. 'Name's Vulpis.'

The name fitted him, or more likely it was a nickname: he was small, wiry, sharp-featured, red-haired and generously freckled. Definitely fox-like. Probably, like Tarquitia, a north Italian with Gallic blood. They might even be related.

'Marcus Corvinus,' I said.

He nodded. We had, at least, contact. 'Well, then, Marcus Corvinus,' he said. 'If you want to talk to the boss, you'll have to come back when we're open. He's generally in just before sunset, but it varies.'

'No, that's OK,' I said. 'At least I think it is. If you can help me yourself, that'd be great.'

'I'll do my best. Tarquitia, you said.'

'Yeah.'

'She hasn't worked here for nigh on a year now. Took up with some old nob she met at a dinner party. At least, he was a guest and she was part of the entertainment.'

'Yeah, I know,' I said. 'His name was Naevius Surdinus. He's been murdered.'

He stared at me and gave a low whistle. 'And Tarquitia's involved?' he said. 'Directly, as it were?'

'Not necessarily. Why would you say that?'

'No particular reason. But you wouldn't be round here asking questions about her if she wasn't, right?'

Fair enough. 'You knew her well?'

'Sure. She was on most nights. Not a bad voice, good little

dancer, very fair juggler and acrobat. The punters we get in here
don't expect too much, but they recognize talent when they see
it. She had it and she was popular. Easily the best of the bunch.
The boss was sorry to lose her.'

'You know anything about her background?'

'Not a lot. She's from Padua originally, like me, although that's
just coincidence. Worked there for a year or so before coming
to Rome. That'd be four or five years back. She did an audition
for the boss and he took her on straight away. That's about all I
know. Anything else, you'd have to ask her husband.'

'Her *husband*?'

'Sure. Titus Otillius.' He frowned. 'You didn't know about him?'

Jupiter! 'No, I didn't. They been married long?'

'Two or three years. He works as a porter in the market, and
he was one of our regulars. That's how they met.'

Two or three years. So she'd been well and truly spliced when
she took up with Surdinus. Yet another thing that the lady hadn't
told me.

Also very relevant, where the terms of the will were concerned.
Interesting . . .

'He know about Surdinus?' I said.

'Naturally.'

'And he didn't mind?'

Vulpis laughed. 'Yeah, well, that's something I can't tell you,'
he said. 'Me, I'd mind like hell, particularly since Tarquitia wasn't
that sort of girl. A prostitute, I mean. Oh, sure, a lot of the talent
we have here go with men for money – most of them, in fact,
that's par for the course in our business, and there's nothing
wrong with it. But Tarquitia didn't. Oh, she was no blushing
virgin, she slept with some of the customers off and on, but only
by her choice, and money didn't always feature. But after she
married Otillius, all that stopped. He'd've half-killed her if it
hadn't.'

'But taking up with Surdinus was different?' I said.

He shrugged. 'Seemingly. Can't say for sure, myself.'

'You know where I can find him? This Otillius?'

'Oh, yes. Nothing easier. But you don't want anything to do
with Otillius, sir. He's a total head-banger.'

'Come again?'

'Known for it. Why a girl like Tarquitia should take up with someone like that, let alone marry him, I can't fathom. Still, who knows how women's minds work, eh? He punched her around now and again, but she seemed happy enough.'

'They still an item?'

'Again, that I can't tell you. Like I say, I haven't seen her around for almost a year. Otillius drops in sometimes, but it's not a subject I'd risk raising with him, and he doesn't volunteer.'

'So where *can* I find him?'

Another shrug. 'Well, sir, it's your funeral,' he said. 'Don't come back and say you weren't warned. Your best bet's the market. Any of the porters'll be able to point him out to you. And there're plenty of people around in case he does decide to get nasty.'

Shit. Still, it had to be done.

Things were getting complicated. And I was rapidly beginning to revise my opinion of sweet little Tarquitia.

NINE

As a matter of fact, the market was pretty quiet. Unsurprisingly so, really: we were halfway through the afternoon, the morning rush was long over, most of the stalls were tenantless and clear of produce, and there was only a scattering of both stallholders and customers. I couldn't see any porters in evidence, either, so the chances of Otillius still being around were pretty slim. Even so, it was worth asking rather than putting it off and having to take the long hike back here another day.

I tried a couple of the remaining stallholders first with no result, before an old woman selling eggs pointed me towards the edge of the square.

'You might find him over there, dear,' she said. 'It's where a lot of the men go when they've finished for the day.'

I looked. Sure enough, there were some tables and benches with people sitting at them.

'Thanks, grandma, much obliged,' I said, and walked over. It wasn't an actual wine shop, just a drinking area with a canvas booth and a makeshift bar counter. But it was popular enough, and filled entirely, as the old woman had said, with the male element of the market's sellers and porters. I got a few glances as I went up to the counter, but they were curious rather than unfriendly ones.

The guy behind the bar was already pouring me an earthenware cup of wine from the single jug on the counter – basic was right; evidently you took what you got – and I pulled out my purse.

'You happen to know a porter by the name of Otillius, pal?' I said as I paid.

'Titus Otillius?' The man gave me my change. Well, the price couldn't've been lower, anyway. 'That's him.' He nodded. 'The big guy over there in the corner, with the red tunic.'

I took a sip of the wine, decided I'd been grossly overcharged after all, and followed the direction of the nod. 'Red' was an exaggeration, but from the looks of the tunic in question I'd guess it was more or less a permanent fixture that had never seen the inside of a fuller's shop. Maybe our barman here just had a very good memory.

'Big', however, was a gross understatement: Naevius's garden slave, Cilix, came to mind. With added extras. And a head-banger into the bargain, right?

Thank you, thank you, Vulpis. Most appreciated. Still, I had been warned.

Shit.

Ah, well, such are the sacrifices I make in the service of honesty, truth and justice. I sighed inwardly and carried my cup over.

'Titus Otillius?' I said. He looked up but didn't answer. 'Name's Corvinus. Marcus Corvinus.' Still no response. There was another stool at the table opposite him. I pulled it out and sat. 'I understand you're Tarquitia's husband.'

'So they tell me,' he said. 'I haven't seen the little bitch for almost a year.' His eyes went to the stripe on my tunic. 'Who the fuck are you?'

'I said. Marcus Corvinus.'

A hand the size of a ham reached out and grabbed my tunic just below the neck. I jerked forwards, spilling my wine.

'You one of the bastard's relatives?'

I temporized. 'Ah . . . which particular bastard would that be, now?'

'Who do you think? Naevius fucking Surdinus.'

'Uh-uh.' I reached up and slowly, gently, unprised the grip, finger by sausage-sized finger. 'Not me, pal, no way. Perish the thought. No relation whatsoever, not even by marriage. But I am looking into his death. Purely as a favour, you understand.'

'Surdinus is dead?' Otillius took away his hand. He could've been faking it, sure, but the surprise on his face and in his voice looked and sounded real.

'Yeah. As of five days ago.' I was watching him carefully for signs of further imminent head-bangership. Or whatever the phrase is. They were all there, in spades. Bugger. 'Someone dropped a lump of stone on top of him.'

The surprised look slowly turned into a grin, and it broadened.

'Well, bully for them,' he said. 'You know who did it?'

'Not yet. I told you, I'm just looking into things at present.'

'You shake them by the hand for me, then, when you do.'

'So you haven't seen your wife – Tarquitia – for almost a year?' I said, straightening the tunic.

'That's right. Since she took up serious with the old lecher and moved in with him.'

I shook my head. 'She didn't do that. He set her up in a flat somewhere.'

'News to me. Mind you, she'd keep that quiet, to stop me gatecrashing the happy home. Which I would've done if I'd known where the fuck it was.'

'You didn't?'

'Uh-uh. Me, I thought she'd be up at that fancy villa of his on Vatican Hill. She talked about it enough when she met him first, but I wasn't going to try anything there.' He was still grinning. 'You've spilled your wine. Let me get you another cup. Shit, this is the best news I've had in a month.'

'No, that's OK, pal.' The tabletop was the best place for the stuff. I could just see it eating into the wood. 'I'm fine. So you won't, uh, have heard about the property he sold her?'

'What property? And how the hell could Tarquitia afford any kind of property? She hadn't two copper pieces to rub together.'

'Oh, it doesn't matter. Nothing of much value.' I put my empty cup down on the table. Evidently, the worst was over. Hopefully, at any rate. I breathed a quiet sigh of relief. 'You care to tell me how she met this guy? At a dinner party, wasn't it?'

'Yeah, that's right.' He looked over my shoulder towards the counter and lifted an arm. 'Hey, Barrio!' he shouted. 'Bring us a top-up over here, will you? My bill.' Bugger. Then, turning back to me: 'Queer thing, that was.'

'Yeah? In what way queer?' I said. Well, at least he was talking normally. All in all, a promising sign.

'Tarquitia usually works – worked – with a girl called Hermia. She played the double-flute, Hermia I mean, while Tarquitia did whatever other bits they or the customer'd decided on. Singing, dancing, cartwheels, that sort of thing. It was a pretty good arrangement. Hermia's a natural on the flute, but she's no beauty, what with her squint, and she couldn't throw a cartwheel to save herself. Tarquitia's the opposite.'

'So?'

'So they've got a gig arranged for that evening. Only at the last minute Tarquitia tells Hermia that she's done a swap. There's another couple of girls booked for that dinner party I told you about, and she's arranged with one of them to take her place.' He shrugged. 'Didn't make no difference to the two sets of punters, of course; they were both getting what they paid for. Odd thing was, Tarquitia and the other flautist had worked together once or twice before, and it hadn't worked out.'

'Hang on, pal,' I said. 'Are you saying . . .' I paused while Barrio came over with the jug and filled our cups. 'Are you saying that Tarquitia was only at the dinner party where she met Surdinus because she made a switch at the last minute with one of the team who'd originally been booked?'

'Yeah.' He picked up his cup and drank. Inwardly, I winced. 'Strange how these things happen, isn't it? If she hadn't done the swap she'd never even've seen the bastard.'

Strange was right. Or maybe not. Jupiter, what was going on here? 'So what happened then?'

'Way she told it to me, she was throwing a cartwheel that went wrong and she landed up on Surdinus's couch. Pure acci-dent, it happens sometimes, and it was too clumsy to be intentional because she made him spill his drink all over his party mantle. She apologized – not that he'd be complaining, mind – and when they'd finished the act he asked her and the other girl to stay. There wasn't no funny business, at least that's what she said, it wasn't that sort of party, and she didn't start any, either. They just talked. She's a good talker, Tarquitia.' He took another swallow of his wine. 'Leastways, that's what the little bitch told me at the time. Far as I knew, that was the end of it. Only half a month later I come home and she's cleared out, leaving me a note to say they're an item. You seen her?'

'What?'

'Tarquitia. You seen her, yourself, recently?'

'Yeah. Over at the villa, as it happens. The one on the Vatican.'

'She OK? Healthy enough, and that?'

'She seemed so, yeah.'

He grunted and drank again. 'Did she mention any plans she might have? A great little planner, she is. One of the best, and always was. "You've got to have a plan, Titus," she'd say to me. "Plans make the world go round. They make the future. Without a plan, you're going nowhere."'

'No,' I said cautiously. 'She didn't have any plans. Not ones that she talked about, anyway.' I wasn't going to mention the Old Villa, let alone the other stuff. Including the will. Otillius hadn't seemed a bad guy to me, certainly not bad enough to justify Vulpis's description of him as a head-banger. Or not latterly, anyway. But then when I'd given him the news of Surdinus's death I'd obviously been slotted into the 'bosom buddy' category – which had been absolutely fine by me, of course, because as a result he'd blossomed like a rose. However, if he found out that his wife was fair set to owning property worth the best part of half a million, I'd bet that'd be a completely different story. Liar and con-artist though the lady might be – and that aspect of things was pretty much beyond doubt, now – I couldn't be the one to finger her. They'd have to work things out for themselves, if push ever came to shove. That side of things wasn't my business, and I wanted no part of it.

There was always the chance, too – an outside one, I admitted, but a chance none the less – that Otillius had been stringing me along; that he'd been responsible for Surdinus's death himself. He'd certainly had motive, whatever the points against.

'Anyway,' he was saying, 'you tell her. Tarquitia. If you see her again. You tell her that if she wants to come back it'll be fine with me. No problems, none at all. Clean slate. OK?'

'Sure,' I said. 'OK. I'll do that.' I stood up.

'You haven't drunk your wine.'

Fuck; he'd noticed. 'Nah. I'm not much of a one for wine, me,' I said. 'A sip or two now and again. Maybe two cups at the Winter Festival, just to celebrate, if it's well-watered.' I passed the cup over. 'You have it, pal. Enjoy. I'll see you around.'

I left.

Hmm. Quite a lot to think about there. On top of everything else.

Enough for the day. Back to the Caelian.

TEN

'It was a set-up,' I said to Perilla as Bathyllus served us our pre-dinner drinks in the atrium. 'She planned the whole thing.'

'Evidently so, dear.' Perilla sipped her carrot-juice cocktail. The lady was experimenting with vegetables. You do not want to know. 'But what I don't understand is how she did it.'

'How do you mean?'

'Well, if she'd targeted Surdinus specifically then she must have known that he would be at the dinner party. That could be the only reason for swapping places with the other girl.'

'Maybe she didn't. Target him specifically. Maybe she sized him up when she was doing her act, reckoned he was a likely prospect, and took it from there.'

'Marcus, that's nonsense. If that had been the case there would've been no reason to make the swap in the first place. Men who can afford to hire musicians and dancers for their dinner parties are all likely to be wealthy – positively rich by someone of Tarquitia's class's standards. If she were simply planning to hook a wealthy protector, one set of customers would offer as good a chance as another. And Surdinus wasn't even the one giving the party. She might conceivably have known the host's name in advance, but not the names of his guests. No, the plan was aimed at Surdinus from the beginning. It had to be. But, as I said, I can't see how she could've managed it.'

'You're assuming she *didn't* have another reason for making the swap. A good one, not connected with Surdinus.'

'Well, did she? You talked to her husband. What did he say?'

Bugger; she was right, of course. As far as I remembered, Otillius hadn't said in so many words that Tarquitia *hadn't* had a reason for getting the other girl to switch gigs, or at least offered one, but that was definitely the implication. And Otillius himself had called the whole thing 'queer'.

'Yeah, OK, lady,' I said. 'Point taken. Still, puzzle or not, manage it she did. And from there on in, she managed things pretty neatly. Oh, sure, according to Gallio everything was done perfectly legally, with Surdinus himself calling the shots, but six gets you ten that whatever he thought was the case himself, the idea behind the transfers came from her. And the upshot is that Tarquitia is now one seriously rich lady.'

Perilla frowned. 'How could an intelligent man like Surdinus *do* that?' she said. 'He was very wealthy, yes, obviously, but half a million sesterces is a huge amount of money. It must represent a significant part of the estate. And to make a gift of it in the course of a single month to someone who's only been his mistress for a year, with the promise of more to come . . . frankly, Marcus, I find it incredible.'

'Yeah, well, from all accounts the guy was completely besotted.' I topped up my wine cup. 'Besides, there are contributing factors. Sullana told me that he looked on Tarquitia more as a daughter than a mistress. And he'd certainly far more time for her than for his real family. Wife divorced, one son estranged and the other, to his mind, mostly a waste of space.'

'Hmm.' Perilla was twisting a lock of hair. 'You have thought in terms of him, haven't you? Surdinus Junior?'

'As the killer? Or at least the one behind the killing?' I set down the jug. 'Oh, yeah. I'm not stupid, lady. In fact, after what old Gallio told me, I'd say he was a pretty good bet. Certainly far and away the best we've got at present. Tarquitia – well, she's a con artist seriously on the make, and for her to have Surdinus murdered just when the con is beginning to show a real profit wouldn't make any sense. Even if he'd woken up to what she was doing and told her he was pulling the plug, he'd be too late; all the transactions had already gone through, she was legally half a million up and sitting pretty, and if she knew about the will she could afford to forget about that side of things. Murdering him just wouldn't be worth the effort, and she'd be taking a terrible risk for very little reason. Surdinus Junior, now, he's another kettle of fish altogether.'

'Damage limitation,' Perilla said.

'Sure. Gallio told me he'd kept the guy informed about what his father was doing, and was planning to do. In effect, Surdinus Senior was giving away the family fortune hand over fist, and there was nothing anyone could do to stop him. Junior was down a cool half million of his inheritance already. The only way he wouldn't be down a hell of a lot more was if his father were suddenly to die. And – conveniently – die he did. Plug pulled, end of problem.'

'You could never prove it, dear.'

I sighed. 'Yeah, I know. That's what's so frustrating. His hand wasn't on the stone that killed the old guy, so it's not a question of proving he was in the tower at the time. As far as this case is concerned, we can forget opportunity altogether; means, too, because we know how the murder was done and who did it, and anyone could've set that up. So it all comes down to motive, and *that*' – I took a morose swig of wine – 'is a real bugger.'

'We have to find this freedman,' Perilla said. 'Make the connection there.'

'No arguments, lady, none at all. You like to tell me how?' Silence. 'Exactly. If he was acting for Junior, he wasn't one of the family's own, because Cilix would've recognized him. Or Leonidas would've, from Cilix's description, because a birth-marked or whatevered cheek is a pretty fair giveaway. Or some other smart bugger among the bought help would, when Cilix's story became common knowledge, which it would about five minutes after he'd opened his mouth, with the result that by now we'd have the guy's name and address. Plus if Junior had the common sense of a gnat he'd be perfectly well aware of the stupidity of using one of his own men to kill his father on his own estate in broad daylight, when he might be seen. Which, of course, he was. Ergo he's a complete stranger, a once-off, who by now could be anywhere in Rome, or anywhere in the fucking whole of Italy for that matter. Not to mention the rest of the empire. Gods!'

'Gently, Marcus, gently. And don't forget that Surdinus Junior isn't the only possibility. If someone else were responsible for the murder, none of that would necessarily apply.'

'You have any theories, lady? I'm open to suggestions.'

'You don't think it was this Otillius? Tarquitia's husband?'

I shrugged. 'It could've been. He'd have motive enough; he was obviously more than fond of Tarquitia, and he knew where to find Surdinus. Plus he's got enough of a violent streak in him to commit a murder, that much is pretty obvious.'

'But?'

'Right. Definitely but. First of all, he'd've done the killing personally, not sent someone else to do it. Someone like Otillius would want the satisfaction of bashing the old guy's head in himself.'

'We can't be absolutely sure he did send anyone else.'

'Come again?'

'Cilix only said he saw a strange freedman acting suspiciously and coming from the direction of the tower at approximately the right time. He didn't see him actually *leave* the tower, let alone commit the murder. At first he thought the man was a poacher. Why shouldn't he have been right?'

I sat back. Shit. True; absolutely true. We were assuming the freedman Cilix saw was the killer, but that's all it was: an assumption. If he'd been what was effectively an innocent bystander, then the whole thing was up for grabs.

Thank you for that, clever-clogs. Thank you so very much. Just what I needed.

'Even so, lady,' I said, 'Otillius wasn't a planner. He's a porter in the vegetable market, for the gods' sakes.'

'So?'

'Jupiter, Perilla, intelligence in a job like that is a positive drawback. Some of the cabbages are smarter than those guys.'

'Marcus, that is judgmental and completely unfair.'

'Yeah, well, maybe. But he didn't seem much of an intellectual giant to me. And he was genuinely surprised that Surdinus was dead. Either that or he was a bloody good actor.'

'Are you so certain that he wasn't?'

'Come on, lady! Give me a break! Trust me, Otillius isn't the one we want.'

'Very well. What about Naevius Gallio?'

I just stared at her. '*What?*'

'He's a possibility. Not as good a one as Surdinus Junior, I admit, but far better, to my mind, than anyone else. And for much the same reasons.'

'You care to elucidate, maybe?' I tried to keep the sarcasm out of my voice.

'Certainly. His family have managed the Naevius estate finances for three generations, and he clearly takes considerable pride in the fact. How do you think he felt when the current head of the Naevius family started dismantling the estate and effectively giving and continuing to give away large parts of it to a common nightclub dancer?'

Bugger; I could see where she was heading. Put like that, it was obvious. A client/patron link that went that far back would be pretty much bred in the bone, and its loyalties would be to the family as a whole, not to any of the individual members. Furthermore, those loyalties would override everything, absolutely everything, even the moral and legal concepts of right and wrong. *Pace* Perilla, Gallio had a motive that, in its own way, was at least as strong as Junior's.

'Pretty hacked off,' I said. 'Particularly when he was forced to sit on his hands and watch it happening. Or, even worse, organize the transactions himself.' Hell. 'Yeah, fair enough, lady. Add him to the pot. Anyone else, while we're about it? You haven't got an axe to grind regarding Sullana, have you?'

'No, dear. Not so far. But then I'm keeping an open mind.'

I grinned. 'OK. Fair enough. Just get off my back, will you?'

She smiled and ducked her head. 'There's the other son, of course. He's a completely unknown quantity at present.'

'Yeah, right.' I emptied my wine cup and refilled it. 'Actually, I've got him scheduled. He's tomorrow's assignment.'

'Do you know where to find him?'

'Not exactly. Postuma said he's got a place – a workshop or whatever – near the Circus.'

'She couldn't be more specific?'

'I didn't ask her at the time, but I'd guess not. Even so, tracking him down shouldn't be too difficult.'

'Oh, really?' Perilla sniffed. 'Marcus, dear, be sensible! The phrase *near the Circus* covers everything bounded by the Caelian, the Palatine and the Aventine. *That* is an appreciable chunk of the city.'

'Yeah, I know. But he's an artist, right?'

'So?'

'So where do you find artists – artists of a kind, anyway – in the neighbourhood of the Circus?'

I could see the answer registering. Perilla grinned.

'In the arcades beside the entrances to the Circus itself,' she said. 'Marcus, that is *brilliant!*'

'Yeah, well,' I said smugly, and took a modest swig of wine, 'score one for the boys.' Of course, most of the hucksters who sold the cheap pottery models of the top chariot drivers were just that – hucksters, without an artistic bone in their bodies, and a lot of the stalls only opened on race days when there were plenty of punters around, but you did see a few booths run by genuine artists and craftsmen who produced their own stuff, mainly for the quality end of the market. Better, some of them – and I hoped that Marcus Surdinus was one – were fixed up more permanently in ground-floor properties opposite the arcades themselves: potters, sculptors, jewellers, bronze-workers and the like. Even if I struck out there, the art-and-craft community in Rome, as happens with any other trade or profession, is a small world where everyone knows everyone else. If I asked around long enough, someone was sure to know where the guy was based.

I was giving myself another top-up when Bathyllus tooled in to say that dinner was ready. Well, I couldn't really complain about how things were going. There were plenty of possible angles to explore still, and even if Surdinus Junior was our man, maybe we'd strike lucky. In any case, after a day traipsing round more than half of Rome and a lunch that'd consisted of a few olives, a hunk of bread, and a bit of cheese, I was starving.

Time for dinner. Tomorrow was another day.

ELEVEN

In the event, I shouldn't've been so smug: finding chummie wasn't easy after all. Which, I suppose, was fair enough, given that – barring at its ends, where the starting gates and triumphal parade entrance are – the Circus has more access points for the punters along its almost-mile circumference than you can shake a stick at. Naturally, this being a non-race day, most of the souvenir booths and shops that serviced them were closed, but even so by the time I'd worked my way along the Palatine side and back round to the southern edge, I'd asked at a good couple of dozen places with no result. The weather didn't help, either: I'd barely come down off the Caelian before it had started to drizzle, and ten or fifteen minutes later it'd been throwing it down. Not pleasant; not pleasant at all.

When I did finally strike lucky it was in a cookshop where I'd stopped off for a dry-out and a restorative late-morning plate of beans and bread.

'Hellenus?' The guy ladling the beans said when I asked him. 'Young guy, well-spoken. Not a freedman; free-born, yes?'

'That'd be him,' I said. 'Artist, right?'

'Sure.' The cookshop owner nodded in the direction of one of the side walls. 'That's one of his over there.'

I turned and looked. Not a mural as such, just a small painting that was part of a more simply decorated wall: a still life with a loaf of bread, various dried pulses, and a few assorted vegetables. The subject was suitable for a cookshop, sure, but even so a piece of decoration like that was a lot more upmarket than you'd expect in a place like this. It was well done, too; not one of your cack-handed amateur's daubs.

'It's good,' I said.

'Isn't it?' The guy beamed and passed me my bowl and hunk of bread. 'He did it cheap, too. That's his thing, painting, he doesn't touch this souvenir tat. Me and the wife, we was thinking of having him do a portrait of us. He does a lovely portrait, Hellenus. Tasteful, you know? Maybe for the wedding anniversary, something to hand on to the kids. Twenty-five years, that'll be, come January.'

'Congratulations.' I picked up the spoon. 'So where would I find him?'

'Practically next door. Three or four doors down. He rents part of the old Luccius place.'

'You know him well?'

'He comes in now and again for a takeaway, like most of the locals. But no, except to exchange a few words with, even when he was doing the picture. Not that he's standoffish; he's friendly enough but he keeps to himself, does Hellenus. Ask me, he's a nob that's down on his luck. Or maybe he's had a spat with his father and got himself thrown out.'

'Yeah,' I said. 'Yeah, that's likely enough.' I spooned up the beans. They were not at all bad; not the usual anonymous mush but carefully cooked with oil and sage. 'So you wouldn't know anything about his friends? People he sees a lot?'

'Nah. Like I say, he keeps himself to himself. There's no one regular.'

'Girlfriend? Singular or plural?'

'I've seen a girl around the place from time to time, yeah. Nice looker. Whether she's his actual girlfriend or not, though, I can't say. She's not a live-in, at any rate, and she's not from around here.'

I'd've asked if he could give me a name, but I was getting suspicious looks already. Besides, I'd found the man himself. I ate my beans in silence, paid and left.

The Luccius place turned out to be one of these old revamped properties where most of the internal wall between the street-side shops and what was once completely separate domestic ground-floor living space has been taken away, leaving what is in effect living quarters with a commercial outlet in open plan. Me, I'd've felt that having your living room open out on to a public street was a pretty uncomfortable arrangement, but the two sections were divided off by a curtain that was currently drawn for privacy, so I supposed it worked well enough.

There was no one immediately in evidence, but judging from the artwork hanging up on the available wall space and propped against the counter itself, I'd come to the right place. I was idly looking it over – it was a mixture of still lifes, topography, mythological subjects and portraits, all painted on board, obviously displayed to give potential customers thinking of commissioning a work an idea of what was on offer – when the curtain was pulled back and a youngish guy in his mid to late twenties came out.

'Morning, sir,' he said. 'Can I help you?'

Well-spoken, like the cookshop owner had said, and a very good looker. A bit under medium height, but well-built and even-featured, with tightly curling black hair. He radiated confidence, too; I was reminded of Tarquitia. Right; his mother had said he was personable. In looks and manner, he definitely had the edge over his elder brother, that was for sure.

'If you're Marcus Naevius Surdinus, yeah,' I said.

He blinked. 'That's my name, yes, but I don't use it. Call me Hellenus. Everyone does.'

'Fine by me. I'm Marcus Corvinus.'

'Was it about a commission?'

'No. I've come about your father. You know he's dead?'

'Yes. I had a message from his lawyer to that effect two or three days ago.' Interesting: there'd been the hint of a hesitation before the words 'his lawyer'; no more than a smidgeon, but I wasn't mistaken. 'An accident on his estate, I understand. So?'

'It wasn't an accident. He was murdered.'

'*What?*'

'Your cousin Postuma asked me to look into it.'

That got me an incredulous stare, followed by a laugh.

'Then you can forget it, Corvinus,' he said. 'The lady's barking mad. She tell you where the idea came to her from? I'll bet you a gold piece to a dud sesterce it was the spirits. Am I right?'

'Someone climbed the tower where your father was found and pushed down the stone that killed him.'

'You're kidding.' The laughter had gone from his voice.

'Uh-uh. I checked it out for myself.'

'Shit.' He frowned. 'You'd better come in, off the street.'

He led the way through the curtain. Sure enough, behind it was what had been part of the original house, not the atrium itself but one of the larger side rooms. Now it'd been fitted out as a live-in studio, dominated by a big table covered with pots of paint and brushes, the paraphernalia for grinding pigments and the like, and the remains of a meal. There was an easel with another still life on it – this one of a couple of dead partridges, plus fruit of various types – and a stack of unused canvas boards beside it. The walls were painted, but the work looked like it'd been part of the room's original decoration; certainly it was nothing special, just a colour wash above false-wooden panels. Which made sense, of course: the guy was a jobbing artist, and he wouldn't get paid for decorating his own living room. There was a bed and a clothes-chest in one corner – so presumably he only had this one room – but not much else. It looked more as if Surdinus's younger son was camping out temporarily, rather than actually living there full time.

'I'm sorry about the mess.' Hellenus cleared a couple of stools. 'I wasn't expecting visitors. Sit down, please. You want a cup of wine? There'll be some somewhere.'

'No, that's OK.' I sat. 'So your father's lawyer has been in touch?'

'Venullius?' I filed the name away for future reference. 'Yes. Four days ago. Two days after my father died.'

'He knew where to find you?'

'Certainly. I've never been lost.' A half-smile. 'Not in those terms, anyway. He came himself, as a matter of fact. Since he knew I wouldn't go to him, or have anything else directly to do with the family or its adjuncts.'

'But you're, ah, still your father's son, as it were?'

'Meaning he hasn't disinherited me?' Hellenus shrugged. 'No, seemingly not. That was the reason for Venullius coming at all. To say that I was still included in the will.' He gave me a direct look. 'That's your reason for asking, is it? Considering it transpires that my father was murdered.'

I could be straight, too. 'More or less,' I said.

He grunted. 'Well, then, you'd probably like to know that I come in for a third share of the estate. That's about three million, by Venullius's estimate. Not a bad return for killing the old bastard.'

'Did you? Kill him?'

Again, the long stare. Then he looked away. 'I could've done,' he said finally. 'I felt like it often enough, before I left. But no, I didn't.'

'Even so, you'll take the money?' I kept my voice neutral.

He turned back. 'Even so, I will. Oh, yes, you can bet your

sweet life I will, particularly if it means Lucius doesn't get his well-manicured hands on it. You've met my brother, Lucius?'

'Yeah. Yeah, I've met him.'

'There you are, then. I'd take it even if it meant dropping the whole load of it *in specie* into the Tiber. As it is' – he smiled – 'things are a bit hand-to-mouth, even if I am living like this out of choice. I could use a bit of cash. To travel. The Greek cities, Athens, Pergamum, Alexandria, where all the good artwork is. At least, what there is of it that we Romans haven't looted.'

'You've never been there before?' In wealthy families – particularly when they're political ones – the sons finish their education by being packed off east for a year or so, usually to Athens, to study the art of public speaking and, incidentally, to soak up a bit of badly needed culture before they take up their tribuneship in one of the legions and get their foot on the first rung of the political and social ladder. Me, I'd spent my gap year boozing, gambling and chasing the local talent, which explains a lot, really.

'No. My father – and my mother – thought I'd absorbed too many Greek ideas already for my own good. They wanted to send me to a teacher of rhetoric in Surrentum. *Surrentum*, for Hermes' sake! They said Campania was quite Greek enough to be going on with.' He chuckled. 'So I told them where to stick it and left. I haven't been back since.'

'You've no contact with the family? None at all?' I knew this already, from the other side, but it was just as well to get confirmation.

'No. None. So I'm afraid I can't help you in any way.'

I shrugged and got up. 'That's that, then. I'll be going.'

'Fine. I'll see you out.' He followed me back through the curtain. I stopped at the counter outside, where the sample artwork was displayed, and took a proper look.

'This is pretty good,' I said. 'Especially the portraits. You self-taught?'

'There was an old man in my father's household. One of the slaves. He taught me the basics, and I took it from there. Now, Corvinus, I'm afraid I'll have to rush you off. I've got work to do.'

'On a commission?'

'On a commission. Which, as you know, is my bread and butter.'

'Not for much longer, though, pal.' I gave him my best smile. 'After your father's will goes through probate, you'll be pretty well-off, right?'

'Yes, I suppose I will. Nonetheless, it's a commitment, and I promised the customer it'd be finished by the end of the month.'

'Fair enough.' I turned, then turned back again. 'Oh, one more thing. An address for the lawyer, can you let me have that? Venullius, wasn't it?'

'Titus Venullius. That's right.' He frowned. 'He has an office next to the Aemilian Hall.'

Just beyond Market Square itself. Yeah, well, checking with him would be easy-peasy, although I didn't expect any surprises from that angle. 'That's great,' I said. 'I'll see you around.'

I left, but with my brain buzzing. There'd been a reason for that sudden rush, and for Hellenus's obvious nervousness, sure there had: the guy had wanted me gone, and quickly. Gone, specifically, from the neighbourhood of the artwork that was on display. Which wasn't surprising, really, because when you looked at it closely, it was clear one of the portraits was of Tarquitia.

Interesting.

TWELVE

The rain had slackened off again to a drizzle, but the sky wasn't looking too cheerful: a solid iron-grey lid that, as far as I could see, covered the whole city, with some ominous-looking black bits over to the west that were getting steadily closer. Bugger. I reckoned a couple of calls – a quickie at the Five Poppies off the vegetable market, just to confirm a suspicion I had, plus one on Lawyer Venullius – and that would do me for the day. Certainly not a trip all the way over to the Vatican, which was the only other thing I had on the cards at present; I wasn't going to risk getting caught out in the open proper when Jupiter chose to send down the mighty flood, and in any case I didn't know for sure that Tarquitia would actually be in residence. That I could only hope for, because if she wasn't – if she was still keeping up the flat that Surdinus had got for her in the dizzy early days of their romance, for example – then I was screwed.

I made my way back along the south side of the Circus and up through Cattlemarket Square to the veggie market and the Poppies. Fortunately, Vulpis was around again, and he gave me the confirmation I needed. Not that I'd been in much doubt that he would, because it fitted in too neatly, and it was the only explanation.

I was heading for Market Square and the Aemilian Hall when the heavens opened in earnest. Bugger. Double bugger. I had on my hooded cloak, of course, but it was wringing wet already, and the dampness was beginning to reach my tunic. Time for another wine shop, at least until Rainy Jupiter decided not to piss down on poor quivering humanity quite so hard. There was one place I knew, Tasso's, at the foot of the Palatine's Market Square edge, that catered for the imperial and senatorial admin staff from the government offices round about. Pretentious and overpriced, sure, and normally I'd've avoided it, but beggars – especially wet ones – can't be choosers. At least they served decent wine, albeit at twice the price of anywhere else. I found it, pushed open the door and went inside.

'Marcus?'

I'd been taking the cloak off to hang on one of the pegs by the door, where it could drip in solitary comfort. I turned round.

Gaius Vibullius Secundus and I go a long way back, practically to childhood. We didn't see a lot of each other these days, mainly because he's a big wheel in army admin and our lives have pretty much diverged, but we bump into one another occasionally. I hadn't seen him for a couple of years, mind, not since I'd picked his brains about Gaetulicus and the German frontier legions. A nice guy, Secundus. And, of course, since he was based at Augustus House on the Palatine, this was his local.

'Hi, Gaius,' I said. 'How's it going? Skiving off work early as usual, are you?'

'I'm on a flexible lunch break.' He indicated what was left of a plate of cheese and olives in front of him. 'Boss's privilege. Pull up a stool and join me.' I did, and he raised a hand towards the bar. 'Hey, Quintus!' he shouted. 'Let's have a half-jug of the Massic over here, OK? And another cup.' He turned back to me. 'So. How are you doing? How's Perilla?'

'She's fine. You, uh, got a replacement for Furia Gemella yet?' Gemella was Secundus's ex-wife. Ex as of a month or so before I'd last seen him. Loud, brash, went in for large earrings. We hadn't got on. Mind you, she and Secundus hadn't, especially, either.

'Not as such, no,' he said. 'At least, no one official. I might keep it like that. Makes things much simpler.' The wine came, and he poured. 'Help yourself to the cheese and olives. I've had enough.'

I took a bit of cheese. 'You in the same job?' I said.

'More or less. I've moved up the ladder a notch, mind, since old Curio got his wooden sword, but yeah, more or less.' He took a swallow of the Massic. 'How about you? Still bumming around with the sleuthing?'

'Off and on.'

'Which is it currently? Off or on?'

'On, as it happens. Old guy had his head flattened by a lump of falling masonry.'

He set down his cup. 'Naevius Surdinus?' he said.

'Yeah, that's him. You heard?'

'Sure I heard. But I heard it was an accident.'

'Yeah, well.' I took a swig of the Massic. Beautiful. 'It wasn't. Most definitely not. Even so, I'm surprised the death is common knowledge. From all reports, he'd been out of the loop for years.'

Secundus shrugged. 'He was an ex-consul, Marcus,' he said. 'Suffect, sure, only for six months and that ten years back, but a consular none the less. A consular's death gets noticed, and when it's as unusual as Surdinus's was, it gets talked about as well. And out of the loop the guy might have been, but when old Aulus Plautius told him it came as a real shock to his ex-colleague, at least, I can tell you that.'

'Ex-colleague?'

'In the consulship. Cassius Longinus.'

'I thought Longinus was Asian governor at present,' I said.

That got me a sharp look: Secundus might not be the brightest button in the box, but he wasn't stupid by any means. Despite having made it, in his time, to city judge's level.

'You developed a sudden interest in who's who in current politics, Marcus?' he said. 'Or does Longinus figure somewhere in that case of yours?'

'Neither,' I lied: friend or not, I wasn't going to tell him about Cornelia Sullana's little admitted indiscretion. Besides, it was probably just coincidence: bed-hopping, in the circles people like Sullana and Longinus moved in, was pretty much taken for granted as a fact of everyday life. 'I just happened to know, that's all.'

'Mmm.' Secundus swallowed some of his wine. 'Yeah, right. He was, certainly.'

'Was what?'

'Asian governor. Not any more, though. The emperor recalled him ahead of time, so as of ten or twelve days ago, he's back in Rome.'

'Recalled him? Why would he do that?' Governors were governors; they were fixtures, at least until their term of office expired naturally. Plus, Asia was one of the senatorial provinces, in fact the plum appointment. Oh, sure, ever since Augustus's day the emperor has had overriding proconsular authority where appointments and removals are concerned throughout the empire, no matter what kind of province is at issue, but it's not been used all that often, certainly not blatantly, and never without a reason in the case of a senatorial governor. Senatorial provinces are the concern of the senate; imperial ones – where most of the legions are – are the concern of the emperor, and neither treads on the other's toes. At least in public. If Gaius Caesar had shoved his oar in and removed one of the senate's prime appointees from office ahead of time, then he must have given a reason. A bloody good one, too.

Secundus shrugged again. 'Jupiter knows,' he said. 'No cause that I'm aware of. Or anyone else, for that matter. Including – or so he claims – Longinus himself. All he got was the order to get his arse back to Rome asap, and that's been that.' He moved his head closer and dropped his voice. 'Mind you – and naturally I'm not implying any criticism here – Caesar's been acting a bit . . . well, a bit arbitrarily these past few months. Longinus is just another example.'

Arbitrarily. Oh, sure: like *tired and emotional* was a euphemism for *pissed as a newt.* Yeah, well, there were no surprises there: in my long and not inconsiderable experience of the neurotic, overbred bugger who was currently our emperor, he'd always been several sandwiches short of a picnic. In many ways, he couldn't've mustered the hamper. 'That'd be a bit more arbitrarily than usual, I assume?' I said.

I'd spoken at normal voice level, and I saw a few heads at the nearest tables – senior civil service types to a man – turn to look at me. Secundus glanced around, grinned nervously, and lowered his voice to a whisper through clenched teeth.

'Gods, Marcus, you stupid bastard, either shut the fuck up or keep it down, right?' he hissed. 'I know most of those guys, and they're safe, but one or two I don't. And these days you do *not* kid around where talking about the boss is concerned. Get me?'

The hairs rose a little on the back of my neck. Shit, he was serious; deadly serious. This wasn't the Gaius Secundus I knew.

'Yeah, OK, pal, I'm sorry,' I said. I lowered my voice to match his. 'Arbitrarily like what?'

'Well, for a start there's the business of the statue in the Jerusalem temple.'

'I thought the Jews were dead against that kind of thing. Having statues of gods in temples. God, singular. Whatever.'

'Damn right they are. Only this wasn't one of theirs; it was one of ours.'

'*What?*' I'd raised my voice, and he winced. 'Sorry, pal. Won't happen again.'

'Caesar wanted to set a statue of himself up in the Jewish holy of holies and make them burn incense to him.'

'But that's crazy!'

'Tell me about it. Offend those touchy stiff-necked buggers and you'd have a mid-east war on your hands before you could say "zealot". Caesar's advisors managed to talk him out of it, luckily, but the idea was there. Rumour is, he's planning to do much the same thing here, in the city. Establish a formal cult, temples, priests, sacrifices, the lot. That's "cult" as in personal cult.'

'Shit.' I was appalled; even for Gaius, this was going too far. Oh, yeah, sure: worshipping a living person as divine has been standard and accepted in the East for centuries – witness Postuma's pal, Alexander – and every provincial town, outwith the Jewish bounds, of course, has its statue of the emperor to whom it's only polite to offer a pinch of incense, but he's there in image to represent the power of Rome, not *propria persona*. And within the city boundaries we like our deified mortals to be comfortably dead first. 'He'll never get away with it.'

'Who's to stop him? He's the emperor.' Secundus took a swallow of his wine and raised his voice a fraction. 'Anyway, all this is by the way. Leave it. What's your interest in Cassius Longinus?'

'I told you. I don't have one.'

'Come on, Marcus! Give me a break! With your peerless grasp of affairs I'm surprised you know the names of the current fucking consuls. That's if you do know them; me, I wouldn't risk a bet. And yet you come straight out with the fact that Longinus is the governor of Asia. He has something to do with the case you're working on, hasn't he?'

I grinned. 'Yeah, OK. His name just came up in passing, never mind how or who gave me it: that's strictly confidential. And it wasn't mentioned in any sort of way that'd connect him with Surdinus's murder, either. I was surprised to hear that he was in Rome, that's all. Satisfied?'

'Not really. But I suppose it's all I'll get.' Secundus took an olive. 'OK, just to fill you in on the guy. Not that you want filling in, no, of course not, perish the thought.' I said nothing. 'Just for the fun of it. Longinus is an old friend of the family; I mean *old*, long before he and Surdinus had their joint consulate. Which was why Plautius made a point of telling him about Surdinus's death; Plautius had the consulship the year before the two of them, so he's always had a friendly eye for Longinus. Incidentally, he was only appointed Asian governor this year, and he seems to have been doing all right – no major cock-ups, certainly, and as far as honesty goes, word has it you could play the stone-and-scissors game with him in the dark. Shit-hot jurist; he's written books on the subject. Oh, and a straight-down-the-line Stoic, like his great-grandfather.'

The Cassius who'd put a knife into old Julius. Yeah, I got the picture, and by the sound of things great-grandson was out of the same mould: a good old-fashioned damn-your-eyes Roman with an integrity you could bend iron bars round. Interesting that he should be a Stoic, mind: Stoic philosophy seemed to be cropping up pretty frequently in connection with this case. But there again, Leonidas the estate manager had said that most of

Surdinus's friends were on the philosophical side, and he was a Stoic himself, so maybe that wasn't so strange after all.

'You happen to know where I can find him?' I said. 'Should I want to talk to him, that is.'

'Which you don't.'

'Which, at present, I don't.'

He grinned again and filled up my cup. 'Right. He has a place on the Quirinal, off High Path and near the Shrine of Mars. You'll probably find him there, because he hasn't got much else to do at present but stay at home grumbling and twiddling his thumbs. You can tell him . . .' He stopped. 'Oh, hell.'

The door had just opened and a freedman-clerk had come in. He looked round, fixed on us, and came over. Secundus sighed.

'Yes, Acastus. What is it?' he said.

'The departmental accounts committee meeting, sir.' The freedman touched the brim of his cap. 'It's in less than an hour's time. You asked to be reminded.'

'Bugger, so it is.' He stood up. 'Sorry, Marcus, I'll have to go. Finish the wine, OK?' He waved at the barman. 'My tab, Quintus, right?' The barman nodded, and Secundus turned back to me. 'Use my name as an introduction to Longinus if you like,' he said. 'Not that you'll need to; he's a perfectly amiable guy. And you know where to find me. Any other questions regarding the case you don't want to know the answers to, I'll be happy to help. Or, depending what they are, tell you to go and screw yourself. Fair enough?'

I grinned. 'Fair enough. Thanks, pal, the next one's on me.'

'Damn right it is. See you remember,' he said, and left.

I settled down and poured the last of the Massic into my cup. Yeah, well, I didn't know how much of all that had been relevant, but it had certainly been interesting. So Longinus was in Rome, was he? And, from what Secundus had said, he'd arrived back just before Surdinus was topped. Probably coincidence, but still . . .

Plus – and I couldn't see how or whether it fitted in with the murder, or indeed why the hell it should – there was the question of why the emperor had suddenly decided to bring Longinus back. Why should a paranoid bastard like Gaius go over the senate's head and recall their top governor, who was not only holding his end up where the job was concerned, but was by all accounts so squeaky-clean-honest that you could play *morra* with him in the dark?

Yeah, right; there was only one answer to that, really. Whether or not, as I say, it was relevant to the case was another thing entirely. We'd just have to see what the future brought.

Meanwhile, I had Lawyer Venullius to talk to. Then it was home for a bit of a think.

THIRTEEN

'Everything to do with the will checks out,' I said to Perilla when I was changed into a dry tunic and ensconced in the atrium with a cup of wine beside me. 'Apart from a few minor bequests, Surdinus Junior gets the bulk of the estate; Marcus – Hellenus – gets a third, while Tarquitia gets the interest on fifty thousand sesterces and the capital when she marries. Which, of course, we know she's done already. So at least no one's telling porkies there, and there's nothing we're missing.'

'Hmm.' Perilla was twisting a lock of her hair. 'You're sure Hellenus and Tarquitia were working together?'

'Yeah. That's more or less beyond doubt. And everything fits in. Vulpis at the Poppies confirmed that Hellenus did their wall paintings for them about eighteen months ago. That must've been when he first met Tarquitia. Whether or not they're an item sexually – then or now – I don't know, and it doesn't really matter. Business partners, now that's another thing entirely.'

'I'd go for yes, myself,' Perilla said. 'Her husband strikes me as more or less a dead weight, and apart from providing her with a legal claim to the bequest capital, he doesn't really serve any useful purpose. He certainly has no right to a share of the money; that was left specifically to her.'

'Yeah, right.' I took a mouthful of the wine. 'As far as the scam itself is concerned, the whys and wherefores are pretty obvious. The original idea was Hellenus's. He couldn't be sure he wouldn't be written out of his father's will completely; all it would take would be a clause to that effect, specifically excluding him by name from a share in the estate. So he needed a little nest-egg in advance, something up front. Hence the deal with Tarquitia, the purpose being to milk the old man of as much as he could before he hung up his clogs. Plus, naturally, anything he could get would be all the less at the end of the day for Surdinus Junior to inherit. I reckon that figured pretty highly, too.'

'So he arranged the . . . well, we'd best call it the *encounter* between his father and Tarquitia.'

'Yeah. Of course, he couldn't be sure anything'd come of it, but Tarquitia is a very sharp cookie, and I'd say where attracting men is concerned she knows what she's doing.'

'As you proved yourself, dear.'

I grinned. 'Bugger off, lady. Fixing things up wouldn't've been difficult. He hadn't any formal connections with his family any more, sure, but I'll bet you there was someone among the bought help he'd kept in touch with, or who'd kept in touch with him. An old nanny, maybe, or more likely a female slave with a crush. He's pretty good-looking, our Hellenus, and a smooth talker. Me, I'd bet women just fall into his lap. He and Tarquitia make a good pair. It'd just be a case of waiting for the word that his father was going to a dinner party where there'd be dancing girls laid on for dessert and that'd be it. Tarquitia could arrange the switch easy as pie, and the rest would be up to her.'

Perilla put her chin on her hand. 'It's all very cold-blooded, though, isn't it?' she said. 'I mean, on both their parts. After all, Hellenus had made his choice; he'd walked out on his father saying he wanted no more to do with him. And Surdinus couldn't've behaved better towards Tarquitia. His own wife said he treated her more as a daughter than a mistress. The whole thing's completely sordid and shabby.'

'Agreed. I'm not defending them. Far from it. Still, I very much doubt that they're our killers, either one or both together, and that's the important thing at present.'

'Of course, you can make a case for Hellenus. On his own, without Tarquitia.'

'Is that so, now?' I settled down and took another swig of the wine. 'Go ahead, lady. You have the floor.'

'Let's say he did know the details of the will after all. That isn't impossible, given that he was working with Tarquitia. Quite the reverse; we only ever had her word that Surdinus never told her them, and we know what that's worth.'

'Fair enough.'

'Very well. How do you think Surdinus might have reacted if he were to find out there was a connection between his mistress and his younger son? Particularly – and he wasn't a stupid man, remember – if he discovered the nature of the relationship?'

'How would he do that?'

'Perhaps someone told him.'

'Like who?'

'His other son. It wouldn't've been too difficult for Surdinus Junior to arrange for Tarquitia to be secretly followed, to see if she were up to something. In which case she would have led him straight to Hellenus.'

Shit; she was right. It was possible, in fact it was more than possible, and the natural thing for Junior to do when he discovered he was being systematically ripped off by his father's mistress. If he could prove to Surdinus that Tarquitia was nothing but a chiseller on the make – and, worse, that she'd been planted on him by his estranged younger son – then the scam was dead in the water.

'Chances are he'd've confronted her, then gone off and changed his will,' I said. 'Disinherited Hellenus, cancelled the fifty thousand bequest. And, of course, any up-and-coming plans for selling more property to her at a peppercorn price.'

'Exactly. Hellenus would have lost his third of the estate, and while all the property Tarquitia had persuaded his father to make over to her would be hers in law, he'd have no claim on it at all. In effect, he'd be left penniless, with no prospects, and in a far worse position than he'd been in before. Totally dependent on her goodwill. The threat of all that would give him a prime motive for murder.'

Bugger, it would, too. Even so . . .

'I'm sorry, lady,' I said, 'but it won't work.'

'Really?' She sniffed. 'You don't think Hellenus is capable of murdering his father? Of arranging the murder, anyway?'

'Oh, sure.' He would be, too: the guy had been convincing and pleasant enough when I talked to him, but I was too old a hand at this game to let that weigh. And given a viable motive I'd bet he had the intelligence and willpower to think things out and carry them through. 'No problems there.'

'Well, then.'

'Come on, Perilla! Think it through. Junior finds out about the scam and tells his father, with the result that the old man decides to change his will. Very shortly afterwards, Surdinus is dead and I turn up on the doorstep to break the glad news to him that it was murder. So what happens then?'

'Ah.'

'"Ah" is right. Given the circumstances, the guy would be falling over himself to point the finger. Quite understandably so. Only he didn't, ergo he didn't know anything about the scam, ergo the theory's up the creek without a paddle. QED. No, my guess is that Tarquitia's little con – or Hellenus's, if you like – had nothing to do with the murder.'

'Hmm. All right, Marcus. Point taken.' She was looking seriously miffed, and I stifled a grin. If there's one thing the lady hates it's coming off second best. 'So. What now?'

'I confront her with it. Oh, sure, I know it won't do much good, and like I say it probably isn't relevant, but it'll clear the air. Then it's back to furkling around hoping that something comes up.'

'Furkling around where, dear?' Prickly as hell.

'I thought I might pay a visit to Cassius Longinus.'

'Why would you want to do that? And *don't* say, "Because he's there".'

I grinned again, openly this time. 'OK,' I said. 'You want the theory? To put him in the frame, I mean?'

'Certainly, if you have one that's valid.'

Ouch.

I topped up my cup from the jug. 'Sullana claims she had an affair with him twenty-five years ago, right?'

'Yes.'

'She also said that if Surdinus had offered her a divorce any time these thirty-odd years she'd've agreed straight away.'

'So?'

'So if they'd been married thirty-seven years – which they had been – then the gilt must've worn off the gingerbread pretty quickly after the wedding. Certainly long before she decided to look for love and affection elsewhere. Maybe as much as ten years, and that's a long time in a marriage that isn't working.'

'Marcus, dear, what exactly are you getting at?'

'Gaius Secundus told me that Longinus was a very old friend of the family, dating much further back than his and Surdinus's joint consulship. Oh, sure, twenty-five years would qualify him as that, no argument; but me, I was wondering about the gap.'

'What gap?'

'Between twenty-five years and, quote, "thirty-odd".'

'Marcus . . .'

'Wait a minute, lady. Just listen. Say that when she talked to me Sullana was fudging things a little, intentionally so, and the affair happened closer to the thirty-five year mark – there's your "thirty-odd" – rather than the twenty-five. That'd put Sullana in her very early twenties, pre-kids and a couple of years into a bad marriage; Longinus – presumably, given he was consul ten years back – just a bit older. Unmarried, unattached.'

'And how do you *know* he was unmarried and unattached?'

I ignored her. 'The perfect age and conditions for an affair, on both sides. And, well, it fits in pretty neatly with Surdinus Junior's age.'

She was staring at me. 'Marcus Corvinus, you should be ashamed of yourself!' she said. 'That is groundless speculation, pure and simple, and very close to muckraking! You've no evidence for Longinus being Surdinus's father. None whatsoever.'

'Sure I don't. But it's an angle worth considering if Longinus's coming back to Rome at a time just predating Surdinus's death is no coincidence. Sullana says that up to a month ago her husband had never even suspected she'd had an affair, and when she told him she had and who with, he was furious.'

'But why on earth should Longinus kill Surdinus? If anything, it ought to be the other way round.'

'Maybe he threatened to, and Longinus got in first.'

'Corvinus, that is absolute nonsense!'

'Or he was threatening to disinherit his elder son. Who, of course, wouldn't be his elder son at all.'

'That might be an additional reason for Surdinus Junior to kill his father, but it would have nothing to do with Longinus.'

'Oh, yes, it would. If the thing went through, particularly just after Surdinus had divorced his wife of almost forty years, whether he made the reason public or not, people would put two and two together, and the chances are they'd come up with the right answer. Sullana would be disgraced, his natural son would lose

a major inheritance, and the oh-so-honourable-and-upright
Cassius Longinus wouldn't come out of things looking too good,
either. Plus the timing would be catastrophic. The guy's just been
hauled back to Rome, presumably in disgrace for committing
some misdemeanour, anything up to and including treason, but
probably just that, and his career's already enough on the skids
without word getting round that he's the father of his erstwhile
colleague's elder son, when his reputation would go down the
tubes as well. I'd say all that was a good enough reason for
murder.'

'Poppycock.'

'Yeah, well, you can sneer all you like, lady, but at least it
means that Longinus needs checking out. We only have Cornelia
Sullana's version of things to go on. Maybe his will be different.
Or can you suggest another avenue I should be exploring?'

'No, but . . .'

'Fine. Longinus it is, then.' I reached for the jug and refilled
my wine cup. 'After I've talked with Tarquitia.'

FOURTEEN

I was half-expecting no one to be at home in the Old Villa, but
when I knocked – under the watchful and censorious eye of
Surdinus Junior's door slave sitting on a stool outside the
villa's main entrance – it was eventually opened by a youngish
guy in a freedman's cap. No birthmark, though.

'Uh . . . I was hoping to talk to Tarquitia, pal,' I said.

'No problem. They're in the dining room. Come in.' He stepped
aside.

I followed him through the lobby and the atrium. Sure enough,
the place seemed to be a separate house in itself, or maybe
'apartment' would be a better word, because everything was
on a much smaller scale than in the main building. It felt and
smelled disused, though, and what statues or furniture were
present were either covered in sheets or dull from lack of
polishing, while the atrium pool itself was empty barring half
an inch of rainwater from the opening in the ceiling above it,

already turning scummy. A basic house staff responsible for the cleaning and the other usual domestic chores hadn't come with the deal, then. Not that, for five silver pieces, Tarquitia could complain that she'd been short-changed. I wondered who the freedman was.

'You've got a visitor,' the guy said.

Tarquitia and Hellenus were lying on one of the couches, holding wine cups. There was a jug – plain earthenware, like the cups – on the table in front of them, and a third cup half-full. Friend, then, not servant.

'Valerius Corvinus,' Tarquitia said. 'What a surprise.'

'Yeah, I can see it must be.' I was looking at Hellenus. He said nothing, just returned the look and took a slow drink from his cup. 'You know each other, then?'

'Very well. But, of course, that won't come as much of a surprise to you, will it?' She was perfectly relaxed – in fact, she was smiling. 'Marcus told me you'd seen my picture at the workshop, so making that particular deduction wouldn't have been difficult. And presumably you've worked out the rest of it, too.'

'"Marcus"?' I said to Hellenus. 'I thought you didn't use your real name any more.'

He shrugged. 'A condition of the old man's will. I don't mind too much, considering what I've got in exchange. Besides, it'll embarrass the hell out of my poker-arsed brother to have a jobbing artist using the family name. I can get used to it. As can my fiancée here.'

'Fiancée? I thought the lady was married already.'

'Only temporarily.' Tarquitia looked past me at the freedman, who was still hovering. 'Damion, find another cup for our guest here, will you?' She looked back at me. 'It's a celebration, Corvinus, and you're welcome to join us. Sit down, have some wine.'

I stayed standing. 'Too early for me, lady,' I said. 'Thanks all the same.'

'Suit yourself, but it's Falernian. Good Falernian. Damion's brother is in the wine trade, and he supplies some of the best houses in Rome.' I said nothing. 'No? Ah, well, your loss. Damion, could you give us a moment, please? I think Valerius Corvinus would like a word in private.'

The freedman grunted, came over, picked up the third cup, filled it to the brim, and went out.

'So.' Tarquitia was still smiling. 'Would you like to begin, or shall I?'

'The whole business – your affair with Surdinus – was a set-up, right from the start. You and Hellenus here arranged the whole thing.'

'Yes, we did.' She took a sip of her wine. 'Hellenus – Marcus, rather.' She turned to plant a kiss on his cheek. 'I really do need to get used to calling you that, dear. Marcus was doing the artwork for the Poppies and we sort of drifted together. I didn't know he was who he was at the time, mind. Then one day he told me about this brilliant idea he'd had.'

'To screw his rich daddy,' I said neutrally. 'In both senses of the word.'

She coloured slightly. 'If you're going to be unpleasant,' she said, 'then you can leave. We're not greedy. Marcus only wanted to make sure of getting what was his by right.'

'Fair enough,' I said. 'So you waited for an opportunity to, ah, effect an introduction.'

'It wasn't easy.' Hellenus reached for the jug and topped up their cups. 'My father didn't go to that sort of party as a general rule. Oh, he wasn't a prude, he just found it below his dignity, and so did most of his friends. But eventually we struck lucky; one of his younger philosopher pals who was a bit more red-blooded than most. After that it was easy. Tarquitia knew one of the girls who'd been hired, some money changed hands, and that was that.'

'You found out that your father was going to the dinner through one of his household?'

'Yes. Penelope.' He exchanged an amused glance with Tarquitia. 'Faithful Penelope. She was one of Mother's maids. Pleasant little thing, a bit mousey but quite good-looking in her way. We stayed in touch after I left, and she kept me informed about what was going on. Of course, after the divorce, all that stopped, but by that time it didn't really matter.'

'So if your father didn't make a habit of furkling pushy dancing girls' – that got me a glare from Tarquitia, but I ignored it – 'how did you manage to hook him?'

'Oh, that was all my lovely girl's doing.' He hugged her. 'She's a smart little thing, Corvinus. But of course you know that. If she'd been pushy, like you say, thrown herself at him literally, he'd've run a mile. No, she made it look like a complete accident, and she was most apologetic and embarrassed. Weren't you, lover?' He kissed her again. 'The suggestion that the girls stay on after finishing their act, naturally, came from my father's friend, and she went to Dad's couch straight away. With suitable modesty and reluctance, I might add.' Beside him, Tarquitia giggled and buried her face in her wine cup. 'And despite what the friend and the other girl were getting up to on the other couch, there was absolutely no funny business.'

'We talked,' Tarquitia said. 'He wanted to know about my family. I told him my father lived in Padua, where he made cheap jewellery, but he was losing his sight and I'd come to Rome so I could make enough to support him. Complete hogwash, of course; the closest my father ever got to being blind was blind drunk, and we haven't been in touch for years, but Lucius lapped it up. When the evening ended he said he wanted to see me again, and that was it.'

'Did you ever sleep with him?' I asked.

'Oh, yes. Not often, though. Like Hellenus – Marcus – told you, he found the whole sexual thing a bit beneath his dignity. But he thought I'd expect it, so he did it. Tried his best to, anyway.' She frowned. 'Corvinus, Lucius was a nice man. A very nice man indeed; the kindest and most generous I've ever met. I told you that before, and I meant it. Don't go away thinking I didn't see it, or that I wasn't grateful.'

'Certainly not,' I said. 'Perish the thought.'

That got me another glare.

'So, anyway,' Hellenus said, 'here we are. Project successfully completed and, I should point out, perfectly within the law. Like Tarquitia said, we're not greedy, either of us. Tarquitia's sold this place back to my brother for, in effect, the difference between my third of the estate and a full half share, which is, admittedly, on the pricey side, but we had him over a barrel and he would've paid far more to remove the embarrassment. Hence' – he raised his cup – 'the celebration, because she's just signed the contract. *She* has, of course, as the owner, although the money will come to me; the only reason I'm here is that I wouldn't have missed for worlds the look on Lucius's face when he saw us together. The other properties my father gave her – sold her, rather – well, they'll be hers as they already are absolutely. She's certainly earned them, and as far as I'm concerned they're just the icing on the cake. Call it an advance wedding present.'

'What about Otillius?' I turned to Tarquitia. 'By the way, I promised him that when I saw you again I'd tell you he's willing to have you back. There, that's done.'

She laughed. 'Oh, I finished with poor Titus long ago,' she said. 'What I ever saw in that brute, let alone why I married him, I don't know.' ('Beefcake,' Hellenus murmured, grinning, and she elbowed him in the ribs.) 'But I repeat, we're not greedy. If he agrees to a divorce, I'll make over Lucius's bequest to him *in toto*. The whole fifty thousand. We don't really need it, after all, Marcus and me, we have plenty to keep us going, and believe me, Corvinus, he will jump at it.'

Yeah, he probably would. And, to my mind, he'd be getting the best of the deal. Still, it was sad.

'So what happens now?' I said.

'I told you.' Hellenus took a swallow of wine. 'We travel, and we do it in style. Athens, Pergamum, Alexandria, the complete eastern tour, as soon as the shipping lanes open again in spring. Everything should be settled by then. I may even buy a yacht. Hiring is so middle class, and bunking down in a cargo ship isn't to be thought of.'

'Yeah, well.' I turned to go; I wanted out before I threw up. 'Good luck to you both.'

'Corvinus!' He called me back. 'Just remember, we've only taken what's due to us. Tarquitia made the old man happier in his final months than he had been for years. And I reckon as an artist I've made a bigger contribution to society and human happiness than my brother ever did, or ever will. I deserve my share. And I'll make better use of it than he ever could.'

'Right,' I said. 'I'll see you around.'

And I left.

So. That was done, at least for the time being. It was a long hike to the Quirinal, where Longinus hung out, practically the other side of Rome, but I could shorten things by crossing the river on one of the little ferry-boats that plied for hire level with the top end of the Janiculan and then cutting through Mars Field. At least the weather was good, cold but dry, with only a few drifting clouds to remind me that Jupiter was only holding off for the present.

As far as the actual murder was concerned, I had to admit that the home team wasn't doing so well; in fact, we'd hit a stone wall. Oh, sure, with the Tarquitia/Hellenus side of things stitched up – or at least looking that way for now – we'd made some progress, but not all that much. Me, I still fancied Surdinus Junior as the killer; certainly he'd got by far the best motive, in fact he was practically the only person who had a motive at all: *pace* Perilla, I couldn't really see old Gallio as a criminal mastermind out to save the family inheritance at the cost of its current prime representative. Still, time would show. Or maybe – and this was the bummer – it wouldn't. Not unless we could get a lead on Cilix's scarface freedman.

Assuming, of course, that he was the actual perp after all, and hadn't just been after Surdinus's game-birds . . .

Bugger.

Longinus, despite what I'd said to Perilla, I didn't hold out too much hope for. Yeah, well, he could've had a motive in line with the one I'd given him, but the chances that he'd done the deed, or had it done for him, rather, were pretty slim. It'd have to be fast work, for a start, if he'd only been back in Rome for half a month or so, and from Secundus's description of him he didn't seem the killing type. Still, he was all that was on offer currently, and I couldn't turn my nose up at him.

I made my way across the Saepta to the old Sanqualis Gate and onto High Path. Near the Shrine of Mars, Secundus had said, the Armilustrum. A quick stop at a corner baker's shop selling sesame twists and poppy-seed pastries to get final directions plus a much-needed late-morning snack, and I found the house itself.

Very nice, which was par for the area. Own grounds, surrounding wall, gateposts with sphinxes on the top. We were talking serious money here; evidently this branch of the Cassii had taken up the slack in the three generations since *the* Cassius Longinus had blotted the family copybook. Although, in all probability, the family themselves wouldn't see it that way, and the villains of the tale would be old Julius and his parvenu successors. The fact that Great Grandfather Gaius had gone down the tubes of history at Philippi fighting against the guy who would later become the Divine Augustus wouldn't make him, to them, any less of a hero. Quite the reverse.

There was a door slave in a natty blue tunic sitting on the bench outside. I gave him my name, though not my business, and he went to check if the master was At Home.

He was, seemingly, and I was shown through to the study.

Mid-fifties, tall, broad, fit-looking, with strong features and short wiry grey hair going white at the temples. He wasn't alone; there were three other men with him of much the same age, all wearing senatorial broad-striper mantles.

We were in heavy company here. Bugger. Possibly *not* the time to broach the topic of an illicit love affair and an illegitimate son.

'I'm delighted to meet you, Valerius Corvinus,' Longinus said. 'Knew your father well. Fine man. Now. What can I do for you?'

'Uh . . . I'm sorry, sir,' I said. 'You're busy and it's not urgent. I'll call again later when you're alone.'

I half-turned to follow the slave back out, but his hand grasped my shoulder.

'Nonsense, my dear fellow, I wouldn't hear of it!' he said, letting the shoulder go and patting it. 'And my friends certainly won't mind. They only called to welcome me back to Rome. Here.' He pulled up a spare stool. 'Sit yourself down.'

Hell. 'Really, sir, I'd rather—'

'Sit!' I sat. 'I'm forgetting my manners. Julius Graecinus, Anicius Cerialis and Valerius Asiaticus. No relation of yours, I hasten to add. Hails from Gaul originally, poor devil.'

As, from the looks of him, did Graecinus: they both had typically Gallic fair complexions and the tell-tale reddish hair. Cerialis, on the other hand, was pure upper-class Roman. I nodded, and they nodded back. Pretty frostily, I thought. Despite what Longinus had said, they didn't look too pleased at the interruption.

'Right, Corvinus. I'm fully at your service,' Longinus said. 'Fire away.'

'Ah . . . it's about the death of Naevius Surdinus,' I said. 'He was your consular colleague, ten years back?'

'Yes, indeed he was. And before that a good friend of long standing.' Longinus frowned. 'Terrible thing, that accident. Terrible. What a way to go. Poor old Lucius.'

'It wasn't an accident, sir. He was murdered. I'm, uh, looking into it as a favour to his niece, Naevia Postuma.'

Now, I have to be very careful about the next bit. There was shock, yes, that was to be expected. But I had the distinct feeling that there was something else, a stillness and a sharpening of interest, like the atmosphere in the room had changed somehow. Trouble was I couldn't tell where it originated; it could've been with any one of them, or with all four. All I knew was that it was there.

'You're joking,' Longinus said.

'No, there's no mistake. The evidence is quite clear. He was killed deliberately.'

'Have you any idea who did it?'

'Who the actual killer was, yes. One of the garden slaves saw a freedman coming from the direction of the tower at about the right time, and acting suspiciously. A middle-aged guy with a scar or a birthmark on his left cheek.' I shrugged. 'That's more or less all I know at present. Who organized the murder and why, well, your guess is as good as mine.'

'Sweet holy Jupiter!' Longinus was staring at me. 'So how can I help you? I haven't seen Lucius since I left for Asia almost a year ago. And not for a good two months before then, either.'

This was the tricky bit. 'Uh . . . it's rather personal, sir. I think perhaps we'd better talk in private.' I turned to the others. 'No offence, gentlemen.'

'Nonsense, Corvinus. I'm sure you can't ask me any questions that I'd be embarrassed to answer. And Graecinus here was a very close friend of Lucius's as well.' Yeah; now he happened to mention it, I remembered that Leonidas, the estate manager, had given a Julius Graecinus as one of Surdinus's bosom philosopher mates. 'You carry on, my dear fellow; ask away. Anything I can tell you I will, and gladly.'

Well, he'd had his chance. Even so, I wasn't looking forward to this. 'I understand you'd been friendly with the family for a long time, sir.'

'That's right. I told you, for thirty years and more. Lucius and I were quaestors together, cut our political teeth on the same teething ring, you might say. We've kept up the friendship ever since.'

'I, ah, don't mean just with Naevius Surdinus. I mean with the family as a whole.' Jupiter! 'Specifically with Surdinus's wife, Cornelia Sullana.'

That got me a straight look. 'Corvinus, just exactly what are you saying?' Longinus snapped.

I was beginning to sweat. Easy this wasn't, and I could see now how the guy had got to the top of the senatorial appointments tree. Cassius Longinus, for all his good-old-boy manner – or maybe because of it – was no pussycat. I'd imagine he and his great grandfather would've had a lot more in common than just their names.

'I was told that, uh, the two of you had an affair,' I said. 'Some twenty-five years back. Maybe a bit more.'

He was goggling at me. I didn't dare even look at the other three.

Then he laughed.

'Who the hell told you that?' he said.

'Actually, it was the lady herself. Cornelia Sullana. It isn't true?'

'Have you *met* the woman, Corvinus? She has a face like a hatchet and a voice like a bloody saw! Of course it isn't bloody true!'

'But . . .'

'Look, get this through your head once and for all, here and now. I can't stand bloody Cornelia Sullana. Never could. Pompous, overbred, whining. I'd no more take her into my bed than I would my farm bailiff's prize sow. The gods know why Lucius married her in the first place. Oh, she'd name and money, yes; in that sense she was a good catch, but he never liked her. And I was quite definitely his friend, not hers.'

'Then why should she claim you had an affair when you didn't?'

'I haven't the faintest idea. You'd best ask her.' He got up. 'And now if that's all you came for, my dear fellow, we'll call the visit at an end, shall we? Nice of you to come. You can find your own way out, can't you?'

Gods!

FIFTEEN

I t was still a long way from dinner when I got back to the Caelian, and Perilla was working in her study. Or, at least, she had a book-roll open and was taking notes.

'Oh, hello, Marcus,' she said absently. 'Just a moment. I want to get this down first.' I waited while she scribbled a line or two on the note tablet beside her then laid the stylus aside. 'There we are.'

'What's the book?' I said. Not that I was really interested, but it's always politic for a man to show an interest in his wife's little hobbies. Besides, we were on her territory here. Unfortunately. Being in Perilla's study always makes me nervous. Oh, sure, studies should have a book-cubby or two included, no argument, that's what they're for – at least for appearances' sake. But not a good dozen of the buggers stacked full of books whose titles make your eyes water. Particularly when they're there for more than decoration.

'Aristarchus of Samothrace's recension of the "Iliad". Julia Procula lent it to me.'

'Is that so, now?' I paused. 'Uh . . . what the hell's a recension?'

'Oh, Marcus! A critical revision. Sort of . . . well, a bit like cleaning the accumulated grime off a painting and restoring it to its original appearance. Removing all the interpretations and amendments made by later scholars operating on premises based on what was, to them, contemporary usage and getting back to what the author really *meant*. Aristarchus works on the principle that you can only understand what an ancient writer is saying by interpreting the words or sentiments by comparison with other, similar passages in the author's own works, and not by anachronistic reference to present import. Or, of course, with passages in the works of his contemporaries, should these exist. Fascinating!'

'Ah . . . yeah. Yeah.' Jupiter alive! Well, I had asked.

'For instance, did you realize that for Homer the word *phobos* didn't mean "fear" but "rout", as in rout in battle? And the verb *phobeisthai* meant to flee, to be routed?'

'Uh, actually, no. No, strange as it may seem, that one must've slipped past me, lady.'

She grinned, put the note tablet inside the roll to mark her place, laid the book on the table beside her, and sat back. 'Very well, dear. So, how did your day go? I'm all ears.'

I sat down on the other couch, cradling the cup of wine Bathyllus had given me when I'd got back. 'We were right about Tarquitia and Hellenus,' I said. 'They cooked up the scam between them. Or at least Hellenus set things up originally and Tarquitia took it from there.' I told her about the visit to the Old Villa.

'But that's terrible!' she said. 'They ought to be stopped! Isn't there anything you can do?'

'Uh-uh. They haven't broken any laws, they were careful about that. As far as the original property sales were concerned, everything was done in due legal form, with Surdinus's consent all the way down the line. The same goes for Tarquitia's resale of the Old Villa to Surdinus Junior; she was the legal owner, and so long as he was willing to pay the asking price, she could charge what she liked. The will's legal, too, so Hellenus gets his third of the estate and because she's already fulfilled the marriage clause, she has the fifty thousand clear to do as she likes with.'

'At least she's giving that to Otillius. I feel very sorry for him, Marcus.'

'Don't be.' I took a swallow of the wine. 'The guy's had a lucky escape, and if he is genuinely in love with her, he'll get over it. Fifty thousand sesterces is one hell of an incentive.'

'You think she and Hellenus will marry? Really?'

'Yeah. I think they probably will. Oh, sure, they're crooked as they come, both of them, but they go together like fish sauce on beans. And for all they've got a cold streak a mile wide, I think they're honest by their lights. At least, they'd claim to be. In theory, Tarquitia could walk away from the guy with the whole boiling, but I don't think she will, because she knew exactly what she wanted and she's already got it.' I shrugged. 'Anyway, they're out of it. For the foreseeable future, at least.'

'So what about Cassius Longinus? Did you manage to see him?'

'Yeah.' I frowned. 'That was strange, if you like.'

'How so?'

'He claimed the affair with Sullana never happened at all.'

'Interesting. You believe him?'

'Perilla, I don't know. On the one hand, the lady said it did. Unprompted. Why should she invent a thing like that?'

'Where her husband's concerned, the answer's obvious. Like she told you, she'd been trying to get him to divorce her for years, and he wouldn't agree. Confessing to an affair with one of his closest friends might well do the trick, as indeed it did.'

'Surely he'd've checked with the man first? Confronted him in his turn?'

'Marcus, how could he? Longinus was in Asia at the time, and as far as anyone knew, he might be kept in office for years. Governors frequently are, and they're forbidden to leave their provinces without formal permission from the emperor. Besides, if Surdinus's wife confessed to him, out of the blue and unprompted, that she'd committed adultery at some time in the past, why should he disbelieve her? Particularly when their marriage had never been a happy one. Personally, if it was an invention, I think it was an extremely clever one; Sullana picked on someone who was not only a prime possibility in circumstantial terms but whom she knew wasn't in a position to give her the lie. You'd never have known Longinus's side of things if he hadn't been unexpectedly recalled to Rome. And as for repeating to you the lie she told her husband, if Sullana wasn't aware of the current situation – and there's no reason why she should be, since his return is so recent – then the same argument applies. She could be perfectly truthful and at the same time perfectly safe from being found out.'

'She'd've been found out eventually, when Longinus's term expired and he came back to Rome, lady. By Surdinus, I mean, if he'd still been alive and believed his friend over her.'

'Of course she would. But that wouldn't matter, because she'd already have her divorce. My guess is that then she'd simply have told Surdinus the truth, that the whole thing was a fabrication. I mean, what could he do about it? And naturally Longinus himself would be completely off the hook.'

Yeah; fair enough. Even so . . .

'Even so,' I said, 'the guy couldn't wait to get rid of me. That's after welcoming me with open arms.'

'Are you surprised, dear? You'd just accused him in front of friends of seducing the wife of a friend and colleague, not to mention siring her first child. Don't you think, whether the accusation was well-founded or not, he might be just a little peeved?'

'Hang on, lady! I hadn't actually got round to Surdinus Junior. He never let me get that far.'

'Nonetheless.'

'In any case, that wasn't the *really* interesting part of the interview.' I told her about the change of atmosphere when I'd said I was looking into Surdinus's murder. 'That was weird. There's something going on there, I'd bet my back teeth.'

'Who were the men? Do you remember?'

'They were all broad-stripers. Pretty much Longinus's age and class.' I thought for a moment. 'A couple of Gauls . . . uh, Julius Graecinus and Valerius Asiaticus. The third was a guy called Anicius Cerialis. Graecinus is a philosopher pal of Surdinus's, that I know, although whether it's relevant I can't say. The other two I've never heard of. Any bells?'

'I know Graecinus, at least. More than just his name, I mean: he's a philosopher, yes, Stoic, you won't be surprised to learn, and a good friend of Marcus Vinicius's.' Yeah, right: I knew Vinicius, or at least I'd met him. One of the lady's more high-powered literary acquaintances, and despite the fact that he was the husband of the emperor's sister Livilla, he was pretty human on the whole. 'We've talked at one or two of Vinicius's get-togethers. Charming man, very intelligent.'

'Solid?'

'If you're implying, could he possibly be the kind of man who would arrange for a block of masonry to be dropped on a friend's head, Marcus, then he certainly is no such thing. That sort of person, I mean. Absolutely not.'

I grinned. 'OK. What about the others?'

'I can't help you there at all, dear; I've never heard of either of them. I know Longinus himself, of course – or at least I did, very slightly, before he went to Asia, again on the literary side of things, although his prime interest is jurisprudence. He's a recognized expert, with several technical books to his credit. Rather an old-fashioned man, with old-fashioned values.' She smiled. 'That isn't a criticism, by the way, far from it; he's a practising Stoic, in the best sense of the word. Our republican ancestors would have loved him, and for the right reasons, which makes a change.'

'So you don't think he would've dropped a hunk of stone on a friend's head either.'

'No. Definitely not. Nor, for that matter, carried on a clandestine affair with his wife, even when invited to do so by the lady in question. I told you as much when you originally suggested it. The idea's completely ridiculous.'

Bugger. Well, the lady had been wrong before in her assessment of character. Not all that often, mind. We'd just have to see. And there were still the other two to check up on, Asiaticus and Cerialis. I reckoned another visit to Secundus was in order.

There was a respectful knock at the door. Only one person knocks like that.

'Yeah, Bathyllus,' I said. 'Come in, we're decent.'

He did.

'I'm sorry to disturb you, sir. Madam,' he said. 'But a message has just arrived. From Naevius Surdinus.'

'Uh . . . that'd be Surdinus Junior, would it?' I said. Given Naevia Postuma's wacky spiritual interests, it was just as well to check these things.

Bathyllus gave me his best fish-eyed stare; humour is something that the little guy does not believe in. 'Yes, sir,' he said. 'Of course. Naturally. He was wondering if you could drop by tomorrow. Whenever is convenient, but the morning would be best. He has something important to tell you.'

Hey! Maybe things were moving after all. One of his bought help might even have identified our mystery freedman. Although if that was the case then it cast serious doubts on Junior being responsible for the murder himself. Still, we'd cross that bridge when we came to it.

'He supply any more details?' I said.

'No, sir. That was the message in its entirety.' The barest of sniffs: the implication being, of course, that had there been any Bathyllus would bloody well have told me them up front. Yeah, well, fair enough. 'And Meton says that since you're back earlier than usual he is prepared as a great personal favour to bring dinner forwards. Should you prefer it.'

'Good idea, pal. Tell him yes, that'd be great.' Early though it was, I'd covered a fair stretch of Rome that day on foot with

nothing since breakfast but a sesame-seed roll, and I was starving.
'OK with you, lady?'

'Certainly.'

'In about an hour, then, sir.' He went out.

So I'd have to take another long hike up to the Vatican. I was
getting my fair share of exercise on this case, and no mistake.
Still, I wasn't grousing.

This looked promising.

SIXTEEN

I was off and away fairly bright and early the next morning,
except that this time I made sure I had a decent breakfast
inside me first. Normally, unlike Perilla, who can really
sink it, I don't bother much beyond a roll dipped in olive oil,
but this time I had Bathyllus rustle me up a three-egg omelette
stuffed with mushrooms, plus a bit of cheese and a couple of
apples from the store to take with me for later. The weather
wasn't too bad – evidently, fortunately, we'd hit a compar-
atively dry spell, although the sky was pretty overcast – and
the temperature was a bit on the chilly side, but fine for
walking.

So. What did Junior want to see me about? Not to confess to
the murder in a sudden fit of abject guilt and remorse, I was sure
of that, and I reckoned we'd all drawn a line under the Tarquitia
business. Personally, I suspected that although it'd cost him an
arm and a leg in the end, he'd simply be relieved to see the back
of her and his brother and get on with his everyday boring life.
And, looking on the bright side of things, foreign travel was
always a risky business. There was always the chance that, when
he did set out on his eastern tour, Hellenus would be lost at sea
or get himself fatally pirated. I couldn't see that causing too
much grief in the family.

So there wasn't much left for him to tell me about. I was
really, *really* keeping my fingers crossed that he'd found our
freedman friend. If so, then how he'd managed it I didn't know,
but with Cilix having provided a description and the bought-help

network on to it, that was at least a possibility. And if we were going to crack the case, then finding the guy was crucial.

I crossed the river at the Sublician and made my way through the immediate built-up area towards the Janiculum and the open countryside. By the time I'd reached it and taken a right along the road to Vatican Hill, what with the increased gradient I was sweating; now the sun was properly up it was beginning to feel positively warm, and the sky was clearing fast. Well, I needn't've bothered bringing my cloak, need I? I took it off, removed an apple from the inside pocket, bundled it up and tucked it under my arm.

I'd only gone a couple of hundred yards further when three men came out of the bushes ahead and fanned out across the road, waiting for me. Two of them – the ones at the sides – had knives in their hands, and the guy in the centre was hefting a nail-studded club.

Shit; muggers, in Rome, don't usually work during daylight hours, but of course out here in the wilds there was no reason why they shouldn't put in a bit of overtime. And they'd chosen their spot well: no villas in sight on this stretch, with inconvenient gate guards who might decide to step in and spoil the fun, while the chances of another pedestrian turning up and complicating matters were practically zilch.

I reached for my purse, unfastened it from my belt, and threw it towards them.

'OK, guys,' I said, 'you've got me fair and square. Drinks are on me. Enjoy.'

The man with the club grinned and took a step forwards. The other two followed him. None of them had even glanced at the purse. I felt a chill run down the back of my neck.

'Fuck that for now, Corvinus,' he said. 'We'll leave it until after you're dead. Right, boys.'

They moved forwards again; not quickly, but like they had all the time in the world and meant to enjoy themselves. The guys on the wings moved slightly further out to cut me off if I made a dash to one side. They were professionals, I could tell that from the relaxed, confident manner and the way they held their weapons. All in a day's work, then.

Fuck. Double fuck. Running wasn't an option, since they'd be on me before I'd got five yards; I'd no knife myself, and the ground round about was spectacularly empty of hefty branches that I could use as a club of my own, or at least to fend them off with. The best I could do was wrap my cloak round my left arm as a shield and trust to luck . . .

Something whirred past me two or three feet to my left, and the guy on that side went down like a poleaxed ox, his forehead, suddenly, a pulped mess of blood and bone. The other two stopped, complete astonishment on their faces. Me, I must've looked the same.

There was another whirring sound, this time to my right. The other knifeman jerked backwards, slumped to his knees and slowly collapsed. The left-hand side of his face had gone, and I could see his cheekbone protruding through the mangled flesh.

Chummie with the club glanced sideways at him, then shouted and launched himself at me. I threw the apple I was holding straight into his face, and he flinched and ducked; not much of a movement, but the distraction had been enough to break his stride and his speed and let me get inside his guard. I got in one good punch to the throat and a not-so-good one, with my cloak-wrapped left hand, to his chest, then wrapped my arms round him and pitched myself forwards. He went down with my full weight on his ribs, and I heard the thud as the back of his head hit the gravelled roadway. He slumped unconscious.

I stood up, breathing hard, and looked round. A big guy, easily six foot four and built to match, was coming towards me. There was a sling tied to his wrist, and a shot-pouch plus an efficient-looking knife attached to his belt.

'Thanks, pal,' I said. 'You arrived just in the nick of time.'

He ignored me, and without even a glance at the two dead men reached down and hefted my live one into a sitting position. Then, still without speaking, he knelt behind him, took a firm hold of his head with both hands, and gave it a sudden twist to the side. I heard the neck-bone snap.

The slinger let go of the body and stood up.

I'd been watching in horror.

'What the fuck did you do that for?' I said.

'It's neater that way.' He unfastened his sling and put it in the pouch.

'I'd got the bastard cold,' I said. 'He wasn't going anywhere. The other two, fair enough, but that was murder.' He shrugged and began to walk away back the way he'd come. 'Hey! Come on! We need to report this!' No answer; he didn't even slow down. 'I need your name, for a start!'

I was talking to his back, and for all the reaction I got he could've been stone deaf.

Shit.

Well, at least I was alive, which was something that I wouldn't have bet on five minutes ago. I lugged the three corpses off the road and into the undergrowth; you can't have bodies promiscuously impeding the public highway and, like I'd said, I'd be reporting the whole thing to the local Watch commander on my way back, so no doubt they'd be cleared up eventually. I'd had a good look at their faces in the process, to check for birthmarks. The club man and the guy who'd been on my left and got it in the forehead were clean, but of course I couldn't tell where the one on my right was concerned because the whole left cheek was missing. I hadn't noticed any distinguishing marks while he was a viable entity, sure, but there again at that point I'd had other things to occupy my attention.

Once they were decently housed, I picked up my fallen purse, reattached it to my belt, and carried on up the road.

I was thinking hard. They'd been no ordinary muggers, that was obvious: muggers don't usually bother to learn the names of their victims beforehand, and unless they're complete headbangers (it does happen), they're usually quite grateful when the punter surrenders with good grace and without giving them any trouble. I mean, why piss the Watch off more than you need to? And zeroing a purple-striper unnecessarily really tends to get you noticed.

So they'd been waiting for me, presumably because they'd been paid to. The first big question, of course, was who by? And, equally of course, the answer was obvious. The only person who'd known I'd be out in the wilds of Transtiber this morning, because he'd arranged it himself, was Surdinus Junior.

When I got to the villa I'd nail his fucking hide to the door.

The other big question was who was my pal with the sling? Not a passer-by, obviously: you don't get many passers-by on the west side of the Janiculan Hill. When you do, they don't carry slings loaded with seriously injurious military-grade lead shot, and they don't break unconscious men's necks for them with no more compunction than a priest killing a pigeon. Plus there was the fact that he'd appeared out of nowhere; there hadn't been anyone on the road behind me, that I knew, because I'd turned round a couple of times on the straighter stretches just to see if I'd got any company. So he'd been tailing me, keeping out of sight, probably off-road, which wouldn't've been difficult, given the terrain. As to why, or who for, or how the hell he knew I'd be out this way, I hadn't the faintest idea.

Not that I wasn't grateful, mind.

I reached the villa, and this time I went straight to the main entrance.

'The master's in his study, sir,' the door slave said. 'If you'd like to wait a moment I'll have someone take you.'

Bought-help number two led me through the labyrinth; not upstairs this time, but to a room on the ground floor at the back, overlooking a small garden. Surdinus Junior was there, sitting behind a desk, talking to Leonidas, the estate manager. They both looked up as I came in.

'Valerius Corvinus!' Junior said. 'This is a surprise!'

'Yeah, it probably is, at that.' I nodded my thanks to the slave as he went out. 'Because I should be lying by the roadside somewhere between here and the Janiculan with either my throat cut or my head bashed in, right?'

'*What?*' He was staring at me.

'Come on, pal! You set me up. You sent me a message saying you wanted to talk to me this morning and then you had your tame thugs lie in wait to take me out.'

Surdinus turned back to Leonidas, who was looking on open-mouthed.

'You can go, Leonidas,' he snapped. 'We'll deal with the rest later.' The little Sicilian got up, gathered together the pile of wax tablets on the desk in front of him and moved to the door; never taking his eyes off me, and edging past like I was some sort of dangerous wild animal. The door closed behind him. 'Corvinus, I sent you no message.'

'Is that so, now?'

'Certainly it is. What would I want to talk to you about? I gave you all the information that I had last time we met.'

'Yeah, well, that side of things wouldn't matter, would it? Because I shouldn't've got this far. And when the question of the message was raised you could tell whoever asked it just that; that it hadn't come from you.'

He was almost purple with anger. 'For the last time, and I give you my solemn word on this, *I did not send you any message!* Now what's this about an attack?'

I frowned. Well, it could be an act, of course, but if it was it was a bloody good one. And I didn't think Surdinus Junior – unlike his brother – had either the nous or the panache to brazen something like this out successfully. Still, if it wasn't him, then who was it?

'There were three of them,' I said. 'Professionals. They'd've had me, too, if I hadn't had a bit of unexpected help.'

'We do get the occasional footpad out here.' He was calming down now, losing his colour. 'But not often during the day. This is disgraceful; the Watch are lax, very lax. When I'm appointed as a city judge I shall certainly make it my business to look into the problem.'

'They weren't robbers,' I said. 'They weren't interested in my purse. All they wanted was to kill me. And they knew my name.'

That got me another stare. 'I beg your pardon?'

'I told you. I was set up. Presumably by whoever sent the message. I don't suppose you have any idea who that might have been?'

'No, of course not. None whatsoever.'

'Uh-huh. Ah . . . one last question, pal, before I go and let you get on with things. Four names. Cassius Longinus. Julius Graecinus. Valerius Asiaticus. Anicius Cerialis. Any bells?'

'Of course. They're all senators. Longinus is – was, I suppose, now the emperor has recalled him to Rome – the Asian governor. Graecinus is currently a praetor. Asiaticus is from Narbonese Gaul; he's a consular, suffect consul five years back. Cerialis – well, nothing special. A bit of an also-ran, really.'

'They all friends of your father's?'

'Longinus and Graecinus, certainly. Intimate friends, you could say. The other two, no, not at all. He'd know them, naturally, as I do, but you couldn't call them friends by any stretch of the imagination.'

'Enemies, then?'

'Good gods, no! That's not what I meant at all! Simply that

he had no particular dealings with them, of any nature.' He was frowning. 'Corvinus, what is this about?'

I shrugged. 'Probably nothing. But I thought I'd ask. I'm sorry for the interruption. I'll see you around.' I half-turned to go, then paused. 'How're your brother and his girlfriend doing, by the way?'

He stiffened. 'Well, I assume. But now our business is done we have no further contact. Or are likely to have in future.'

'Fine, fine.' I grinned. Cheeky, sure, and completely unwarranted, but I hadn't been able to resist it. 'Thank you, Naevius Surdinus. Don't disturb yourself, I'll find my own way out.'

'The slave will be waiting out of earshot.'

'Great,' I said, and left.

Back to the centre, with a brief stop-off at the Fourteenth District Watch house. To the Palatine this time, for another word with Gaius Secundus, if he wasn't too busy, regarding the senatorial quartet. If the set-up hadn't been Surdinus Junior's doing – and I'd be very surprised, now, if it had been – then one or all of these guys was in the frame: it couldn't be coincidence that I'd been attacked practically right after I'd mentioned to them that I was investigating Surdinus's death and knew, in essence, who to look for as the actual perp. Someone, somewhere, didn't want things to go any further.

Why any of them would want to kill a quiet-living man like Naevius Surdinus, mind, I couldn't think.

Still, you can't make tiles without clay. We'd have to start by finding out as much as we could about the buggers, and see if anything gelled. With luck, Secundus would be able to help there, and I was sure he'd be amenable enough. Besides, I owed him a half-jug of Massic.

There was still the matter of the phantom slinger (by the gods, there was!) but he, like the birthmarked freedman, was currently a piece of the puzzle with no context. No doubt that'd come in time; I could only work with what I'd got.

I set off back to the Sublician Bridge and the Palatine.

SEVENTEEN

Secundus, it turned out, was free, and like he'd said, being the boss had certain perks, so we adjourned to a corner table in Tasso's. I ordered up the Massic and a plate of nibbles, and hit him with the four names. He asked me the same question Surdinus Junior had asked.

'What's this all about, Marcus?'

I shrugged and gave him the same answer. 'Probably nothing. Even so, I need some background here, pal. Anything you can do to help?'

'Well.' He settled down with his cup of wine. 'Longinus you already know about, I've nothing to add there. Appointed Asian governor just under a year ago, been back here for less than half a month.'

'And you've no idea why he was recalled.'

'No. I told you. The emperor gave the order personally, and if he didn't care to offer a reason, that was his privilege. There was nothing obvious, though, at least as far as I know; like I said, Longinus seemed to be doing a good job, and he'd kept his nose clean. He's well-connected, too; his brother Lucius was married to Julia Drusilla.' Gaius's favourite sister – dead, now, these two years. 'He's a pretty straight-down-the-line guy, Longinus. But of course, if you've met him, you'll know that.'

'Yeah.' He'd given that impression, anyway, and it chimed with Perilla's opinion of him. Still, I'd've liked to know why he'd had his governorship revoked. I had my suspicions, sure, but that was all they could be without hard confirmation from an external source. 'What about the others? Graecinus, for example?'

'I don't know much more about him than you probably do.' Secundus took an olive from the dish. 'He's from Narbonensine Gaul originally; Fréjus, to be exact. This is his first year in the senate, as one of the foreign judges. Again, from what I hear he's pretty straight. A bit too straight for his own good, perhaps.'

'How do you mean?'

'You remember Junius Silanus?'

'Sure I do.' Gaius's erstwhile father-in-law and advisor, who'd been charged with treason three years before and forced into suicide.

'Word is' – and here Secundus glanced around and lowered his voice; I remembered the last time we'd talked – 'Caesar wanted Graecinus to handle the prosecution, and he wouldn't do it. Silanus was a personal friend, he said, and it went against his principles. Not many people have the guts, or maybe you'd call it the stupidity, to say no to the emperor, but that's just what the guy did. Didn't make any difference in the end to Silanus, of course, but Graecinus had blotted his copybook good and proper. A lot of people were surprised he was even allowed to run for praetor after that, but evidently the emperor's decided to forgive and forget after all.'

Uh-huh. I was beginning to get a glimmer of something here, not that where Surdinus's murder was concerned it made any kind of sense. And it definitely wasn't the sort of glimmer I wanted to see being encouraged.

'Asiaticus,' I said.

'Another Narbonese Gaul, from Vienne. Family's big among the Allobroges, which is the local tribe. Quite a trailblazer in his day; he was the first Narbonesian to make it as far as the consulship. That was five years ago; suffect, sure, but even so. Since then, a bit like Surdinus, he's tended to stay out of things, which is fair enough, because he's already rich as hell – he owns the villa and gardens that once belonged to old Lucullus – and very well-connected socially. Or at least he was; his wife's Lollia Saturnina, Paulina's sister.' Gaius's third wife, married four years before but divorced six months later. 'He's still well in with the emperor, though. Or again, so I believe. I've heard nothing to the contrary, anyway. And he's also pretty thick with the Claudians, for what that's worth. He's been a close friend of Caesar's Uncle Claudius for years.'

Shit; we were certainly moving in high society here. Which fitted, unfortunately. I was beginning to get a very bad feeling about this. 'OK,' I said. 'Last one. Anicius Cerialis.'

'Can't tell you much there, I'm afraid. I know the name, and I might even be able to fit a face to it at a pinch, but that's about all. Oh, he's a senator all right, but he's pretty much a

backbencher. Certainly nothing special.' The same phrase as
Junior had used. Obviously not someone who got himself noticed,
was Anicius Cerialis. 'I'm sorry, Marcus, but if you want to know
anything beyond the surface stuff, you'll have to ask someone
more qualified.'

I'd been beginning to think that myself. As a likely if probably
reluctant informant, my muckraking acquaintance Caelius Crispus
came to mind.

'That's OK, Gaius,' I said. 'Don't worry about it. You've helped
me a lot. Thanks.'

Secundus grunted, picked up his cup and, instead of drinking,
turned it round and round in both hands and set it down again.

'Marcus,' he said finally. 'Level with me, right? Is this thing
getting political?'

Bugger; he might be slow, but like I said, Gaius Secundus was
by no means thick. I crossed my fingers, hoped like hell I wasn't
lying, and said: ''Course not. Why should it be? It's just a
straightforward murder enquiry, that's all.'

'Only the situation's changed these past few months.' He
lowered his voice again, so I had to lean right forward just to
hear him. 'I told you. About the emperor. You can't take anything
for granted now, and all the bets are off. Messing around with
politics, shoving your nose in and asking too many questions,
it's just not safe any more. You get me?'

I grinned. 'Has it ever been?'

He didn't grin back. 'A hell of a lot safer than it is at present,
boy, I'll tell you that,' he said. 'You can get hurt, seriously hurt,
maybe even fatally if you *really* step out of line. You remember
the Sejanus years, don't you? Well, read my lips, because I know
what I'm talking about: this is fucking worse.'

I could feel the icy knot forming in my gut, but I forced myself
to hold the grin. 'Come on, pal!' I said, topping up our cups.
'That's enough! Lighten up and forget it! Tell me all about Furia
Gemella's temporary successors.'

We shot the breeze for another half hour or so and finished
the wine and most of the nibbles, by which time Secundus had to
get back to running the empire.

Yeah, well, I thought, as I chewed on the last olive, since I
was in this part of town anyway I might as well go the whole
hog, get it over with and pay that call on Caelius Crispus at the

foreign judges' office. See what dirty linen my four possibles were hiding under the bed. If any.

I hadn't liked the sound of Secundus's warning about the dangers of furkling around in the grey areas of current politics, mind. I hadn't liked it at all. Unfortunately, and *pace* what I'd told him, I had a very strong suspicion that was the way this case was going.

Things, to put it mildly, were *not* looking good.

'Oh, shit,' Crispus sighed as the public slave who'd taken me to his office opened the door and stood aside for me to pass. 'What is it this time?'

'Hi, Crispus,' I said, as the slave closed the door behind me. 'How's the boy?' Then I noticed the purple stripe on his squeaky-clean mantle. 'You're an *equestrian*?'

'As of a few days ago, yes, as it happens. The emperor has graciously agreed to my elevation to that rank.'

Gods! The whole fabric of society was beginning to unravel. If I needed any more proof that Gaius was completely out of his tree, then this was it. Yet another rung of the ladder – and not an inconsiderable one – achieved in the slimy bastard's climb towards social respectability and, indeed, eminence. Or maybe another few inches on the greasy pole would be putting it better.

'Congratulations,' I said.

'Thank you,' he said. He picked up a stylus from the desk. 'Now, I'm extremely busy, Corvinus. Please state your business in as few words as possible so I can tell you to fuck off out of my life.'

I went over to the desk, pulled up a stool, and sat down.

'Come on, sunshine!' I said. 'Is that any way to treat an old friend and neighbour?'

'Neighbour?'

'More or less. Of the family, anyway. How're you enjoying your new property?' The year before, Crispus had bought a villa in the Alban Hills not far from Castrimoenium, where our adopted daughter Marilla and her husband Clarus lived. 'You been down there recently?'

'Not recently, no. Pressure of work, you understand.' He cleared his throat. 'I am, however, giving a select house party at the Winter Festival. My superior in the office and his lady wife have kindly indicated their willingness to be the guests of honour, and I have also prevailed upon several professional acquaintances within the senate to attend. It should be quite a lavish affair.' Absently, his fingers brushed the stripe on his mantle, and he beamed. 'Somewhat of a personal triumph, in fact.'

'Hey, you know, pal' – I crossed my legs – 'that is *really* a coincidence, because we'll be in Castrimoenium for the festival again this year ourselves. Perilla and me, I mean.'

The beam disappeared. 'No!'

'But yes! Long-standing invite. Our daughter and her husband have a baby due around that time, and naturally Perilla wants to be on the spot when it's born. Me too. First grandchild and all, big occasion.' All, by the way, perfectly true: according to Clarus – and as a doctor he should know – the kid was due on the first day of the festival itself, and we'd arranged to be there a few days in advance and stay for the duration. 'Maybe we could drop in on you and your friends. Just to say hello and wish them Happy Festival.'

Crispus was definitely pale now, and licking his lips nervously. 'Look, Corvinus,' he said. 'We had an agreement, right? When we talked last December, you promised that you and that wife of yours wouldn't come anywhere near me. Particularly when I had company.'

'Well, that was last December, wasn't it? Eleven months ago.' I gave him my best smile. 'It wouldn't be polite to ignore you altogether, would it, pal? And I'm sure your guests wouldn't mind, because after all you and me go way back. They might even be interested to hear a few personal anecdotes in that regard. I'd keep them clean, of course.' I paused. 'Reasonably clean, anyway. As clean as possible, certainly. Where and when I could.'

He was staring at me in horror.

'Corvinus, you *bastard*! You complete and utter *bastard*!'

'Well, we'll see,' I said. 'What with everything else going on, we may not be able to spare the time. In any case, that's all by the way. I was wondering if you could help me with some information here.'

Pause. Long pause. Eventually, he said suspiciously: 'What kind of information?'

I uncrossed my legs and gave him another sunny smile. 'Nothing complicated,' I said. 'Just the kind of thing that you do so well, and I really would be most awfully grateful.' Smarm, smarm. 'Simple background stuff, on four members of the senate.' I gave him the names.

'This is blackmail.'

'Sure it is. Of the blackest kind. No arguments there.'

'You promise you'll come nowhere near my house party?'

'Absolutely. See it wet, see it dry.'

'And you'll stay well clear of me in future?'

'Come on, pal, be fair, I'm not promising that! One sale for one payment. Call it insurance, if you like. Besides, admit it, you'd miss the little frisson you get sharing some of the dirty little secrets you've come across, wouldn't you? You don't get much chance any more now you've become respectable.'

He didn't actually smile, but his lips twitched a fraction. Yeah, well, it had to be tough for someone like Crispus to play the establishment game, life decision or not. Sure, he always complained like hell about being held over a barrel, but I had more than a sneaking suspicion that it was largely for appearances' sake: the truth was he was a born gossip-monger, and the dirtier the linen he could pull out of the basket for display, the better he liked it. His sharp civil servant's mantle with – now – its purple stripe were just the surface covering for the metaphorical ragged underpants beneath.

'All right, Corvinus,' he sighed. 'Where would you like me to start?'

'With Longinus. Why was he recalled, do you know?'

'Because the emperor's tame fortune teller told him he should be careful of a man called Cassius.'

I blinked. '*What?* You mean that's all? Longinus was hauled all the way back to Rome just on the word of a fucking *fortune teller?*'

'So I'm told.'

'No proof of any sort of guilt or malfeasance whatsoever? Zero? Zilch?'

'Not that I'm aware of.' He shrugged. 'You asked, Corvinus. That's your answer. At least, it's the only one I can provide.'

Jupiter! Gaius had to be out of his tree right enough. Still, it fitted in with what Secundus had told me: we weren't talking rational here any longer. Which was seriously worrying on all counts.

'He, uh, wouldn't've been involved in an affair with a Cornelia Sullana at one time, would he?' I said. 'Longinus, I mean?'

'Again, not that I know of. And I think it's very unlikely.'

Yeah, well; that shot that one right out of the water, anyway: if Crispus went to the lengths of adding *it's very unlikely* to *not that I know of*, then we were in flying pigs territory.

'OK. Fine. Moving on. Julius Graecinus.'

'Close friend of Junius Silanus. Refused point-blank the emperor's request to undertake the prosecution.'

'Yeah, I knew that. Gaius was seriously pissed off, right?'

'*Caesar* –' Crispus emphasized the word – 'was most definitely not pleased, and stayed so. Graecinus, however, is an extremely able man, and the fact that he's an outsider, Gallic, largely self-made and with no political axes to grind, has made him quite a few friends in the senate. They persuaded the emperor, last year, not to oppose his appointment as praetor.'

'Uh-huh. So no apology from him personally, then?'

'No. I'm afraid that Julius Graecinus' – a sniff – 'is a man of principle.'

Not a positive phrase, that, in Crispus's vocabulary; it had the force of 'complete political no-brain with probable suicidal tendencies'. Which, I supposed, was fair enough, really.

'How about Anicius Cerialis?' I said.

'Frustrated wannabe, with as much flair for politics as a newt. Known in government circles, in as much as he's known at all, as the Tongue.'

'Ah . . . the Tongue? We talking sexual proclivities here?'

'Oh, no! For completely different reasons. Cerialis has only got as far as he has through gross flattery of the emperor. Emperors, I should say, as I'm including Tiberius. That's "gross" even by senatorial standards.' Gods! 'Mind you, up until recently it's worked quite well.'

'So what happened recently?'

'Gaius—' He stopped. 'I'm sorry, *Caesar*, promised him the suffect consulship for the second half of this year. In the event, the place went to Terentius Culleo, and Cerialis was not a happy bunny.'

Uh-huh; we were definitely seeing a pattern here.

'Last one,' I said. 'Valerius Asiaticus.'

'Ah.' Crispus smiled, like a gourmet squaring up to a plate of roast flamingo with larks' tongue sauce. 'Asiaticus is rather special.'

'In what way?'

'You know his wife Saturnina is Caesar's ex Lollia Paulina's sister? And that as a consequence they're invited to the best parties up at the palace?' I nodded. 'It seems that a few months back, Caesar, ah, developed a certain fondness for the lady.'

'You mean he's screwing her.'

'No. He *was* screwing her, only because she was putting on such a mediocre performance, he gave it up. Caesar has been pointing out this fact loudly to Asiaticus and complaining of his wife's failings on a regular basis. At the palace dinners, when the couple are both in attendance. *Compulsory* attendance.'

Ouch. 'Pattern' was right.

Fuck. Well, you took what you were given and liked it. Or, as in this case, maybe you didn't: what I was hearing was really, *really* bad news. I stood up.

'Thanks, pal,' I said. 'Very thorough and informative, as usual. I'll leave you to get on.'

'All this is strictly confidential, right, Corvinus?'

'My lips are sealed.'

'And you'll stay the hell clear of my Alban villa?'

'Of course. My word is my absolute bond. Perilla'll be seriously disappointed, mind, but—'

'*Out!*'

I left, grinning.

EIGHTEEN

So. Back home to the Caelian, for a serious think.

The lady was definitely *not* going to like this. In view of what Secundus had said about pussyfooting round the fringes of current politics, I didn't like it more than half myself. Four guys, all highly placed, all with a grudge against the emperor, couldn't be any sort of coincidence. Oh, sure, when I'd gone round to Longinus's I might've been gatecrashing that common thing in Rome, a group of senatorial soul-brothers getting together to whinge in private about how rotten the emperor had been to them and what a despicable cad the bounder was; in which case as far as I was concerned they could get on with it and do all the whingeing they liked. Even so, particularly when you factored in the arranged ambush near the Janiculan, I had a horrible suspicion that I'd stumbled into something a whole lot nastier: we were looking at treason here, or potential treason, anyway, and it had something to do with the death of Naevius Surdinus.

Not that the prognosis was total doom and gloom. For a treason plot to be a viable proposition – if this *was* a treason plot – then the guys behind it had to have something in the bank that, when push inevitably came to shove, they could lay on the table. So far, at least, I couldn't see that being the case. Oh, they were all senators, sure, but even in respect of that toothless shower they were lightweights: Graecinus was a newcomer from a no-account provincial family; Asiaticus might be a consular but he'd been out of the loop for five years; Cerialis hadn't even been able to muster the support he needed to make suffect; and after his recall, Longinus was effectively a spent coin. Asiaticus had an in with Gaius himself, certainly, but from what Crispus had told me it was more as a figure of fun than anything else. Longinus . . . well, as Asian governor with three legions under him, he might've had some military clout at one time, but even if he'd hung on to that somehow after his recall, it was very localized, and nothing when measured against the rest of Rome's armed forces.

Of course, there still remained the wild card of an assassination – taking out the emperor personally – but the chances of success there were about the same as a snowball's of making it through hell. Even given the opportunity, there'd be Gaius's Praetorian bodyguard in the assassin's way, for a start, and these buggers you do not mess with. And when they were off duty he had his personal contingent of Germans, who by reputation were an even worse proposition because they were complete head-bangers and would just *love* the chance to dice up one of the Roman master race with no comeback. So any senator stupid enough to try anything on, either in public or private, wouldn't get within five feet of his target before he was carved up six ways from nothing like a Spring Festival chicken.

No worries there, then.

Maybe . . .

Like I said, I was heading back along the Sacred Way in the direction of the Caelian. I'd just reached the junction of Fabricius Street when I felt a hand on my arm. I turned.

'Valerius Corvinus?'

'Yeah, that's me,' I said, frowning.

The guy was young, in the mid-twenties or so, with a narrow-striper tunic showing under his cloak. And he looked scared as hell.

'I'm sorry, sir,' he said. 'I've been following you, looking for a chance to . . .' He stopped, glanced behind him, then went on in a rush: 'We have to talk.'

'About what?'

'Naevius Surdinus.'

My stomach went cold. 'Sure. No problem, pal,' I said. 'There's a wine shop I know a bit further on. We can—'

'No, not now. I haven't the time, I have to get back.' He was terrified, almost gabbling.

'Back where? And who are you, exactly?'

He shook his head in a quick, nervous movement, and his hand gripped the edge of my cloak. 'Tomorrow, right? Anywhere you like, but it can't be before the seventh hour. I'll be . . . I can't come until then.'

'OK. That wine shop I mentioned. Pollex's, about a hundred yards on the right. You can't miss it.'

'I know it. Pollex's it is, an hour after noon.'

And he was gone, walking quickly back towards Market Square.

Gods. What was that about?

One thing, though. I'd noticed, when he'd turned round, the red mark between his chin and his throat; nothing permanent, not a scar or a burn, but the kind of mark made by something that's been rubbing a lot against the skin. Something, for example, such as a helmet strap. And, taking that together with his age and the narrow purple stripe on his tunic, that could only mean one thing.

My young pal was a military tribune. A Praetorian.

Shit.

Perilla was in the atrium when I got back. She had a book unrolled on her lap, but as soon as I came in she put it aside, and I had the distinct impression that she hadn't actually been reading it. Taken together with the fact that she had her serious look on, the omens here were not good.

'Marcus . . .' she said, and stopped. She frowned, and shook her head. 'No. You first. How was your day?'

I put Bathyllus's cup of wine on the table and lay down on the couch next to it. I was beginning to get seriously worried.

'Sod that for now,' I said. 'You OK? You're not ill or anything?'

'I'm perfectly well, dear,' she said. She didn't look it: *death warmed up* was the phrase that suggested itself. The worry went up another notch; for Perilla, this was *not* normal behaviour.

'But something's happened, right?' A horrible thought struck me. 'How's Marilla? You had a message from Clarus?' Like I said, our adopted daughter was in the last stages of pregnancy, always a dangerous time, particularly when it's a first child.

'Marilla's absolutely fine, as far as I know. No, we've had no messages from anywhere. And nothing at all has happened. At least, nothing involving the family. It's just that . . .' She stopped again. 'Look, I may be completely wrong about something. I hope I am, but I need your opinion.'

'Come on, lady! Just forget all the mystery and spill, will you?'

She ignored me. 'You talked to Surdinus Junior?'

I took a deep breath; we might as well get this over with. I wasn't going to tell her about the attack on the Janiculan, mind you. 'No. That turned out to be a wild-goose chase. Forget it, it's not important. But I did end up having another word with Gaius Secundus. And with Caelius Crispus at the foreign judges' office. It seems that Longinus isn't the only guy out of the four to have something against the emperor. In fact, all of them do, of one kind or another.' I gave her the details. 'Plus I'd a run-in with a youngster on the way back. Although *run-in* isn't exactly the phrase; nothing violent. He wants to talk to me tomorrow about Surdinus's death.'

'What was his name?'

'He wouldn't tell me. No name, no details up-front whatsoever. But the kid was jumpy as hell and seriously scared, and I'd bet my boots he was a Praetorian tribune.' I paused. 'And if that's so, then I'm afraid we have a completely different ball game.'

She nodded; she was looking paler than ever.

'Yes,' she said.

'You're not surprised?'

'No.' She gave a brittle smile. 'My turn, dear. I'll take this step by step, because I really, *really* do want to be told that I'm mistaken. You remember Aristarchus of Samos, that Julia Procula lent to me?'

'The "Iliad" guy, yes?' I was frowning: Perilla *wanting* to be proved wrong? That wasn't normal behaviour either, very far from it. I was beginning to get a very bad feeling about this. 'Sure. So?'

'Well, I thought I might apply his principle, or something like it, anyway, to Surdinus's bequest and his letter. That we shouldn't look at things through our own eyes but through the writer's.'

'Sorry, lady, but you've lost me.'

'Actually, when you have the trick of it, it's quite simple. Horribly so. First of all, the book he left me – Hipparchus's Commentary on the *Phaenomina* – was in Greek, so I thought perhaps that although Surdinus's letter was in Latin he wanted us to keep the idea of *Greek* in mind when we read it. You see?'

'Gods, Perilla . . .'

'Just bear with me, dear, please. It sounds complicated, I know, but it does all make perfect sense. Unfortunately. Start with the author's name. Hipparchus. Does that ring any bells?'

I sighed. 'Look, lady, you're the academic in this household. Until I saw his name on the book-tag, I'd never even heard of the bastard.'

'No, not Hipparchus of Nicea, an earlier one. Much earlier, much more well-known. Historical, not literary.' Then, when I looked blank: 'Oh, *Marcus*! I told you, I need confirmation of the train of thought. Or, preferably, refutation. Athens? Just over five hundred years ago? *Don't* make me say it myself, please!'

I'd my mouth open to say that I hadn't heard of that bastard either, when I realized I had. About twenty-five years previously, thanks to a particularly vicious rhetoric teacher who'd beaten the name into me, plus the details of how he'd ended up, as an encouragement to morality achieved through abstention from drink and loose women. And with the name two things happened. The first was that I saw where the lady was headed; the second was that I felt a cold ball of ice forming in my gut.

I was now hoping that she was wrong, too. But I didn't think she was.

'The Athenian tyrant,' I said. 'Got himself—'

'Yes. But leave it there for the moment, dear. Moving on to the letter. Surdinus calls your father "agreeable" and "the best of neighbours".'

'Yeah.' I was frowning again. I remembered thinking at the time that that made no sense, because making himself agreeable wasn't exactly Dad's thing, and he sure as hell hadn't lived anywhere near the Vatican. Where, I'd discovered early on, the Naevius family had been fixtures for generations. 'So?'

'So what would the Greek for that be?' Perilla said. '"Agreeable" and "the best of neighbours"?'

'*Harmodios* and . . .' I stopped as the implication hit me. 'Oh, shit! Oh, holy fucking Jupiter! Harmodius and Aristogeiton.' Those two names you couldn't *not* know, certainly not if you'd spent much time in Athens, as we had, because statues to them were all over the place, particularly where there was a good chance that a Roman or two would stroll past on a regular basis and get the intended message: the two tyrant killers, who'd done for Hipparchus and laid the foundations of Athenian democracy. 'Surdinus was telling us there's a plot to kill the emperor.'

'Yes. It all makes sense, doesn't it?' Perilla said. She was perfectly calm now. 'On your side as well.'

'Yeah.' Oh, sure, like I'd said, an assassination had always been on the cards, given the treason scenario, but it hadn't been likely. However, if I was right about the guy who'd stopped me on the Sacred Way being a tribune, then six got you ten that the local military were involved, and in that case the conspirators' chances of success had taken a spectacular hike. If some – or all – of the troops that were supposed to be acting as Gaius's body-guard were actually his potential killers, then this was a completely new ball-game right enough. 'He has to be warned,' I said.

'I know.'

Bugger; this was *not* going to be easy. Or safe. If Gaius Secundus was right – and I'd no reason to disbelieve him – then the time when I could simply make an appointment with Gaius, stroll down to the palace and have a pleasant chat regarding conspiracies and homicidal Praetorians was over. I'd nothing against the guy, sure, nor him against me. If anything, it was the reverse: I'd done him quite a few favours over the years, and we'd always rubbed along pretty well together when our paths had crossed – but after all he was the most powerful man in the world who could have me chopped on the spot just for the fun of seeing what my insides looked like, and the terrible thing was that that eventuality was no longer remote enough for me to discount it, let alone laugh it off.

If I were to go to the emperor – or even bring myself to his notice indirectly – I'd have to do it with more proof than I had at present. Even if it meant I was too late.

Hell. Hell and damnation.

Well, we'd just have to see what my Praetorian pal had to say.

NINETEEN

It was just shy of the seventh hour next day when I got to Pollex's. Not one of my favourite wine shops: the wines are only so-so in quality, seriously overpriced for what they are, and the décor's Early Empire grunge. The Sacred Way being what it is, you get a mixed clientele, sure, but because it's not too far from the city's administrative hub, there's always a fair sprinkling of broad- and narrow-striper mantles on their lunch break chortling over how old Marcus or Titus or Decimus has screwed up yet again over the stationery order. *Good lad, Marcus or Titus or Decimus, but a bit past it these days, yah?*

Still, wine and ambience wasn't what I was here for. Luckily, the place was fairly quiet for a change, possibly because the bad weather was encouraging the mantles to stick closer to the Market Square area itself. I couldn't see my tribune pal around yet, so I bought a half-jug of Massic and a plate of sliced sausage and took them plus two cups to a secluded corner table and sat down to wait.

The whys and wherefores of the meeting were pretty obvious, or at least I thought they were. Either the guy, in the course of his duties, had heard something that seriously worried him and wanted to pass it on, or he was involved in the conspiracy itself and had got cold feet. The second was by far the most likely, because it would answer the question of why me. He'd've had to get my name from somewhere, and the most likely source, given that I'd accidentally shown my hand as an interested party and potential problem at Longinus's get-together, was an inside one. If he'd been a pure innocent who'd just stumbled across something that made him suspicious, I wouldn't've figured as an option at all, and he'd just have passed the information on up the line, to someone he could trust.

Assuming, of course, he still knew who he could trust . . .

The problem was that I was working in the dark here. If there was a military component to this – and that, now, was pretty well beyond doubt – then what level were we talking about? Given that the only necessary criterion for success was that the assassin was within easy reach of the target and legitimately armed with a sword, it could just be the one guy. Oh, sure, under those circumstances it'd be suicide, but the world's not short of fanatics, death-and-glory boys who'll willingly sacrifice their own lives for an ideal. And since we already had a definite Stoic element figuring in this case, that was by no means impossible. It fitted with Surdinus's Harmodius and Aristogeiton clue as well, because if I remembered the story correctly, they'd both ended up chopped.

On the other hand, if the conspiracy was at a fairly high level – and again, given that there definitely had to be at least one broad-striper involved, that was more than likely – then the chances of success *and* survival were a lot higher. Duty rotas could be arranged, the right men chosen, the situation stage-managed so the target was in a minority of one. In which case, if it got that far then Gaius was a dead man walking . . .

The door of the wine shop opened. I looked up, but it was just a couple of ordinary punters, working-tunic types. I frowned and took a swallow of the wine. It was seventh hour now, easy, and chummie was late; which, considering how anxious he'd been to talk to me, was surprising, at best. Oh, sure, he'd probably had duty in the morning, which was why he hadn't been able to come earlier, and something unexpected may have come up; but he'd chosen the time himself, and he'd've factored that possibility in as best he could. I was beginning to get worried.

Half an hour and most of the jug later, the worry had turned into a certainty: for whatever reason, the guy was not going to show. Fuck. So what did I do now? I emptied the last of the wine into my cup, chewed on the last bit of sausage, and considered the options. Not that those were very thick on the ground: carry on waiting, in case he'd just been seriously delayed, or cut my losses and go, in the hopes that he'd contact me again. If he was in a state to contact me again, that was: I had a bad, bad feeling about that side of things.

Of course, maybe I could find him instead. That'd be tricky, sure, but not impossible; most Praetorian tribunes were older career soldiers with as many as twenty years' experience under their belts already, usually ex-auxiliary cavalry commanders making their way up the promotion ladder to an appointment in charge of a legion. Young purple-stripers from good families learning the ropes in good old-fashioned fast-track style would be in the minority. And at least I knew what he looked like.

So, time for another quick word with Gaius Secundus. I finished the wine and set off for Palatine Hill.

He was in his office, going through a list of facts and figures with his chief clerk. He looked up as I came in, and frowned.

'Marcus?' he said. 'What're you doing back?'

'Just a quick question, pal. It won't take long.' I closed the door behind me.

'That's fine, Acastus,' he said to the clerk. 'Give us a few minutes in private, will you?' I stood aside as the guy went out. 'Now.'

'You're sure I'm not disturbing you?'

'No problem. Bread-and-butter stuff, a faulty consignment of hides. It can wait. So what's the question?'

'I need to find a young tribune. Purple-striper, probably Praetorian.' I described him.

'Sounds like Sextus Papinius,' he said. 'Or his brother Lucius. They're both tribunes, with the Third and Fifth Cohorts.' The frown was back. 'What's your interest?'

'We'd arranged to meet today. He didn't turn up. You know where I can find him?'

The frown deepened. 'If he's on duty, then at the Praetorian barracks. But you'd find it difficult to get in there. They're not too keen on civilian visitors.'

'That's OK,' I said. 'Actually, the chances are that he's free at present. You happen to have a private address? At least, some-where I can contact him?'

Secundus hesitated; there was something wrong here, I could see that. 'Marcus,' he said, 'this has something to do with the case, hasn't it?'

'Yeah. As a matter of fact it has. That make a difference?'

'Yes, it does. Quite a big one.' Another hesitation. 'Look, we talked about this, right? Whatever it is, leave it alone. Leave it absolutely alone, because it's too dangerous. I told you, you can get hurt.'

'Warning duly noted, pal,' I said. 'But this is important. Really, *really* important. Believe me, I wouldn't push if it wasn't.'

'And you are pushing?'

Shit, I hated this: Secundus was a good friend – one of my best, and putting the pressure on was something I did not want to do. Still . . .

'Yeah,' I said. 'Yeah, I'm afraid I am.'

That got me a straight look. Finally, he shrugged and looked away.

'You might find him at his adoptive father's house,' he said. '"Him" being either Sextus or Lucius, it doesn't matter which one. That's on Patricius Incline near the junction with Viminal Hill Street.'

'Adoptive father?'

Again, he hesitated. Then he said: 'Anicius Cerialis.'

Fuck.

It was one of the older properties in the street, reached by a gate in a high wall with a small garden behind it. The gate was closed, but above it I could see the tops of three or four palm trees which screened the first floor of the house itself, and ivy had spilled over the wall on the street side. There was a slave sitting in a cubby next to the gate – dozing, rather – and I dawdled in covering the last few yards before taking the final, irrevocable step of waking him and telling him my name and business. Even after thinking it over on the walk from the Palatine, I still wasn't sure what was the best way to play this. If the slave passed me straight on to the master himself, and if – as seemed pretty likely – Cerialis was mixed up in the plot, then breezing in with the news that his adoptive son had effectively been on the point of blowing the gaff but hadn't turned up for the crucial meeting would not be the smartest of moves. There again, what other reason or excuse for visiting would I have? The whole situation was a complete bugger.

In the event, I was saved the trouble. The gate opened, and two of the house slaves came out carrying a ladder and a pile of cypress branches. My stomach went cold. Oh, shit. Cypress branches could mean just one thing.

There had been a death in the family.

The gate slave woke up and saw me staring.

'Yes, sir?' he said. 'Can I help you?' Now we were close up, I noticed his freshly shorn fringe.

'Yeah. Uh . . .' I indicated the other slaves, who'd set the ladder against the wall and were fixing the branches to the gate bars. 'You had a bereavement here?'

'The young master, sir. Master Sextus. It only happened this morning.'

Oh, fuck. 'So how did he die?'

'A fall from his horse, sir. He was out riding on Mars Field. You're a friend of the family?'

'No. Not exactly. But it was Sextus I came to see. At least, I think it was.'

He frowned. 'Pardon?'

'I only knew him by sight. It might've been his brother Lucius.'

'Master Lucius is at home, sir. I could take you to him if you like.'

'Ah . . . is your actual master at home, pal? Cerialis himself?'

'I'm afraid not, sir. He had senatorial business this morning, and he's been out since breakfast. A messenger was sent directly we had the news, but that was less than an hour ago and he hasn't returned yet.'

Well, that was something, at least. And if I was really, *really* lucky then Lucius was the one I wanted after all, and his brother's death was just a horrible coincidence.

On the other hand, there weren't any flying pigs overhead.

'That would be great,' I said. 'Thanks.'

I hadn't given my name, intentionally, and I had my fingers crossed that the guy wouldn't ask it. Which for a wonder he didn't. Maybe, in view of the circumstances, the usual niceties of announcing a visitor had slipped his mind, or maybe we'd just got beyond that point with the exchange over the death. In any case, he led me through the gate and the garden to the house.

Whoever had brought the news, they'd brought the body as well. Sextus Papinius was lying on a couch in the atrium, and evidently the undertakers' men hadn't been yet because he hadn't been properly laid out, simply covered feet to chin with his military cloak. He was my tribune, all right: his face had been washed clear of mud, but there was still a trace of it at the hairline. The head lay at a slightly crooked angle.

Gods!

I'd been looking at the corpse, and I hadn't noticed the other guy in the room, who was sitting on a folding stool in the corner. There was a jug of wine and a cup beside him. He got up and came towards me, swaying slightly.

'Who're you?' he said.

Lucius, obviously, and I could see why Secundus had thought my description could go both ways. He was slightly older and more broadly built, but he had the same features.

'A friend of your brother's,' I said. 'We'd arranged to meet today for a cup or two of wine, but he didn't show. I thought I'd drop round, see what the problem was. What happened, exactly?'

The guy was more than half-cut, but apart from a poached-egg-eyed stare he was holding it well. He shrugged and looked away, and I drew a small breath of relief.

'He was out riding on Mars Field,' he said. His voice was dull, mechanical. 'His horse shied at something and threw him; he landed on his head and broke his neck. That's all I know.'

'He was on his own?'

If he'd thought about it, it was a pretty odd question to ask, but I reckoned that Lucius here wasn't exactly in thinking mode at present. In the event, he didn't even blink.

'No. Bassus was with him,' he said. 'He was the one who brought him back.'

'Bassus?'

'His quaestor friend. Titus Bassus.' This time I did get an oddish look; maybe Lucius wasn't as drunk as he appeared. 'You say you're a friend of Sextus's, and you don't know Bassus?'

'Yeah, well . . .'

'They were practically inseparable, been friendly since they were kids. Bassus is more like an older brother to him than a friend.' Now his expression was definitely suspicious, and there was something else there as well; a spark in the eyes that looked very like incipient panic. 'Just who are you, exactly? What's your name?'

Shit. 'It's not important, pal,' I said, turning to go. 'I'm sorry for your loss, and I'm intruding. You'll have things to see to, and I won't take up any more of your time.'

'Fuck that! You're going nowhere!' His hand grasped my shoulder. I shook him off, maybe with more force than I'd intended, because he stumbled and fell heavily against the couch. Before he could recover himself, I was out and away.

Jupiter!

TWENTY

So. That had been illuminating, if you like.

Accident, nothing; that was obvious. Sextus Papinius had been rumbled and his mouth shut before he could blab. I remembered that, when he'd talked to me on the Sacred Way, he'd not only been scared out of his wits, but he'd also been constantly looking over his shoulder like he suspected he was being watched. Which the odds were he had been, and it had effectively done for him. The *modus operandi* was interesting, too: where had a broken neck figured already in this case?

Right.

I really had to talk to Bassus. He'd be needed, naturally, to provide the circumstantial evidence of an eyewitness, but the corollary of that was that, once you knew damn well it was murder, he had to be lying through his teeth. And *that* meant he was involved in the plot himself. What got me – sickened me, to tell you the truth – was that there was a better than good chance that Lucius Papinius was in it as well, maybe even to the extent of collusion over his brother's death. He had to be – why else would he spend the hour after the body was delivered to the front door in getting systematically smashed? Plus there had been the dead-voiced account of events, like he'd been told exactly what to say when someone asked for them, and that weird business at the end: the guy had finally put two and two together, realized who I was, panicked, and lost the plot completely.

Gods, the more you went into this thing, the worse it got, like some sort of hydra sprouting extra heads. And Lucius, like his brother, was a military tribune, with all the implications that brought with it. I had the horrible feeling that we'd only just scratched the surface.

So how did I find Bassus? I couldn't go knocking on Secundus's door again, that wouldn't be fair. I'd twisted the poor guy's arm right up his back once already in the name of friendship, and unless I absolutely had to, I wouldn't be doing that again in a hurry. The same, in a way, went for Crispus: he wasn't exactly a friend, but I reckoned I'd pretty well shot my bolt in that direction for the time being. Anyway, there was no need: Lucius Papinius had told me that he was one of the quaestors, and a visit to the Public Finance Office would net the information, no problem. After all, as far as they'd know, there was no skulduggery involved, just an innocent request for information.

So that's where I went.

Like every organization in a position to allocate and monitor their own expenditure, the Public Finance Office had done themselves proud. Oh, sure, the quaestorship is the lowest rung of the senatorial magistracies' ladder, and the quaestors only serve for a year, but the faceless administrators who staff the offices – mostly freedmen – do most of the work, and hold their young masters by the hand as they guide them through the maze of contract legislation, building regulations, fire-prevention requirements and the like. They are a permanent fixture, and they do like things to be *nice*. Especially the décor.

At least it'd been tastefully done, with the mural in the entrance hall showing a neutral lake scene complete with an architecturally complex villa rather than the rampant crowd of topless maenads that the clerks who had to sit there all day would probably have preferred, but that's government thinking for you.

I went up to the freedman on the nearest desk.

'Excuse me,' I said. 'You have a Titus Bassus as one of your officers?'

'Certainly, sir. Titus Herennius Bassus, that would be. I don't

know if he's around at present, though. If you'd like to wait, I'll
go and check for you. Your name and business?'

I had my mouth open to answer when a young guy in a smart
mantle with a senatorial stripe came down the stairs. He must've
caught the freedman's last few words, because he said, 'What is
it? Anything I can do?'

'The gentleman's looking for Herennius Bassus, sir.'

He turned to me. 'Oh, gods, it's not about the bloody replacement finials for the Temple of Jupiter Stayer-of-the Host, is it?'
he said.

'No, I'm—' I began.

'Thank the gods for that. Titus isn't in today; he's out riding
in Mars Field, the lucky beggar.'

'Yeah, I know,' I said. 'Only, ah, something came up and he
had to cut it short. You happen to know where I'd find him now?'

'Not a clue. He isn't back on duty until tomorrow morning.
Was it urgent?'

'Pretty urgent, yeah.'

'Damn.' The young man frowned. 'You could try his father.'

'His father?'

'Up at the imperial offices on the Palatine.' I must've looked
blank, because he said: 'Herennius Capito. He's one of the imperial procurators-fiscal. He might know.'

'Thanks, pal, I'll do that,' I said, and left.

Interesting; so Bassus's father was in government admin on
the imperial side of the fence, was he? And pretty highly placed
at that. Some procurators are freedmen – the name, of course,
means nothing more than *agent* – but the imperial procurators-
fiscal have the direct management of the emperor's personal
income and private estates, and they tend to be much bigger fish
– knights, not senators, but no less important or influential for
the thinner stripe. Quite the reverse, because it's on the imperial
side of the fence that the real governmental power lies, direct or
indirect. And 'fence' it is: ever since old Augustus divided the
government and everything connected with it between himself
and the senate, the two sides have been as separate as the two
faces of a coin. Oh, sure, they come into contact now and again
where and when necessary – the empire couldn't function if they
didn't – but essentially they're two distinct worlds operating in
parallel. Which was very relevant indeed. Granted, I might be

leaping to unwarranted conclusions; just because young Bassus was implicated in the plot didn't mean that his father had to be. But if he was then we had a third strand here: first the senate, represented by Cassius Longinus and his pals; then the military, by the two Papinii; now the imperial household itself.

Heads of the hydra was right.

Imperial admin officers – the ones on the private side, anyway, like Capito – have their offices in the administrative wing of the palace itself. So up to the Palatine I went, passed unchallenged between the two Praetorians on guard, and was directed by the clerk on reception to a room on the mezzanine floor. I knocked, opened the door, and went straight in.

There were two guys there. The one sitting behind the desk was late-middle-aged, in a narrow-striper mantle; the other, standing in front of it, had a senator's broad stripe. He turned round sharply as the door opened, and I saw that he was much younger, in his late twenties. They were obviously, from the facial resemblance, father and son.

They were obviously also, from the expressions on the faces, in the throes of a family conference. A fairly urgent, unpleasant one, at that.

'I'm busy,' Capito snapped. 'What is it?'

Fair enough; if that was the way he wanted to play it, fine with me. It'd save a lot of pussyfooting around, certainly.

'Actually, pal' – I closed the door behind me and set my back to it – 'I wanted a word with your son here. About the death this morning of a military tribune by the name of Sextus Papinius.'

I was watching the younger man's face when I said it, and I couldn't miss the flash of panic – the same look I'd got from Sextus's brother, Lucius. He glanced back at his father.

'Dad—' he began.

'I'll handle this,' Capito said. He hadn't taken his eyes off me, and his face was set. 'Who are you? And what makes you think you can barge in here without an appointment?'

'The name's Corvinus. Marcus Corvinus.' Definitely a flicker there; if I'd had any doubts that Herennius Senior was involved I didn't have them any more. 'I understand from his brother that the quaestor here was with Papinius when he died.'

'That's correct. In a fall from his horse on Mars Field. They were out riding together, and young Sextus's horse shied and threw him. A terrible business, terrible.'

'Was there anyone else around?'

'No, as it happened. They were in the top corner of the field, near the river, beyond Augustus's Mausoleum.' He was frowning. 'What's this about? And what has it to do with you?'

'I'm looking into the death – the murder – of Lucius Naevius Surdinus.'

He blinked; that name had registered, too.

'So?' he said.

'Papinius told me, yesterday, that he had certain information he thought I should have. We'd arranged to meet this afternoon, only of course he never turned up.'

'That was unfortunate, but—'

'He never turned up because your son here killed him. Or rather, probably, he engineered things so that someone else could do the job.'

'That's a lie!' Bassus was white with anger. 'Sextus was one of my best friends! We grew up together! If you think—'

His father reached out and put a hand on his wrist. He was still staring at me, but he'd gone noticeably pale. His Adam's apple bobbed.

'Corvinus,' he said, 'that accusation is not only nonsensical, unfounded, and unwarranted, but actionable in a court of law. Which is where I and my son will see you as soon as I can lay a charge before the city judge. Now, get out of my office.'

Weak. I recognized bluster when I heard it, and I could see a bead of sweat on his forehead. I didn't move. 'You haven't asked why,' I said.

Capito's brow furrowed. 'Why what?'

'Why he did it.' I shrugged. 'Oh, sure, you know the answer perfectly well already, but I'll give you it nonetheless. There's a plot to kill the emperor. Papinius was involved; your son Bassus here's involved. You're involved yourself. How Surdinus fits in I'm not sure yet, but that's why he was killed, and Papinius knew about it. Go ahead, tell me I'm wrong.'

They were both staring at me: Capito like an actor who'd suddenly lost his place in the script, his son in pure wide-eyed terror.

'That's . . .' Capito stuttered.

'The simple unvarnished truth,' I went on easily. 'Right. Of course, you're wondering just how much I know in the way of detail, and who else knows besides me. Whether it's enough to take to the emperor himself, and whether I'm in a minority of one. Maybe whether I *have* taken it to the emperor already, in which case you're all dead men walking. That includes your pals Longinus and Cerialis, plus the two Gauls. No doubt quite a few others that I don't yet know about, yes, but never mind, because once you're in the bag, the emperor has ways of getting the names out of you. Not very pleasant ways, but there you are. And believe me, if you are thinking of passing the fact that we've had this little talk on to your heavies so that they can take appropriate action, the secret isn't a secret any longer. The horse is out, the stable door's wide open, and you're living on borrowed time. Trust me on this, absolutely.' They were grey with fear now, both of them. 'So the good news is that I'm cutting you some slack. Not much, but it's the best offer you'll get.' I folded my arms and leaned back against the door. 'As far as I know, Gaius doesn't—'

I'd been half-expecting it, so it didn't come as a complete surprise; besides, Bassus was no fighter. He came at me swinging, but I ducked and planted a fist in his midriff, then when he doubled up I followed it with a sock to the jaw. He folded like a wet rag and lay there groaning.

Capito had got to his feet, but he didn't move.

'Like I was saying,' I continued, 'as far as I know – although I may be wrong – all this'll come as news to the emperor. Me, well, I'm an outsider, a nobody, but if someone he trusts, one of his own senior admin staff, say, were to go to him off his own bat and tell him the whole story up-front, first to last, he might just decide to overlook the details of where the guy had got his information. He might even be grateful, although I wouldn't count too much on that possibility, myself.' I shrugged. 'It's a gamble, sure, but I'd think the odds would be pretty good. Better, certainly, than if you let things slide, or if you're stupid enough to stay on the losing team, because if you do and you are, then you have no future at all. Your decision completely, pal, and you might be lucky. Think about it.' I opened the door. 'As for the mechanics of the thing, well, Gaius couldn't be more handily placed, since you're virtually neighbours, so I'll only give you until tomorrow morning before I make an appointment myself. I'll see you around. Hopefully.'

I left.

That had been risky, sure, but it'd been a calculated risk, and I reckoned it would pay off because those two were no hardened conspirators – that had been obvious practically from the first. Someone with backbone like Longinus, or even Graecinus, would've laughed in my face and brazened it out, then quietly arranged to have me chopped. Them, I'd never have tried it on with, not in a million years, because it would've been just too damn dangerous. Capito and his son, though, were running scared, particularly the son, and if I'd been bluffing when I'd implied that other people were in on the secret, it'd been in the certainty that they wouldn't call the bluff and arrange for the chopping themselves. Besides, I'd been totally honest about their options. Spilling the beans voluntarily to the emperor wasn't by any means a guarantee that they'd live through this, especially in the current climate, but the chances of it were a hell of a lot better than if they'd just been two more names on the list. And given my deadline of tomorrow morning, which allowed them no time to think, it would be by far the best and fastest way of letting Gaius know what was going on; I could spend months putting a water-tight case together, and whatever the plot's timetable was, months were something I'd bet I didn't have. Nowhere near it.

So, a good day's work, and if I was lucky the first real crack in the case. I hadn't lost sight of the fact that my remit was to find whoever had killed Surdinus, and a little thing like unmasking a conspiracy against the emperor was just an incidental feature. Oh, yeah, sure, there was a connection; there had to be. The simplest explanation was that, like Papinius, Surdinus had been involved in the plot himself, got cold feet, and taken the best indirect way he could of blowing the whistle. Or ensuring, rather, that if he were to die prematurely, the whistle would still be blown. Still, I didn't actually *know* that, not yet, and there were factors militating against it. Like – given the other conspirators were either serving senators or Praetorians, or had strong imperial connections – why should an apolitical sort like him be mixed up in it at all? However, if I was lucky, when the whole boiling were hauled in for questioning, the case would solve itself. You might not like them – I didn't, particularly – but as I'd said to Capito, Gaius had ways of getting even the most reluctant suspect to talk. And with a planned assassination in the pipeline, he wouldn't pull his punches, either.

Anyway, I reckoned we'd call it a day. I headed through the Palatine complex towards Staurian Incline, the flight of steps that was the quickest way, if you were on foot, of getting from Palatine to Caelian. The easiest, too, because especially at this time of day they were pretty quiet. There was a punter a flight or so ahead of me, and another about the same behind, and that was about it.

I'd got almost to the foot, where there was one of the public litters parked with its two litter-men leaning against it shooting the breeze, when I noticed that the guy ahead of me had stopped and turned round. He reached into his belt and drew out a knife, while the two off-duty litter-men stopped lounging and did the same.

Oh, shit. I turned – or half-turned, rather – just in time to see that chummie behind me had closed the gap . . .

Which was when something that felt like a decent-sized marble column smacked me behind the ear, and I went out like a light.

TWENTY-ONE

I woke up with my back to a wall, a thumping headache, a definite no-go area on the back left-hand side of my head where I'd been clouted, and my slinger pal from the Janiculan looking down at me. We were indoors, I could see that much, although vision wasn't exactly my best feature at the moment and my eyes were actually telling me said slinger pal was overlapping identical twins. I could see we were somewhere with no windows, because the only light came from lamps.

I reached up and gingerly touched the no-go area on my head. There was a lump there the size of a goose egg, but my fingers came away dry. A sandbag, then, or a blackjack – chummie had been careful, which, considering the knives his three mates had been carrying, was interesting.

'You're awake,' the big guy said.

Nine out of ten for observation, with one point deducted for stating the totally bloody obvious.

'Yeah,' I said. 'More or less.' I felt like something the cat had dragged in, and woozy as hell, but apart from the pain in my head and the double vision, everything else seemed OK. 'Why am I still alive? Not that I'm complaining, mind.'

He grunted and stood up. 'Not by my choice, friend,' he said. 'If I'd had my way you would be fucking dead. You *prat*!'

Yeah, well, I wasn't going to argue: I hadn't exactly covered myself with glory here. Which reminded me . . .

'So where exactly am I?' I said. 'If it's not a stupid question.'

'In a wine cellar.'

Great. Very informative. 'You care to elaborate a little, chum?'

'No. That's all you need to know, Corvinus. Except that it's under a house that's been empty for the past six months and that there's only the one way in or out, through a three-inch-thick reinforced oak door with a lock and a couple of iron bolts on the other side. So this is where you fucking well stay.'

Uh-huh. That would just about do it; curiosity satisfied. 'Until when?'

'Until it's all over. Boss's instructions. As I said, me, I'd've gone for the more permanent option and left you back there on the Stairs with your throat cut.'

Ouch. Well, at least I could be thankful that I was still breathing. 'The boss?'

He ignored me. 'Up you get.' He pulled me to my feet and I felt my head explode. 'Just don't try no fucking funny business, right? Killing you might be out, but the boss didn't say nothing about loosening a few teeth or breaking a couple of fingers. And believe me, after the trouble you've caused, I'd whistle while I did it.'

'Pal, the way I'm feeling just now, I couldn't get past your white-haired old grandmother.' I wasn't kidding, either; the room was swimming round me, and the inside of my skull felt like someone was hitting it with a mallet. Wine-cellar the place might be, but it looked more like a prison cell. Which, evidently, was what its present purpose was: no more than ten feet square, with a table and stool against one wall, a cot and blankets against another, and a chamber-pot in the corner with a bucket and sponge-stick beside it. Right; at least we had all the amenities. No windows, of course, and like the guy had said a door that looked like it'd need an army battering-ram to get through.

So much for any dramatic escape plan I might think up. Hell. The table, mind . . .

It wasn't empty, not by a long chalk. There were three loaves of bread, a whole chicken, three or four covered pottery bowls, a couple of jugs, and the full complement of tableware. Plus a mixing bowl and strainer, and – leaning against the wall beside it – two sizeable flasks in their iron foot-rests.

I certainly wouldn't starve, and given the presence of the flasks, the mixing bowl and wine strainer, I wouldn't go thirsty, either. The accommodation might be pretty basic, but I couldn't complain about the catering. The boss, whoever he was, had done me proud.

What the hell was going on?

Chummie walked across to the table, filled a cup from one of the jugs and brought it over.

'Here,' he said.

It was wine. I tasted it . . .

Shit, that was Caecuban! *Good* Caecuban! The best, in fact, that money couldn't buy, because it all went to the one place. I took a proper swig, and it kissed my tonsils on the way down like liquid velvet . . .

Things began to make sense.

'You should be OK now,' he said, turning away and moving towards the door. 'The oil for the lamps is in the corner by the latrine. Enjoy your stay.'

And he was gone, slamming the door behind him. I heard the key turn in the lock and the bolts slide home.

Damn!

Yeah, well, I might as well see what I'd got here, because there was bugger all else to do. The loaves and the chicken were self-evident, but I took the lids off the bowls. Cold bean stew, braised mixed vegetables, assorted pickles and some dried fruit and nuts for dessert. Not bad, well beyond the bread-and-water stage. Not up to Meton's standard, of course, but better than I'd get in most cook shops. I topped up my wine cup and investigated the other jug and the flasks. Water and – whoopee! – more of the Caecuban.

There was a leather case for book-rolls beside the bed. I opened it up and took out the first roll. Plautus's *Captives*. Oh, hah; someone had a sense of humour, anyway. I put it back and pulled out the others: Cato's *On Farming*, the first couple of books of Ennius's *Annals*, and Cicero's *Tusculan Disputations*. Good solid reads, all of them, bloody dry as dust, except for the Plautus, and I've never found that bastard particularly funny. Boredom, I could see, was going to be a major problem. If it'd been the lady stuck down here for the duration, then . . .

Oh, fuck. Perilla. I hadn't thought about her. She'd have no idea where I was, let alone whether I was alive or dead, with the probability being the latter.

Well, there was nothing I could do about it now. Except worry, of course, about her being worried. I settled down to wait.

I'd no way of measuring time exactly, but I estimated there were three days between the door shutting and it opening again. By which point – leaving aside the fact that I was practically climbing the walls – I'd more or less worked everything out: when you're faced with a choice between ratiocination and Marcus Porcius bloody-skinflint Cato rabbiting on about how to squeeze as much oil as you can out of an olive or work out of a slave, suitably anaesthetized beforehand with Caecuban or not, it's no contest.

So. After three days of solitary confinement, the door finally opened. Not my slinger pal this time; instead through it came a little guy wearing a freedman's cap and a sharp lemon-coloured tunic. The boss in person.

No surprises there. It just had to be him, didn't it?

'Hi, Felix,' I said. 'How's it going?' He was alone, which, I supposed, was a safe enough risk to take, given that I knew who he worked for, although even knowing that after three days of being banged up in a cellar with only an increasingly pervasive latrine smell and Cato and his jolly mates for company, I could cheerfully have beaten the little bugger to death with his own chamber pot.

Which, given who he was, would not have been a good idea. I hadn't seen Gaius's freedman sidekick – spymaster, intelligence chief, whatever you liked to call him – for three years, not since the last conspiracy against his master had gone down the tubes, but he hadn't changed. Still the fastidious, dapper little bugger we had grown to know and love for his unfailing cheerfulness, ruthless efficiency, and bacon-slicer brain.

'Things are going very well indeed, sir,' he said. 'May I sit down?'

'Sure. Why not? Make yourself at home.'

Sarcasm is lost on Felix. He never even batted an eyelid.

'Thank you.' He sat on the bed. 'And do let me say what a pleasure it is to see you again, Valerius Corvinus. You haven't been too uncomfortable, I hope? Had everything you needed?'

Stupid bloody question, but I took it in the spirit it was meant.

'I could've done with a razor,' I said. 'Apart from that – and of course apart from the fact that my wife will be worried fucking sick about where I've got to – no, not too many complaints. You total sadistic bastard.'

He looked pained. 'Really, sir, give me some credit for humanity, please! That is *most* unfair! I sent a message right away telling the Lady Perilla that you were perfectly safe and well. As for the razor, that was an oversight, and you have my most abject apologies. I will speak to Trupho about it in no uncertain terms.'

'Yeah, well.' At least I was glad that I could stop worrying about Perilla. She'd've been anxious, sure, but I had to admit that under the circumstances, Felix had done his best. 'Couldn't you just have told me to lay off?'

'Would you have done it?'

'I might have, if you'd asked nicely and explained the situation.' Still, it was a fair point, and we'd been there before in our past dealings together. Plus the chances were that, no, I wouldn't have, and we both knew it. 'Trupho's the big guy who brought me here, yes?'

'Indeed. An ex-auxiliary, and one of my best men. Rather a rough diamond, but he is generally very efficient. Particularly at killing, as you no doubt saw. When did you know, by the way?'

'That the conspiracy was already blown and you had things in hand? Almost straight off. It was the wine. Imperial Caecuban, right?'

He was beaming. 'Oh, well done, sir!' he said. 'I thought that might do it, or at least provide you with a major clue, if you needed one. The flask was from the emperor's own cellars. His idea, not mine, so when you see him, please be appropriately grateful.'

Bugger, that did *not* sound good: the last thing I wanted was a face-to-face with that psychotic bastard. Even so . . .

'So what happens now?' I said.

'Nothing, as far as I'm concerned. You're free to go, of course, absolutely free. The conspirators are all rounded up and in custody.'

'Still alive?'

'Naturally. For the moment, at least. We need a little more information from them first.'

A cold chill touched my spine. 'Is that really necessary?' I said. 'After all—'

'Completely necessary, sir,' he said primly. 'As you're quite well aware.'

Shit. Execution, yeah, that went with the crime. But torture, that was something else. Oh, sure, I couldn't really expect any different, and nor could they. Even so, the thought of it turned my stomach.

'The two Herennii, father and son?'

'In the bag, shortly after you left them.'

Well, I'd tried to give them an out, at least, and I felt better for that. Not a lot better, mind.

'Lucius Papinius?'

'He wasn't involved, as far as we know.'

I frowned. 'You sure?'

'As sure as one can be, yes. He accepted Herennius Bassus's word that his brother's death was an accident in good faith.'

I left it at that. For the moment. 'So Bassus killed young Sextus? To stop him talking to me. Or manoeuvred him into a position where he could be killed?'

'Yes again. The precise details aren't clear, but no doubt they will be before long.'

Shit. Yeah, I guessed they would be, at that; Gaius's torturers were pretty efficient. The chill touched my spine again, not so much at the thought this time as at the matter-of-fact way Felix referred to it. He was a cold bastard at heart, Julius Felix.

'What about the father? Adoptive father, that is. Anicius Cerialis.'

'Cerialis has left Rome.'

'You mean he's escaped?'

'Not exactly, sir.'

I frowned again. 'So what, exactly?'

'Anicius Cerialis was working for us.'

'*What?*'

Felix smiled. 'Latterly, at any rate. After a small amount of persuasion. It's called *turning* in the trade. Oh, you couldn't have guessed it, not in the short time you had, and of course his fellow conspirators had – and have – no idea of the truth. Although I must say, before I forget, how impressed I was that you got so far so quickly. To be frank, it was downright embarrassing. Trupho was most put out.'

'Yeah, I noticed that,' I said drily. 'He was keeping an eye on me right from the start, wasn't he? On your instructions.'

'That and keeping an eye out *for* you, sir. Fortunately, with regard to the Janiculan incident.' Yeah, well, I'd give him that, and I was grateful. 'But not exactly right from the start; only when you began to show an interest in Cassius Longinus and his friends. That was *most* unexpected; worryingly so on my part. The poor dears really started to panic, and there was a genuine danger that they'd decide to cut their losses and run. Which would, naturally, at the end of the day have made things far more difficult. As it was, we had to bring our plans forward by almost half a month and get you out of the equation spit-spot. Could you tell me why, by the way?'

'Why what?'

'Why your interest in Longinus.'

'Cornelia Sullana – my victim's ex-wife – claimed she'd had an affair with him years back.'

'Really? And did she?'

'No. At least, I very much doubt it.'

'So it was simply a coincidence? An unfortunate one, as I say, for both of us.'

'Longinus was involved, then?'

Felix hesitated. 'As to that, Valerius Corvinus,' he said, 'as you would say, the jury is still out. Certainly he was taken along with the rest, as was Valerius Asiaticus, who is, albeit for different reasons, in a similar situation to his. But he's simply being detained on suspicion, no more. The emperor thinks it's unlikely, or at least that things were only at the recruitment stage, and is willing to give him the benefit of the doubt. After all, the conspiracy has been in progress for several months, he only returned very recently to Rome, and he wouldn't be here at all if Caesar hadn't recalled him.'

'Because his fortune teller warned him to beware of a guy called Cassius?'

That got me a sharp look. 'Who told you that?'

I shrugged; I wasn't going to finger Gaius Secundus, no way; I'd caused him enough trouble already. 'Someone. That doesn't matter. Is it true?'

'As a matter of fact, it is.' Felix hesitated. 'Corvinus. A small warning of my own, and to you. The emperor is . . . not quite his normal rational self these days.' I kept my mouth firmly shut. 'You'd do well to remember that when you talk to him.'

'So how does Surdinus fit in?'

Felix's brow furrowed. 'Surdinus?'

'Naevius Surdinus. My victim. The guy whose death I'm looking into.'

'Oh, yes. Of course. That, I'm afraid I don't know. He wasn't on our list, certainly.'

'That's odd. Me, I'd bet it was mentioning that I was investigating Surdinus's murder – not his accidental death, that was the point – that had me targeted. And he knew about the conspiracy, that's for absolute certain.' I told him about the Hipparchus business.

'Ingenious,' Felix said. Yeah, well, I'd thought the little guy would like that bit; it'd appeal to his warped, labyrinthine brain. 'All I can say is he comes as news to me. Which isn't surprising, really: you and I approached things from different directions, and as I said we still don't know the names of everyone who was involved, just as there are several guilty parties you never found out about and whose names would mean nothing to you. Still, if the man's already dead then the whole thing's academic.'

'Well, maybe so, but—'

'I'll tell you what.' He was beaming. 'If it's still important, then why not sit in on the interrogations? I'm sure Caesar won't mind, although naturally I'd have to clear it with him first.'

'Ah . . .'

'In fact, I insist. I know how you feel about leaving loose ends, and I really do want you to be satisfied. You can ask the question at first hand. I'd suggest Julius Graecinus, since he was one of your four original suspects. I'm certain he'll come up with something useful.'

Gods! 'Listen, Felix . . .' I said.

'That's settled, then.' He stood up. 'Shall we say tomorrow, at the palace? Not too early; no doubt you have private business to attend to, and you deserve a little time to yourself. The seventh hour will be fine. Just give your name to the officer on duty at the gate and he'll bring you down. And now I won't keep you any longer. Can I get you a litter? We are, incidentally, just on the edge of the Subura, near the Temple of Tellus.'

'No, that's OK. I'll walk. I need the fresh air and exercise.'

'Very well, sir, as you like. You may get a little wet, though, because it was raining when I came in. My best regards to Rufia Perilla, and, of course, my apologies, both to her and to you. Until tomorrow, then.'

Jupiter!

TWENTY-TWO

Bathyllus's eyes widened when he opened the door for me, and for once there was no cup of wine waiting on the lobby table.

'Sir, are you . . .?' he began.

'Yeah, Bathyllus, I'm fine. Still a bit of a headache, but no bones broken. Perilla at home?'

But she was already there, practically flying through the atrium entrance. I might've been wrong about the *no bones broken*, because she was hugging me so hard I felt my ribs creak.

'Hey, lady,' I said. 'Pull back a bit. I'm pretty bristly.'

'Marcus,' she said, the words muffled against my shoulder, 'I will *kill* you!'

Ouch. Nothing like a touching reunion when you've been away on business for a couple of days.

'Felix told me he'd sent a message,' I said.

'Of course he did.' She hadn't let go. 'Three days ago, to say you were at the palace and being taken care of. Just that. There hasn't been anything since. What was I to think?'

The bastard. Oh, sure, he'd done as he'd said, all right, but although it was accurate enough as far as it went, the wording left a lot to be desired: *taken care of* would've worked pretty well as a euphemism. If the words were Felix's, that was.

'Uh . . . who was the messenger, lady?' I said. 'You see him?'

'Yes. He insisted on telling me personally. A big, rough-looking man. Could have been an out-of-uniform soldier.'

Trupho. Right. And he'd done it deliberately. I promised myself that if I ever met that particular bastard again I'd do a little negative dental work on my own account.

'It wasn't the palace exactly,' I said; she'd stopped hugging me now, and I massaged my ribs. 'But the other bit was true enough. Felix just wanted me kept out of the way.'

'Out of the way of what?'

I explained.

'So the case is over?' she said.

'Not . . . exactly,' I said cautiously. 'Look, can we go somewhere a bit more comfortable?' I turned to Bathyllus. 'Let's have that wine, little guy. Oh, and see that the furnace is properly fired up. I'll want a bath.' Too right I would; I wasn't particularly aware of it myself, but after three days in the cellar I'd bet I stank. Still, expecting Felix to provide bathing facilities might've been pushing things a bit.

'Yes, sir. Certainly. And let me say that I and the rest of the staff are delighted to have you back safely.'

He buttled off, although I had caught the slight, possibly this time involuntary, sniff before he did: accumulated body odour was right.

We went through to the atrium and settled down on the couches.

'What do you mean, not exactly?' Perilla said.

'Yeah, well, we don't know who killed Naevius Surdinus yet, do we? And there are some puzzling points that need clearing up. We've got some unfinished business here.'

She was glaring.

'Marcus Valerius Corvinus!' she snapped. 'You listen to me! These last three days have been appalling. I *never* want to go through that again. Is that very clear?'

'Ah . . . yeah. To be fair, mind, it wasn't exactly my—'

'We were going down to Castrimoenium in any case within the next few days—'

'Come on, Perilla, hardly the next few days! Before the Winter Festival, we said, and that's half a month off!'

'But I'm sure Clarus and Marilla won't mind if we make it earlier. Such as tonight, or first thing tomorrow morning at the latest. Marcus, please read my lips here: I am *not* going to have you faffing around in Rome in the aftermath of a conspiracy. It is just too – bloody – *dangerous*. Now, do you understand, or do I have to get Bathyllus to tie you hand and foot and throw you into the carriage?'

I grinned. 'You think he'd be up to that?'

'I'll make sure that he gets all the help he needs. Look, I am *serious*! This time, no arguments. *Do you understand?*'

'Fair enough,' I said. 'So will you tell the emperor or shall I?'

That stopped her. 'What?'

'Gaius – or at least Felix, but it comes to the same thing – wants me round at the palace tomorrow just after noon. He was pretty insistent.'

'What for?'

'Just a chat,' I said easily. I wasn't going to tell her about the interrogation-under-torture side of things, no way. I felt bad enough about it myself without inflicting it on her as well.

'A chat?'

'It shouldn't take long.' I had my fingers firmly crossed that it wouldn't. 'An hour or two, at most. And then I promise we'll go straight to the Alban Hills and stay there as long as you like.'

She was looking at me suspiciously. 'So I can tell Lysias to get the carriage ready for early tomorrow evening, yes?'

Lysias was the coachman. 'Sure,' I said. I couldn't approve of Felix's means, to put it mildly, and I certainly wasn't looking forward to seeing them in operation, but the odds were we'd have the rest of the case stitched up by then. Besides, when Perilla was in this mood, rational argument went out of the window; she hadn't been kidding about Bathyllus, for a start. And it'd only take a few hours to cover the distance between us and Clarus and Marilla's place. 'Go ahead, lady. Make what arrangements you like.'

'And I have your absolute firm commitment that you won't be sloping off back to Rome at the first opportunity?'

'Cross my heart and hope to—'

'*Don't say that! Don't* ever *say that!*'

Jupiter, she *was* serious. The lady was shaking.

I got up, went over and kissed her. 'We stay as long as you like,' I said. 'That's a promise. You make the decision. After all, Clarus's estimate of when the kid's due might be out. The birth might not be for another month, at least.'

She smiled weakly. 'I hardly think so, dear.'

'Yeah, well. Medical science has been proved wrong before.'

Bathyllus shimmered in with the wine in one of our best dinner-party cups, with more of the same in the matching jug.

'I thought the Special, sir,' he said, 'since it's an occasion. And Meton says that after your unscheduled absence he will make a particular effort where dinner is concerned. That will be immediately after your bath. Say in two hours' time?'

'That'd be great, Bathyllus.' I took the wine cup and sipped. Not the imperial Caecuban I'd been getting used to (I should've had the nous to lug the rest of the jar with me, even if it'd meant taking Felix up on his offer of a litter; too late now), but very nice all the same. And *a particular effort*? Now there was a phrase you didn't hear very often from Meton. If to my suspicious mind it hadn't had a certain Meton-ish ambiguity about it (a particular effort in which direction?), especially taken with the *after your unscheduled absence* bit, I would've been quite touched.

It was good to be home.

I lounged about the next morning and went down to Market Square for a proper shave before turning up prompt at the palace at the seventh hour, wearing my best tunic and mantle. I wasn't exactly sure of the sartorial code where attending torture sessions was concerned – let's not mince words here, and I wasn't looking forward to it, to put it mildly – but a visit to the emperor was a visit to the emperor, and I couldn't've done any less. I gave my name to the Praetorian tribune on duty and he delegated a squaddie to take me in.

We bypassed the usual state apartments and went down a plain stone staircase to the vaults. Shit, it was a different world down here; not a pleasant one, either. When we walked along the bleak, torch-lit, evil-smelling corridor past a row of cells (some of them, judging by the sounds I tried to ignore, obviously occupied), I felt the bile rising to my throat.

Not that it seemed to faze the squaddie, mind, but then maybe, for him, it was all part of the job. We reached a low, iron-bound door, and he stopped.

'In here, sir,' he said. He pushed the door open and stood aside.

Oh, bugger. Here we went. I moved past him, ducking my head to clear the lintel. The smell – a mixture of human shit, urine and vomit, plus the flat-iron tang I recognized as old blood – hit me straight away. That and the heat: the place was like a furnace. Or maybe an antechamber to hell would be a better parallel.

I retched.

'Marcus, petal! How lovely to see you again! So nice of you to come!'

Oh, gods! The man himself!

There were things in the room. And people, one of them fastened naked to a table in the centre and barely recognizable as such. Graecinus, evidently. Him, after that first glance, I tried not to look at. I tried not to look at anything, and not to breathe through my nose.

'Caesar,' I said.

'You're just in time, dear. We were going to start without you.' He was wearing a light tunic, crisply laundered, and he looked like he'd just stepped out of the bath. In that room, he was as out of place as a flowering rose in a latrine. 'You know Julius Graecinus, I think?'

'Yeah.' I was still keeping my eyes off the thing on the table. 'Yes, sir, we've met.' Not, I was sure, that when I did look at him I'd recognize the poor bastard for the dapper figure I'd seen at Longinus's villa. I felt suddenly angry.

'Oh, jolly good. Splendid.' Gaius gave me a sunny smile. 'Off we go, then. Felix? Your department, I think. Don't mind me, I'll just keep Marcus company here on the sidelines.'

'Sir.' Felix stepped forward. 'Valerius Corvinus.' He turned to one of the other two guys in the room: a slave, stripped to his loin-cloth. 'The hot iron, I think. Nothing major, just enough to get his attention.'

The slave put on a leather glove and picked up a poker from the charcoal brazier while his partner freshened up the coals with a pair of bellows. He touched the tip of the poker to Graecinus's thigh; it was no more than a touch, but I could hear the hiss as it made contact and smell the burning flesh.

Graecinus screamed.

There was a bucket next to me. I bent over it and was lavishly sick.

Gaius tutted. 'Oh, Marcus!' he said. '*Really* now, petal, don't be such a big girl's blouse! If you're to be allowed to stay then you must behave.'

I didn't answer. I couldn't have.

'If you'd like to ask your questions, sir?' Felix murmured. Then, more loudly: 'Sir! Valerius Corvinus!'

'Yeah. Right.' I wiped my mouth with the back of my hand and forced myself to look at Graecinus's face rather than at the scarred, twisted and scorch-marked obscenity that the rest of his body had become. I'd been right in thinking I wouldn't recognize him, but then the condition he was in, I doubted that even his closest friend would. He stared back; one eye was almost completely shut, and from the look of it possibly missing altogether, and his face was a solid mass of bruises. 'Graecinus, I'm sorry about this,' I said. 'Really, really sorry.' No answer, just the one-eyed stare, with pure panic behind it. 'Only two questions, and if you know the answers, please tell me them. Who had Naevius Surdinus killed, and why?'

His head moved slowly from side to side. Then he cleared his throat and mumbled: 'Don't . . . know.'

Just the two words, and I had a struggle recognizing them, too. Shit; he'd lost his teeth, or most of them, maybe part of his gums as well. A thin trail of blood trickled from the corner of his mouth and ran down his cheek.

Sweet immortal gods!

'Graecinus!' I said. 'Come *on*! It can't matter now!'

'Don't . . . know.'

'Again,' Felix murmured to the slave with the poker. 'On the testicles. Leave it there for longer this time.'

I turned away before the scream came, but I could still smell the stench and hear the hiss, counting in my head to stop myself thinking. The count went to ten before the hissing sound stopped, by which time I was biting down hard on my lower lip and clenching my fists so tightly the nails pierced the palms.

'Corvinus, sir?' Felix said calmly. 'Try again, please.'

I nodded, and turned back, forcing myself to bend down with my lips close to the man's ear. 'Graecinus, for the gods' sakes!'

I whispered, 'I don't want this either, but there's nothing I can do to stop it. Just tell me, OK?'

'Don't . . . know,' he gasped. 'Swear. Don't . . . *know!*' The look in his eye now was a mixture of pain and sheer animal terror, and the words were almost unintelligible. 'Don't . . . know . . . any . . . more. Ask . . . them . . . kill . . . me. *Please!*'

Shit, I couldn't take this, not even with the emperor involved. I raised my head and tried to keep my voice steady.

'Felix, give this up, right?' I said. 'There's no point. The poor bastard doesn't know anything about Surdinus's murder. You've had all you'll get from him already.'

Felix glanced at the emperor.

'Marcus, dear, you are so terribly, transparently *squeamish*,' Gaius said. 'Gullible, too. Yes, I know, he *says* he knows nothing about the man's death. Of course he does. But they can be such persistent liars, the naughties. That's the whole point of torture. To get behind the lies to the truth in as short a time as possible. Simple but so beautifully effective.' He smiled. 'Which reminds me. I must show you something quite amusing that my predecessor had made. A modification, rather, and one of the old man's better ideas. Watch and enjoy.' Then, to the slave: 'Just two turns, I think, to begin with. To take up the slack, as it were.'

The slave bent down and turned a wheel set into the table's side. The table creaked and moved, lengthening, splitting apart in the middle along a line cutting across Graecinus's back. Graecinus moaned and shifted, tugging at the bands holding his wrists and ankles which were shackled to iron staples nailed to the wood.

The gap widened to a hand-span, the creaking stopped, and the slave straightened. Graecinus lay rigid, arms and legs fully extended. He said nothing, but his one good eye was staring at me, flecked with madness.

'That's lovely.' Gaius moved to the side of the table with the wheel, and the slave stepped aside. 'My turn.' He giggled, and twisted the wheel sharply. The gap widened by the space of two fingers and Graecinus screamed. 'It's a pun, you see, Marcus. *My turn.* I always say it, so it hasn't exactly much freshness to it any longer, but it is so *apt*. Don't you think?'

'Yes, Caesar,' I said. I felt like retching again and fought the bile down. 'Very amusing.'

'But I'm forgetting my manners. You'd like a turn yourself, of course.' He moved back. 'Go ahead, enjoy yourself. Felix won't mind, will you, Felix?'

Sweet Jupiter!

'Ah . . . I'd rather not, Caesar, if you don't mind,' I said.

There was a sudden silence. Out of the corner of my eye, I saw Felix shift, and he cleared his throat. Gaius was frowning.

'Marcus, petal,' he said slowly and carefully. 'You've been told, we all have our turn, and this is yours. I absolutely insist. Now don't be tiresome, there's a love.'

I was beginning to sweat. Oh, sure, common sense told me that I was being a complete fool, that whatever I did or didn't do, the poor bastard on the table was booked for the urn by the slowest and most painful route imaginable, and that one word from Gaius would mean I was the next one lying there. But I knew I couldn't turn that wheel. No way. Never.

The silence lengthened. Gaius and Felix were both looking at me; the two slaves, too.

'Uh . . . Caesar, that sort of thing's better left to the experts, don't you think?' I said at last. 'Me, the chances are that I'd just screw things up.'

Gaius was still frowning, and I could almost hear Felix and the brought-in help holding their collective breaths.

Hell. Yeah, well, it'd been sheer bloody stupidity and I'd only myself to blame; still, it was done now, and I'd had a good life on the whole. Not that that was much consolation, mind. I swallowed . . .

Then, suddenly, Gaius's frown lifted. He laughed, came over and hugged me round the shoulders.

'*Screw things up!*' he said. 'Marcus, that is utterly, totally *brilliant*! Oh, I really must remember that one. Don't you agree, Felix?'

'Yes, sir. Absolutely.'

'You're still a big girl's blouse, though, petal; don't think I don't see that. And I have more than a sneaking suspicion that the pun was accidental. Not that it matters, of course.' He grinned at me, but I said nothing: the guy might be a cold-blooded amoral sadistic killer and a cartload of tiles short of a watertight roof, but there was nothing wrong with his intelligence. 'Oh, fuck it, I'm bored anyway, and I need a drink. Let's call it a day, shall we? Felix, you carry on, please.' Another giggle. 'And try not to *screw things up* too much, won't you, because we need Graecinus here alive for just a little longer. Oh, yes, find out about Marcus's Surdinus by all means, if you've time, but I'm sure he has lots of other more important secrets to tell us.' He turned back to me. 'Now, Marcus, dear; come upstairs for a cup of wine and a chat. You can manage that? No pressing business elsewhere, hmm?'

'Yes, Caesar. I mean no. Of course; I'd be delighted.' Slight exaggeration, but not necessarily a complete lie; I was as grateful for the escape as I was worried about the chat, and more than relieved to be walking out with all of my bits still attached. Even so, I remembered what both Secundus and Felix had told me, or implied, anyway, about not relying on the emperor's prior goodwill any longer.

'Follow me, then.' Gaius opened the door and we went out into the fresh air. Or at least that's what the corridor smelled like now, after the stench in that hellish room. 'We'll take the short-cut.' He turned right rather than left, the way I'd come, and almost immediately up a set of narrow stone steps. 'Tiberius had this stair put in, and it is *so* convenient. He did enjoy a good torture session, the bloodthirsty old buffer. Personally, I've always wondered whether that wasn't partly the reason why there were so many traitors around in those days – make your own amuse-ments, as it were – although of course the staircase wasn't used much after he went to Capri. There again, he did have other ways of amusing himself there, didn't he?' He flashed me a sunny smile over his shoulder. 'But I'm prattling. Marcus, come *on*, you slowcoach, you're puffing like an absolute grampus, whatever that might be! You really should do more to keep yourself fit.'

Well, at least the bugger was his usual chatty self so far. I kept my fingers crossed; this Gaius I could cope with. Or hoped I could, anyway. At present I wouldn't have trusted him any more than I would a rabid dog that happened to be wagging its tail.

We came out, at last, through a door at the top which opened on to a room in the private imperial apartments. At least, from the décor, I assumed that's where we were; after the vaults, not to mention the torture chamber itself, it was Olympus compared to Tartarus. There were a couple of slaves in matching natty green tunics putting the room to rights. They stopped when they saw Gaius, bowed nervously, and edged over to stand by the wall.

Gaius ignored them. He threw himself onto a couch and indicated the one opposite.

'Make yourself comfortable, Marcus,' he said. Then, to the slaves: 'Wine. After that you can bugger off.' One of the slaves went to a corner table, poured two cups of wine from a glass decanter and brought them over. I sat. 'It is *so* nice to see you again after all these bum-faces I'm usually surrounded with. When Felix told me you were mixed up in this nonsense, it came as quite a tonic.'

'Thank you, Caesar,' I said. I sipped the wine. Caecuban. After the events of the past half hour I could've swallowed the whole bloody cupful, but I didn't want Gaius to know that; it might've implied criticism, and I reckoned I'd sailed too close to the wind enough already today without risking it twice. 'By the way, I should thank you for that flask you left me.'

'Oh, tush! Tush!' He waved it aside. 'The least I could do. But you were becoming quite a nuisance, you know. At first I thought it might be better on the whole if I got rid of you altogether, sad though that would've been, but Felix talked me out of it and suggested the cellar instead. What *would* I do without Felix?' He smiled. 'No hard feelings, I hope?'

My stomach had gone cold. 'No, Caesar, none at all,' I said.

'That's good. Water under the bridge. Let's forget about it, shall we?' He took a swallow of his own wine. 'So. Another case, wasn't it? Felix told me the connection with Graecinus and his friends was purely coincidental.'

'He . . . concluded that, yes. Graecinus happened to be a friend of the murdered man. Naevius Surdinus. And Surdinus's wife said she'd had an affair with Cassius Longinus. Which turned out not to be true.'

He'd frowned at the mention of Longinus's name, but the frown cleared.

'Longinus and Graecinus were together when you visited Longinus's house, weren't they?' he said.

'Yes, they were.' I was cautious. 'With Anicius Cerialis and another man. Valerius Asiaticus.'

'And you thought they might all be in it together? *It* at the time simply being Surdinus's murder?'

'Yes, Caesar. More or less. It was a possibility, anyway.'

'Only *it* turned out to be a conspiracy against me?'

I was beginning to wonder where all this was leading. It was leading somewhere, that was for sure: like I said, there was nothing wrong with Gaius's intelligence. Mad or not, the emperor was a smart cookie.

He smiled. 'Well, I can set your mind at rest there, anyway, to a certain extent. Regarding the conspiracy if not the murder. Cerialis you know about; Felix told you, he was our man on the inside. Longinus . . . a conspirator in embryo, maybe, but not a de facto one, fortunately for him. He's had a shock, and if he's wise he'll learn from it. Asiaticus, now . . . oh dear, oh dear, oh dear!' He laughed. 'Marcus, cherub, you cannot *possibly* suspect Asiaticus!'

'Why not, Caesar?'

'The man's a joke. A fat cuckold with the backbone of a slug. You know why he resigned his consulship five years ago? He said he couldn't take the pressure, told me so himself. Fact! Marcus, I ask you, common sense, now: what sort of politician does that make him, let alone a conspirator or a murderer? These cold-minded bastards in the senate, they thrive on pressure, they eat it for breakfast, lunch and dinner. All Asiaticus cares about is his belly and swanking around his fancy gardens. Take him off your list, petal, is my advice. I'd as soon suspect my idiot Uncle Claudius.'

Yeah, well, fair enough: Gaius knew him, and I didn't. And Gaius, in that sense at least, had his head properly screwed on to his shoulders.

'You're probably right, Caesar,' I said.

'Of course I'm bloody right! Oh, I've had Felix pull him in along with the others, but it was just for fun, to tickle him up, give him a little shock, have him pissing in his pants, the tosser.' He swallowed some more of his wine. 'Moving on. What put you on to Herennius Capito?'

'Nothing, sir. Or nothing as such. It was his son I was interested in. He was the last person to see Sextus Papinius alive, and I thought – still think – that he'd had him killed to prevent him talking to me.'

'Hmm.' Gaius was frowning again. 'I could've seen you far enough over that business, Marcus. You lost us a good source of information there. He'd still have been alive if it hadn't been for your cack-handed faffing about.' Yeah; and downstairs having his dick burned off with a red hot poker. Somehow I didn't feel too guilty about that. I kept quiet. 'Even so, we've got the father. Or had, anyway.'

'Had?'

'Capito's dead. Died under torture. It should never have happened; sheer damn carelessness on the slaves' part. After all, what do I keep those jumped-up butchers for?'

Well, at least he was out of it, and again that was a relief rather than anything else. 'He say anything useful?'

'Useful to you, you mean, about your man Surdinus?' Gaius got up, went over to the table where the wine was, brought back the decanter and topped up both our cups. 'Of course not. If he had I would've told you, petal. Not all that useful to me, either, as it turned out. Load of bloody nonsense. But then Capito was a coward; he'd say anything to avoid the pain, and he was babbling at the end so badly you couldn't make out the half of it.'

'You were there?'

The frown deepened.

'He was one of my own,' he said. 'Been with me from the start, and Tiberius before me. I thought he was loyal, I'd trusted the fucker, and that's how he repaid me. I wanted to watch him bleed and hear him scream. Of course I was bloody there!'

'So what did he say?'

A sudden smile. 'Nonsense, like I told you, cherub. Not that it started like that, mind, because the first name he came up with was his immediate boss, Callistus. No surprises there, on the surface: Callistus is one of my freedmen, Capito's a knight, so the seniority should've gone the other way. It didn't, at least de facto, because Callistus is a shit-hot accountant, which Capito isn't. Capito has always hated his guts, so if he knew he had to go, he might as well take Callistus with him. You see?'

'Yeah. Yes, Caesar, I see.' Fair enough.

'On the other hand, Callistus is a scheming, ambitious bastard who'd take to conspiracy like a duck takes to water.'

'Ah. Right.'

Gaius grinned and set down his wine cup. 'You know, Marcus, petal, I *do* enjoy talking to you,' he said. 'Even when you're doing the careful *Yes, Caesar* and *No, Caesar* bit and answering in monosyllables, I feel that I'm dealing with a working brain, not just a ragbag collection of petty ambition, half-baked prejudices, vested interests and self-serving *tat*. Believe me, that's what I get in this job, most of the time, and it is just *so* boring you would not *believe*. I'm glad I didn't have you killed.'

I half-smiled myself, despite the touch of cold on my spine at the offhand tone. Yeah, when you got Gaius on a good day – or maybe a good half-hour might be more realistic, given the pace of the mood changes – there was something there apart from the monster that I could identify with and even feel sympathy for. It was buried pretty deep, mind you, and the rest of the psychotic bugger was a walking toxic nightmare you wouldn't want to get within a mile of, no arguments, but there it was.

'Me, too, Caesar,' I said.

'Ah, the monosyllables again. Well, well.' He sighed, picked up the cup and drank some more of his wine. 'So. Callistus was a definite possible, and so was the next name. Arrecinus Clemens.'

'Who's Clemens?'

'One of the Praetorian prefects.'

'Ah.'

Another grin. 'As you say, dear, and justifiably so, *ah*. Again, perfectly possible and believable. Certainly that, yes, but no more: I've nothing in particular against Clemens. He's a knight, of course, although from a nothing of a family, and he's good at his job. He's loyal, or if he isn't he's given me no reason to suspect it, and more important he's neither ambitious nor a risk-taker. Very god-fearing, although his god-fearing-ness, if there is such a word, does take peculiar forms.'

'Such as?'

'He seems very taken with the Jews, poor lamb – don't, please, ask me why, cherub, the silly stiff-necked buggers – and them with him. In fact, they call him just that, "The God-fearer", although in their case they're being quite specific. Still and all, I thought he was one of my prefects, top of the Praetorian tree, and if you're organizing a conspiracy then who better to have on your side than a Guard commander? No, I was perfectly prepared to believe in Clemens as a conspirator. Particularly because, as far as I knew, Capito didn't know him from Romulus.'

'So where did the nonsense come in?'

'Oh, that! The third name he came out with was my wife's.

Caesonia's. Now don't laugh, petal.' I wasn't going to. 'But really, it's ridiculous, isn't it? Caesonia wouldn't conspire against me. She hasn't a conspiratorial bone in her body or thought in her fluffy little head. To tell you the truth, she hasn't got all that much in her fluffy little head to begin with. Great little body, though. Anyway, that's where he lost me. I mean, credibility's one thing. Callistus and Clemens, fine, in theory, but did he take me for a gullible bloody imbecile? So no, I decided we could forget friend Capito. Then of course the treacherous sod went and died on me, and that was that.' He suddenly yawned and stretched. 'Marcus, dear, I wonder if you'd excuse me? I know it's only the middle of the afternoon, but these sessions downstairs are *so* tiring, and I had quite a heavy night last night. A nap, I think. You don't mind if I throw you out now?'

'Not at all, Caesar.'

'I have enjoyed our little chat. As I say, I've found it very refreshing. We must do it again sometime. Or perhaps you and your lovely wife – Rufia Perilla, isn't it? – would like to come to dinner one evening soon. Nothing too formal, just a few friends.'

'Thank you, Caesar. But we'll be going through to the Alban Hills tonight to see our adopted daughter and her husband, and staying until after the festival.'

'What a shame! Perhaps when you come back. We must arrange something.'

'Certainly.' Not if I could help it. 'I look forward to it.'

'I'll let you know. Do have a nice time, and a happy Festival. My regards to Perilla.' He stretched out on the couch and closed his eyes. 'Goodbye, petal. The slaves'll show you out.'

I left, and he was asleep before I reached the door.

Interesting, yes? Certainly there were avenues there that needed exploring. Even so, I'd given my word to Perilla, and besides, the conspiracy per se was dead and buried and so was the case: Surdinus, like Papinius, had been killed to stop him blabbing, and the identity of his actual killer was academic because the bastard was already dead or soon would be. If the itch was still at the back of my mind then I'd just have to live with it. In any case, Gaius was probably right about Capito's evidence being useless; Felix had the business completely in hand, and everything else was a mare's nest.

Possibly.

Or, there again, possibly not . . .

Fuck. Well, like I say, I'd just have to make the best of things. I went home.

TWENTY-THREE

We took the carriage through to Castrimoenium that evening. Perilla had sent a skivvy on ahead, so at least we were expected; meaning that, when we rolled up well after midnight, we didn't get the locked door and the dogs set on us. The hellhound Placida excepted, naturally, but then with her you stood more chance of being drooled to death than anything else, and she meant well.

Childbirth, of course, is a risky business at the best of times, but where Marilla was concerned I needn't've worried; she was blooming. Clarus said the pregnancy was going as it should and the sprog looked like being on time. Which, in the event, he was. After several days of nail-biting tension and a couple of false alarms, young Marcus Cornelius Clarus came squalling into the world bang on the button an hour after dawn on the first day of the festival. He was introduced to the household and the household gods; Juno the Light-Bringer had her post-natal sacrifice and set of thank-you clothes, and after he'd thrown his ninth-day party and sicked up all over Perilla's shoulder, life settled down into an easy holiday pace.

Oh, yeah, sure, I'd thought about Surdinus and the rest of it from time to time, but there'd been enough going on to keep my mind occupied. Plus the fact that being away from the city and completely out of things had given the whole boiling a sort of mental distance as well. By the time Perilla had finally had enough of playing the doting grandparent and given the thumb's-up for heading home, I'd virtually drawn a line under it.

Until, that is, sixteen days into the new year and halfway through our second morning back, Naevia Postuma rolled up.

* * *

This time, both of us were at home. Perilla laid the book she'd been reading down on the table beside her couch and gave the lady her best smile.

'Naevia Postuma,' she said. 'Well, this is a surprise.'

'Then it certainly should not be.' Postuma glared at Bathyllus until the little guy had wheeled out one of our broadest and strongest chairs and set it behind her. She sat; the chair creaked in protest. 'Valerius Corvinus, you gave me your word of honour that you would find my uncle's killer.'

'Ah . . . in actual fact . . .' I began.

'Don't prevaricate! That was certainly the impression I formed during our last interview, and you know perfectly well that you have done nothing of the kind. It's an absolute disgrace!'

'To be fair, Naevia Postuma, it wasn't entirely Marcus's fault,' Perilla said. 'How was he to know that the death was going to link in with a plot against the emperor? After which, of course, the whole thing was taken out of his hands.'

'Stuff and nonsense. Uncle Lucius was no traitor.'

'No one's claiming that he was,' I said patiently. 'Quite the reverse. My guess is that one of the conspirators tried to recruit him, he was about to blow the whistle on the business and the guy panicked and had him killed. End of story.'

'Which conspirator?'

I shrugged. 'I don't know. I hadn't got that far. But the question's academic because the conspiracy is busted, the emperor had everyone responsible in the bag well before the festival, and by this time they're all dead as mutton. Like Perilla told you, as far as I'm concerned the case is closed.'

'That it most certainly is not.'

I blinked. 'Uh . . . I beg your pardon?'

'Granted. The case, as you call it, Valerius Corvinus, is most definitely still open. Very much so. Alexander has given me his most firm assurance to that effect.'

Gods! I was prepared to make some allowances, sure – after all, the lady was right, in a way, and I hadn't delivered in full in terms of the contract, if contract there had been – but my patience was wearing thin here. Besides, I couldn't see what else she expected me to do. Not with the real professionals on the job and an emperor in the background who was as mentally stable as a rhino with a migraine.

'Look, lady, you can tell Alexander from me that he can take a flying—' I began.

'*Marcus!*' Perilla snapped.

'Leap.'

Postuma stood up. 'I repeat, young man, the case is *not* closed. Very far from it. Furthermore, because of your inexcusable shilly-shallying—'

'My *what*?'

'—time is of the essence. According to Alexander, you have only until the Palatine Games to do as you promised. Should you fail, the consequences will be disastrous; Alexander was most clear on that point as well. Now that is all I have to say, and the rest is up to you. I'll see myself out. Good day to you both.'

And she left.

Bugger.

'So, dear,' Perilla said when the room's vibes had settled and we were alone again. 'How do you think that went?'

'Come on, lady! What did she expect? And whose side are you on, anyway?'

Perilla sighed. 'Yours, of course,' she said. 'I'm sorry. And you're quite right, there's nothing more you can do.'

'Isn't there?'

She stared at me. 'Marcus, I distinctly heard you telling her that there isn't. And you are *not* taking this any further. For one thing it's not safe.'

True, unfortunately. Still, although I hated to admit it, the safety angle was only one factor in all this, and not necessarily the most important one, either.

'Agreed,' I said. 'No argument. Only, if we're being totally honest here, the lady's VIP pal is right about the case not being properly closed; there're too many loose ends dangling around. And I didn't like that bit about the Palatine Games much above half, either.'

'Marcus Valerius Corvinus, you are not telling me you *believe* that nonsense about Alexander the Great? That is just silly!'

'Yeah, well, maybe. Stranger things have happened, and me, I like to keep an open mind.'

'I told you, it's just a harmless eccentricity. Postuma's been claiming he talks to her for years. No one pays any attention any more.'

'Even so, the guy was bang up to scratch originally about Surdinus's death being murder when all the evidence pointed towards an accident. And the Palatine Games are only eight days away. Plus there're no prizes for guessing what the disastrous consequences will be, not when we've already got a conspiracy on the books.'

'A failed conspiracy. You said it yourself.'

'Let's assume it hasn't. Failed, I mean, or not completely. That it's still up and running.'

She'd picked up her book when Postuma had stormed out. Now she set it down again.

'Marcus, I will get really angry with you in a minute!' she snapped. 'The conspiracy is *dead*! Whatever else Gaius is, he's no one's fool, and your friend Felix certainly isn't one either. Besides, they used torture on the poor men that they did catch. Don't you think that if there were any other people involved they'd've had the names out of them long ago?'

I thought of Graecinus, or what Felix and his pals had left of him, anyway. I hadn't mentioned that side of things to Perilla – as far as the lady was concerned, I'd just gone to the palace for a chat with the emperor – but she was no one's fool, either, and where treason was concerned, torture was normal practice.

'Maybe they didn't know them,' I said.

'Of course they did! They must have done!'

I let that one pass for the present; Perilla wasn't in any mood for a prolonged argument, and I wasn't chancing my luck where getting mauled was concerned. 'OK,' I said. 'Then maybe they just decided that protecting them and giving them a chance of getting rid of Gaius after all was more important than saving their own lives. Or saving themselves pain, rather, since the poor buggers'd know they were for the chop whatever they said. Where they got the courage from, the gods know, but it happens sometimes.'

'Not very often, I would imagine. If anything, I'd expect things to go the other way. The temptation would be to give the names of people who were completely innocent, simply to suggest that you were cooperating.'

'Yeah, like Capito did. OK, fair enough. Good point.'

'Who's Capito?'

Oh. Right. She wouldn't know about that side of things. Capito – or rather his evidence, relayed to me by Gaius – had fallen by the wayside in the rush to get down to Clarus and Marilla's, and naturally once we were clear of Rome, anything to do with the case had become a no-go area. 'Herennius Capito,' I said. 'The imperial procurator. You remember? His son Bassus was with Sextus Papinius when he had his riding accident and I found them both together in Capito's office. Felix bagged them just after I left.' I was frowning; there was an itch somewhere at the back of my mind, just where I couldn't quite get to it. 'Gaius mentioned it, that day at the palace. Capito claimed there were more people involved than he knew about, and the names he came up with were pretty impressive.'

'Such as who?'

'Arrecinus Clemens. He's one of the two Praetorian prefects. And an imperial freedman, a guy named Callistus. One of the emperor's top civil servants, seemingly a whizz kid on the financial side. Both good possibilities, according to Gaius.'

'Then why weren't they arrested? Or were they?'

'No. Capito gave Gaius's wife Caesonia as the third conspirator. At least, the third one he knew about, anyway. Gaius decided that he was doing just what you said, implicating innocent people in the hope of stopping the torture, so he didn't take the matter any further.' The itch was there again. 'In any case, Capito died on him practically straight away, so that was the end of that. Of course . . .' I stopped. Bathyllus had slipped back in and was doing his hovering-with-intent act. 'Yeah, little guy, what is it? Postuma nick the best spoons on her way out?'

'No, sir.' He was looking self-important as hell. 'A dinner invitation. From the palace.'

'*What?*' Perilla was up like a rocketing pheasant.

Oh, fuck, this I didn't need! I swallowed.

'Ah. Yeah, right,' I said. 'Sorry, lady, my fault. I'd completely forgotten about that.'

'How on *earth* could you *possibly* . . .'

'Gaius did say when we met that he'd have us round to dinner when we got back. I hoped at the time he was just making polite noises.'

'Marcus, you absolute *idiot!*' She turned to Bathyllus. 'When's the invitation for?'

'Tomorrow evening, madam.'

'Oh, gods! *Tomorrow* evening?'

'Yes, madam. The emperor's social secretary apologizes for the short notice, but he says to be assured that the occasion will not be a formal one.'

'There you are, Perilla,' I said. 'Informal. No worries.' That just got me a Look, after which she was up and moving in the direction of the stairs. 'You going somewhere?'

'I am going,' she said over her shoulder, 'shopping. Just as soon as I've changed and collected my cloak.'

'Shopping for what?'

'A new mantle, of course. If, that is, thanks to you it's not too late to find a decent one.'

'Come on, lady! The invite said informal and you've got dozens of the things already!'

That didn't even get an answer. 'Bathyllus, I need the litter,' she said. 'Inside of five minutes, please.'

'Yes, madam.'

'And Marcus, if you ever, *ever* do anything like this again I shall kill you in the slowest and most painful manner I can think of. I may even do it anyway, after I get back. Particularly if I can find nothing suitable. Is that clear?'

'Yeah, well . . .'

But she was already gone. Sometimes I wonder about that lady's sense of priorities.

'Hey, Bathyllus,' I said before the little guy buggered off in his turn. 'A half-jug of wine, please. No hurry. After you've broken the bad news to the litter slaves will do fine.' It was throwing it down outside, which was why I was hanging around the house, and no doubt our matching set of lardballs were toasting their toes in front of a brazier somewhere. Plus, knowing Perilla's hyper-picky approach to shopping, they were in for a good few hours of lugging her round most of the mantle shops in the city. Fun, fun, fun. 'Make it the Special.'

I might as well use the lady's sudden absence to put in a bit of constructive thinking regarding the case. Because case it undoubtedly still was; Postuma's Alexander had been right about that. And there wasn't a better way of lubricating the brain cells than a cup or two of the Special.

Five minutes might have been pushing it, but she was back down in short order, dressed for a cold, wet January tour of the clothes shops. I got a distinctly acid look as she passed me going in the direction of the lobby. A couple of minutes later, the front door slammed hard enough to shake the paint off.

Well, that one certainly wouldn't go down in the annals of How to Keep the Shine on your Marriage, would it?

I sighed. Bathyllus brought in the half-jug and cup, and I took a contemplative swallow.

Right. So where did we start? First, and *pace* Perilla, with the assumption, crazy as it might seem, that Postuma's Alexander was more than the product of a slightly nutty middle-aged woman's fevered imagination; that, in fact, imaginary or not, dead over three hundred years or not, the guy was worth listening to. Alexander had been fairly insistent throughout that what I was looking for was a solution to Surdinus's murder, not the uncovering of a conspiracy against the emperor. Oh, sure, the two were bound up together, no arguments there – and in the end I'd bet that it came to the same thing – but even so there had to be a reason for the preference.

So. Given the ongoing impossibility of tracing the actual perp – our freedman friend with the scar or birthmark or whatever – it was back to my four original suspects for the role of murderer-by-proxy, the guys at Longinus's house: Cassius Longinus himself, Valerius Asiaticus, Anicius Cerialis and Julius Graecinus. Graecinus was dead, of course – at least I assumed and hoped he was – but I'd've taken him off the list anyway. Conspirator or not, if he'd been lying when he'd sworn under torture that he knew nothing about Surdinus's death then he had a lot more courage and strength of mind than I could ever have mustered. So not Graecinus.

Not Cerialis, either. Given the theory – and I could see nothing wrong with it – that X, the killer, had had Surdinus murdered because he was threatening to expose the conspiracy to Gaius, Cerialis had no motive, because he was working for the emperor himself. Oh, sure, running the chance of having their clandestine operation put in jeopardy by a premature whistle-blower might've been an inconvenience – I only had to think about what had happened in my own case to see that – but it surely didn't warrant taking the guy out. He'd've shown himself a loyal and conscientious subject of the emperor, and a quiet word would've been enough. Besides, if for one reason or another that had been the way things had happened, either Felix or Gaius himself would've made no bones about telling me so straight out.

So not Anicius Cerialis, either. Which left Longinus and Asiaticus. And given the likelihood that the story of his adultery with Cornelia Sullana, which had provided Longinus with what paltry scraps of motive I could hang on him, was so much moonshine, plus the fact that having only been in Rome five minutes – and that by Gaius's own doing – made him an unlikely conspirator, Cassius Longinus was a definite also-ran.

Asiaticus it was, then.

Right; what did I know about him? Seriously wealthy, ex-suffect consul but not currently political, at least according to Gaius. Had resigned his suffect-consulship five years back prematurely because – again according to Gaius – he couldn't take the pressure. Well-connected socially: married to the sister of Gaius's ex-wife. Whom Gaius had proceeded to seduce, then get tired of and treat her cuckolded husband as a figure of fun, giving him a very personal motive for wanting to see the emperor in an urn.

Not a lot to go on, to put it mildly. Nor did Asiaticus – as far as I knew – have a direct connection with Surdinus. In fact, if I remembered rightly, when I'd talked to Surdinus Junior he'd told me specifically that his father hadn't known Asiaticus except by name. Still, he'd certainly been a friend – or at least an intimate – of Julius Graecinus, who was one of Surdinus's closest pals, and given that Graecinus was a co-conspirator, it'd explain why . . .

I stopped, frowning. Hang on; things didn't add up here. The theory was that, for reasons best known to themselves, and forget the whys and wherefores, the conspirators had decided to recruit Lucius Surdinus – mistakenly, as it turned out, because the guy turned out to be a loose barrel in the hold and had to be got rid of. Now if Asiaticus was our man X – the murderer-by-proxy – then we had a major logical problem. The original decision to bring Surdinus on to the team could only have been made by someone who knew him well enough to decide that he'd be sympathetic to the cause. And that could only be Graecinus, because apart from him, out of the remaining members of our Gang of Four, only Longinus qualified, and even if Longinus was a member of the conspiracy in its latter stages he was out of the country at the time. Logically, then, Graecinus must've known at least of Surdinus's initial involvement, however deeply that went, because he'd've done the recruiting himself. Or at least advised on it.

So far so good.

Only at that point the whole thing gets wobbly, because that's where Graecinus's knowledge of the situation stops. Or ostensibly stops, anyway. Which brought us to three possible scenarios.

First, Graecinus had been telling the truth, and the connection between Surdinus's murder and the conspiracy was a complete mare's nest from start to finish. Possible, sure, but for all kinds of circumstantial reasons as likely as a snowfall in July. File and forget.

Second, that when the guy had sworn to me that he knew nothing about Surdinus's death or the identity of his killer, despite all Felix's torturers could do and the prolonged, unbearable pain, he'd been lying through what few teeth the bastards had left him. If you could credit him with that much sheer persistent courage then that scenario made perfect sense: although Valerius Asiaticus might've been under suspicion at that point, he was a long way from Gaius's sliding table, and one word from Graecinus would've put him on it before you could say 'rack'. Me, I doubt if I could've done the same, given the circumstances, but I had to admit it was a viable possibility.

Third scenario, the *really* interesting one. Back, in a way, to the first: that when Graecinus had said he knew nothing about Surdinus's murder he'd been telling the absolute truth. Not, though, this time because the dead man and the conspiracy weren't connected, but because X was working to his own agenda; the decision to have the guy killed and the arrangements for his actual murder were made on his own authority, without the knowledge and agreement of the others. If that was the case, then we were faced with what could be an entirely new ball-game: unless X – Asiaticus – was playing things off his own bat, which was pretty unlikely, then he was working for or with someone else. In other words, what we had was a conspiracy within a conspiracy, one that was still up and running, and one that neither Gaius nor Felix knew about. And, presumably, I had until the Palatine Games in eight days' time to crack the problem.

Shit. Score one for Alexander.

I took a long swallow of the Special.

So, what did I do now? The most sensible course of action, naturally, would be to take the whole boiling straight to Gaius, or to Felix, at least. Where treason was concerned, they were the experts, and if the plot went ahead and succeeded then it was Gaius himself who'd get the chop. Only I couldn't do that, could I? Not yet, anyway. First, because it was only a theory with nothing to back it up; second because Gaius himself had told me in so many words that as a conspirator Asiaticus was a non-starter, and given the emperor's current mental state I wasn't stupid enough to risk contradicting him. The third reason, though, was the clincher: I'd seen what happened to treason suspects first-hand, and there was absolutely no way I was about to finger Asiaticus – or anyone else – to Felix when I wasn't a hundred per cent cast-iron sure of the bastard's guilt myself. Absolutely *no* way.

Eight days it was, then. Bugger. I took another swallow.

Right. Plan of action. When in doubt, dig and see what turns up that you can use. I needed to find out more about Julius Asiaticus. Also, of course, about the two guys whose names had cropped up in Herennius Capito's evidence, the Praetorian prefect Arrecinus Clemens and the top-notch civil servant Julius Callistus: Gaius could dismiss them if he liked, but me, I couldn't take the risk, and besides, my gut feeling told me they came into this business somewhere along the line.

So a visit to Cornelius Lentulus was definitely in order, because if my pal Caelius Crispus was the expert where the private, seamy side of Rome's Great and Good went, then old Lentulus balanced him where their public and not-so-public roles as political animals were concerned. Balanced, that is, in its purely metaphorical sense: physically Lentulus would've made three of Crispus with a large helping of blubber still to spare, and he wouldn't have balanced anything lighter than a hippo. As a brain, though, and a mine of information, eighty years old or not the guy was in peak condition. Also, he lived just up the hill from us, which, given the current filthy weather was an added bonus. Not even I enjoyed slogging my way through streets with mud and worse up to the ankles, in the teeth of a freezing rainstorm, and in general early January wasn't the time to be out and about in Rome.

Lentulus it was, then, and there was no time like the present. I downed the rest of the wine in my cup and went to change into my outdoor things.

Onwards and upwards.

TWENTY-FOUR

L ike I said, Lentulus lived only a few hundred yards upslope
from us, not far from Mother's and Priscus's place, in a
rambling old property that predated most of the ones on
the hill. It was fortunate that it was close, since I'd been right
about the weather, and the road was a muddy river overflowing
its central guttering. I wondered how Perilla was getting on; not
a wet-weather fan, either, that lady, and although she'd be snug
and dry in the litter, I knew there'd be hell to pay when she got
back. Especially if she hadn't found anything to suit.

Ah, well, it wasn't every day we got invited to an imperial
dinner party. Luckily. Not that I was looking forward to it,
mind.

I gave my name to the door slave and he took me through.
Not to the atrium: Lentulus was holed up in his study, on a couch
big and hefty enough to take half a squad of Praetorians, and
the room was heated like an oven.

'Ah, Marcus,' he said when the slave had closed the door
behind me and left me cooking. 'Come to visit the invalid on
his bed of pain, have you? Good of you, my boy!'

Yeah, well, whatever was wrong with him didn't look too
serious: the table beside the couch was laden with goodies, and
his ancient major-domo was in the process of topping up his
wine cup.

'Hi, Lentulus,' I said, pulling up a stool. 'You're ill?'

'Oh, it's nothing much. Just a cold. A complete stinker, mind;
I wouldn't wish it on anyone.' He sneezed. 'Bugger! Desmus,
get Valerius Corvinus a drink. Not this muck, Marcus, it's hot
honey wine. Poisonous stuff, but my doctor says it's the best
thing for me. Hot and dry to counter cold and wet, or some such
Greek nonsense. The Falernian, Desmus, if you will.' Another
sneeze; he reached for a napkin, blew his nose and tossed the
napkin aside. 'Excuse me. What's it doing outside, weather wise?
Still pissing down hard?'

'Yeah, more or less.'

'Good. No fun being snug as a bug in a rug in here if the poor bastards outside aren't suffering. How's Perilla?'

'Blooming. And we're grandparents now. As of the Winter Festival.'

'Clarus done his duty and young Marilla's popped, then, has she?' It always amazed me that Lentulus had people's names at his finger-ends: the last time I'd seen him had been two years before, when Marilla and Clarus were first engaged, and I'd only mentioned our son-in-law's name to him once. Still, among his erstwhile senatorial cronies, Lentulus's nickname was 'the Elephant', and it wasn't just because of his size, either. 'What is it? Boy or girl?'

'Boy. Marcus Cornelius Clarus.'

'That's good. Girls're too much trouble, in my admittedly limited experience. Give them my congratulations and best wishes.' Desmus was at my elbow, handing me a cupful of Falernian. I sipped: beautiful. Lentulus knew his wines; he ought to, he'd swallowed enough of them in his time. 'Help yourself to nibbles.'

'No, I'm OK, thanks.' I looked at the table: the 'nibbles' included quails' eggs, marinated chicken legs, bean rissoles and a selection of dried fruits and nuts. 'I'm sorry, Lentulus, I'm disturbing you. Early lunch, is it?'

'Nothing of the kind, as you well know, you sarcastic young bugger. Just a mid-morning snack. Feed a cold, starve a fever. Didn't your old grandmother teach you anything?'

From what I remembered of Grandma Calpurnia, she'd've told the slaves to remove the whole boiling and replace it with a bowl of nourishing barley gruel. Still, maybe medical theory had moved on in the past thirty years. 'Obviously not,' I said.

'Clearly.' He grinned, coughed, and selected a chicken leg. 'Right, boy. Social civilities dispensed with, we can get down to business. You're here to pick my brains again, yes? So what's it about this time? Another conspiracy?'

Straight to the point as usual. Another thing I liked about Lentulus. 'Ah . . .'

'Hmm. That bad, eh? Well, in that case don't bother telling me because I don't want to know. At my time of life, the less anxiety I have the better. Or so the doctor says, and this time I'd agree with the po-faced old bugger.' He bit into the chicken leg and chewed. 'Fire away, then.'

'Just some background information on a few names. Starting with Valerius Asiaticus.'

'Asiaticus?' The eyebrows went up. 'Not a star performer, that one, young Marcus. Fella's one of the Johnny-come-lately Gallic crowd. Allobrogian, from Vienne. Good local family, had their citizenship originally from one of your lot about a hundred years back. Valerius Flaccus, that would be, the Transalpine governor. Consul suffect in the old emperor's last year, resigned before his six-month stint was up. Rich as Croesus, owns a house and gardens the other side of the river that used to belong to Lucullus. Wife Lollia Saturnina, our Gaius's ex-wife's sister. Silly woman, too fond of jewellery, thinks that it and good looks make up for brains, and she's possessed of conversational skills that would disgrace a parrot. He's technically a senator, but lazy as hell. Doesn't turn up for meetings very often and steers clear of committee work. Not that I blame him there; it's the bane of existence and boring as hell. That do you?'

'No, I knew all that. Barring the bit about the jewellery.'

'You're hard to please today, you young sod. What, then?'

'His reasons for resigning his consulship, for a start. The emperor told me it was because he couldn't take the pressure.'

That got me a straight look. 'Been talking to Gaius, have you? This must be important, right enough.' I said nothing. 'Well, it's none of my business. Or rather, I don't want it to be.' He downed some more of the wine, tore off another mouthful of chicken and took his time chewing it, not taking his eyes off me all the while. Finally, he swallowed and shrugged. 'Very well, young Marcus Corvinus,' he said. '*Pressure* isn't exactly the word I'd use, although I can see why Gaius chose it.'

'What, then?'

'See if you can get there yourself. What was happening, politically, that last year of Tiberius's life?'

'Uh . . .'

'Come on, Marcus, you're being slow! Put your thinking cap on! I'll give you a whopping great clue. Gemellus.'

Shit. 'Tiberius altered his will. Or the part affecting the succession, anyway.' He was right; I should've thought of that myself. 'Up to then, Tiberius's grandson Gemellus had been his only principal heir, in effect his named successor. Only now he named Gaius and Gemellus as joint heirs.'

'Right. And we're anticipating matters slightly here, but it's relevant. Tiberius died in March the following year. Gemellus being underage and several tiles short of a watertight roof to boot, Gaius became emperor. Come December or thereabouts, what happened?'

'Gaius had Gemellus executed. For conspiring against him while he was ill.' Fuck; we'd been through all this the last time I'd talked to Lentulus, regarding the Macro business: the whole Gemellus plot had been a sham, from start to finish. 'What's this got to do with Asiaticus's resignation?'

'Evidence of intelligent planning, boy, and a nose for the way the wind was blowing. He's a smart cookie in that respect, Asiaticus, always has been. Oh, there was no skulduggery involved on his part, quite the reverse, and at the end of the day it probably saved his life.'

I frowned. 'I'm sorry, pal, you've lost me completely here.'

'Marcus, Marcus!' Lentulus tossed the remains of the chicken leg on to the table. 'Use your brain! We're talking factions. Julians against Claudians, the way it's always been ever since that bitch Livia's day. Asiaticus was and is a protégé and supporter of the old emperor's sister-in-law Antonia, right? Gemellus's great-aunt by marriage, and definitely on the Claudian side of the fence. In fact, he's been a close friend of her son Tiberius Claudius for years. Gaius, of course, is a Julian through and through. So between Gaius and Gemellus, where would his sympathies lie as far as the question of Tiberius's successor went, hmm? Or rather, where would Gaius assume they lay?'

I was beginning to see light here. 'With Gemellus, naturally.'

'Correct. Like I say, Asiaticus isn't stupid, far from it; he could see the way things were going better than most, and a whole lot earlier. It was getting too hot for him, so he cleared out of the kitchen while he still could. Jacked it in completely and went off to prune his roses on the other side of the Tiber. Which is what he's still doing.' He held up his cup for Desmus to fill. 'At least, that's his story.'

'You don't believe him?'

Lentulus chuckled and coughed. 'Now don't you go putting words into my mouth or taking me up wrong just because it happens to suit you, you over-suspicious young bugger,' he said. 'I don't have an opinion one way or the other, and nor should you. All I'm saying is that the man's a survivor, but whether that comes about through deliberate craft or inbuilt nature, I don't know. He was a close friend of Junius Silanus, too, and that wasn't a safe thing to be when the emperor decided he was conspiring with Gemellus and ordered him into suicide. Asiaticus was left alone because he kept a low profile. Head well below the parapet. Best policy to adopt when you're dealing with a paranoid bastard like Gaius, hey?' He caught himself and tutted. 'As you were, Marcus, forget that, I didn't say it. It was the wine talking, right? Or maybe this cold. I'm not at my best.'

'Yeah, sure. Understood.' A survivor. Head below the parapet. Yeah, that had Asiaticus to a T: he'd survived this time as well, whether because, as Lentulus had said, he'd planned things deliberately, or because he was quite genuine and what you saw was what you got. Certainly, he'd convinced Gaius, and like I say the emperor was no fool where judging character was concerned. I thought of those snakes that blend in with their background so perfectly that you don't know they're there until they rear up and bite you . . .

OK, so plenty of food for thought there. And it all fitted. *Pace* Gaius, Asiaticus was definitely in the frame. Move on.

'What about Julius Callistus?' I said. 'You crossed his path at all?'

'The emperor's financial secretary? No, can't say I have.'

'Know anything about him?'

'Only that he's bloody good at his job, like a lot of the freedmen Gaius has been filling the top imperial admin posts with these past few years. Mind you, he'd have to be, especially these days.'

'Why so?' I reached over and helped myself to a stuffed date.

'Because what with one thing and another, Gaius is getting through money like there's no tomorrow. Publicly and privately. It has to come from somewhere, and even those bloody fancy direct taxes he's introduced lately aren't bringing in enough pennies to pay the bills.' Lentulus chuckled and peeled a quail's egg. 'Just shows you to be careful what you wish for, boy. When the emperor started using freedmen, some of my more poker-up-the-arse colleagues down the hill moaned like hell. Ex-slaves with their master's slap still fresh on their cheeks giving the orders and running the empire? What would Sulla have said? Barbarians at the gates, the end of civilization, grouse, grouse, grouse. You know the sort of thing.' He dipped the egg in fish sauce, popped it into his mouth and chewed. 'Only now you don't hear a cheep from them, do you, because the tossers know that if they moan too loud and Gaius hands the job over to them, Rome'll be bankrupt inside of a month.'

'As bad as that, is it?'

'Well, maybe I'm exaggerating a tad. But if it wasn't for Julius Callistus and his ilk over on the Palatine doing their financial balancing act and holding things together, the treasury would be looking pretty bare.'

'Uh-huh.' Interesting. 'OK. Last name. Arrecinus Clemens.'

'Clemens, eh?' Another shrewd look as he reached for the quails' eggs. 'Quite a mixed bag you've got there, Marcus, my boy. Praetorians, now, is it?'

'Yeah, as it happens.' I kept my voice neutral. Not that I had any illusions about being able to pull the wool over Lentulus's eyes. He was no Secundus; he'd been involved in the labyrinthine world of politics all his life, certainly long enough to know how many beans made five, and the pattern that was emerging here was pretty obvious. As were the implications, and so my reasons for asking. If he'd decided to play dumb then it was through conscious choice. 'Anything you've got.'

He grunted and concentrated on shelling the egg. 'Joint Praetorian prefect, equestrian, good provincial Italian family but nothing special – from Arpinum, or thereabouts. Military type to the bone, not a political. Steady, reliable, conscientious. Solid clear through, particularly where his head's concerned. Which of course was why Gaius appointed him.'

Well, again I'd known most of that, and from Gaius himself. But there had to be more. 'Happy in his job?' I said.

Lentulus hesitated. 'Moderately,' he said. 'Chap's got a bit of an awkward bee in his bonnet, though. About the Jews, of all things.'

Yeah; Gaius had mentioned that, too. 'The God-Fearer business,' I said.

He nodded. 'That's right. You'd heard?'

'Not in any detail, no. Why awkward?'

'Because it's producing a certain . . . conflict of interests.' He still wasn't looking at me; all his attention was on the egg. 'You know about the Alexandrian delegation?'

'No. What delegation would that be?'

'From the Jewish community there. Led by a chap called Philo. They arrived in Rome a year ago to petition the emperor to give them equal citizen rights with the Greeks. They're still around, as it happens.'

'After a *year*?'

Lentulus laid the egg aside and looked up. 'Gaius is in no hurry, boy,' he said. 'That's the point. Or partly the point. Philo and his cronies have spent the past twelve months twiddling their thumbs on the other side of the river, and they're likely to stay there indefinitely. Jews haven't exactly been flavour of the month with Caesar ever since the trouble at Jamnia.'

'Where the hell's Jamnia?'

'Palestine. Near Jerusalem, on the coast. The town's part of the imperial estates. Mixed Jewish-Greek, like a lot of those places. Just after the delegation got here, the Greeks in Jamnia set up an altar to the imperial cult. The local Jews rioted and pulled it down.' I winced. *Trouble* was right: Rome's pretty tolerant where religion's concerned – as long as you don't go in for ceremonies involving cannibalism, ritual bestiality or the wholesale sacrifice of virgins, you can worship whatever god you like – but start mixing religion with politics and you're up shit creek before you can say *military intervention*. Pulling down an altar to the Goddess Rome and her earthly representative would qualify in spades. 'When Procurator Capito passed the news on to Gaius, the emperor went spare. He—'

'Hang on, Lentulus,' I said. '*Capito*? Herennius Capito?'

'That's the fella, yes.' He was bland. 'Gaius pulled him back to Rome shortly afterwards. He's dead now, poor bugger. Blotted his copybook good and proper, so I understand. Anyway, I was saying, Gaius decided that if that was the way the intolerant bastards were going to play it, then he'd give them tit for tat and convert their temple in Jerusalem into an imperial shrine, with a statue of himself as Jupiter as the centrepiece. Not that that came to anything in the end, mind, fortunately, because the Syrian governor deliberately dragged his feet over supplying the actual statue itself. By which time Caesar's pal Herod Agrippa had managed to persuade him to drop the idea.'

Yeah, I remembered that Secundus had mentioned the statue

business. I hadn't realized at the time that it was going to be relevant. Which it appeared it was.

'And all this is connected with Clemens, right?' I said.

'Naturally. In a way, at least. I told you: Clemens may not be political as such but he and Philo are pretty thick together. Plus he's a good friend of Agrippa's. Just as well things panned out the way they did, mark you. Things being as they are, if the emperor had had his way it would've caused real trouble. Still might, for that matter, if he's not careful and pulls his horns in. No fan of the Jews, our Gaius, and they know it.' Lentulus picked up his wine cup and took a swig. 'So. There you are, young Marcus. Had enough?'

'Yeah.' I took a contemplative swallow of my Falernian. 'Yeah, that'll just about do it.' Gods, it would at that, and with knobs on! I'd seen the trouble messing with Jewish sensibilities caused myself, at first hand, a couple of years before when we were in Alex. That time we'd been lucky to get out of the place in advance of the rioting, but it had been a close thing, and matters had got a whole lot worse before they were finally settled. If an uneasy truce with Jew and Greek still at daggers drawn can be called settlement. And sure, Alexandria might be the second biggest city in the empire, but it wasn't the only one with a major Jewish population, not by a long chalk. Just the thought that what had happened there could happen on a much wider scale sent a chill down my spine.

If I was looking for a reason for Arrecinus Clemens to be involved in all this, I didn't have to look any further. Lentulus's mention of Capito – and it had been deliberate, I was certain of that – was interesting as well.

'Good. I'm glad. Always pleased to help, so long as you don't quote me.' Lentulus had been reaching for another chicken leg – where the guy put it all, big as he was, I didn't know – and he hesitated. 'By the by, Marcus. One name you didn't mention. Fella called Vinicianus. Annius Vinicianus.'

I gave him a sharp look. 'What about him?'

'What about who?'

'Ah . . . Annius Vinicianus?'

'Oh. Nothing. Nothing at all. Forget I said it, I was rambling.' He picked up the chicken leg. 'Must be going senile. Now, if that's the morning's business over to your satisfaction, we can move on to more important matters. Like the new wine my supplier's trying to foist off on me.'

'Yeah? Where's it from?'

'Place over in Belgic Gaul by the name of Durocortorum. Fizzy stuff, comes in small flasks with the bung tied down. Now don't look at me like that, boy, he says it has a future, although of course he's bloody selling the stuff, so he would, wouldn't he? Probably just a passing fad, but I'd be glad to hear your opinion.'

'Ah . . . *fizzy*?'

'Full of little bubbles. Jupiter knows how they get them in or why they bother, but there you are. Desmus likes to see how far he can shoot the bung when he opens one of the bastards, don't you, Desmus? His record so far's fifteen feet. Ah, well, simple pleasures. Get the rest of that Falernian down you and we'll give it a go.'

Annius Vinicianus, eh?

Senile, nothing; I was being *told*.

TWENTY-FIVE

hadn't been expecting Perilla back much shy of dinner time, but she breezed in only about an hour after I did. In a much better mood than I thought she'd be, too.

'You find what you were after, then, lady?' I said when she came back down from getting changed.

'Yes, thank you, Marcus.' She put her cheek down to be kissed. 'I thought I'd try Fabatus's. You remember? That new shop in the Saepta, the one that Naevia Postuma mentioned when she was here the first time and Calventia Quietina recommended to me.'

'Uh . . . yeah. Right.' I didn't remember any such thing, but sometimes it's safer not to make admissions like that. 'That's nice.'

'Off the peg, of course, but then I didn't have much option, did I?' This time I said nothing: there'd been a definite trace of frost there. 'And it is rather nice. It'll go very well with the over-mantle I got before we went to Clarus and Marilla's.'

'The one young Marcus sicked up on?'

She frowned. 'Oh, damn, so he did. Not that one, then. Never mind, I'll find something else.' Bathyllus was hovering. 'A hot mint and lemon balm with honey, please, Bathyllus. It is *not* pleasant out there.'

'No, it isn't.' I handed him the empty jug. 'Bring me a top-up too, will you, little guy?'

'Certainly, sir, with the greatest of pleasure. Madam.'

He bowed and bustled out. I watched him go, grinning: he'd been like this, oozing smarm, ever since the imperial dinner invitation had hit the mat. Sometimes the little guy was so transparent that it was embarrassing.

'I thought you were staying at home this morning.' Perilla settled down on the couch opposite.

'Hmm? No, I changed my mind. I decided I'd go round to old Cornelius Lentulus's.'

'Really? Why would you want to . . .?' She stopped. 'It had something to do with the case, didn't it?'

'Ah . . .'

'Marcus, I *told* you! Never mind what Postuma said, leave things alone! You did your best where Naevius Surdinus was concerned, and as far as the conspiracy side of things goes, if Felix and Gaius are happy that it's dead, that's the end of it.' She paused. 'And if it isn't then it's no business of yours.'

'Even if come the Palatine Games, Gaius gets himself chopped?'

She looked uncomfortable. 'Well, I don't actually wish the poor man harm, but . . .'

Wish him *harm*! Jupiter! 'Look, lady, we're talking about the possibility of treason and the assassination of a serving emperor here. In under ten days' time.'

'True. Perhaps, anyway. If you believe in Postuma's conversations with Alexander the Great, that is.' The barest sniff: one of Nature's militant realists, our Perilla.

'Yes. Granted. Even so, it could well happen. You want to have Gaius's death and a *coup d'état* on your conscience? Because I don't.'

She was quiet for a long time. Then she said: 'So what did you talk to Lentulus about?'

Hey! This was better! 'I thought he might be able to fill me in on some of the best prospects. Which he did.'

'Namely?'

I told her. 'It looks promising for Asiaticus, at least in circum-stantial terms. The guy's good, so good he has even Lentulus in two minds. And Cornelius Lentulus is *sharp*.'

'How do you mean, good?'

'On the face of it, he's a simple political dropout. No interest in politics, doesn't even bother to turn up at meetings of the senate, let alone get involved in the committee network. Plus the fact that he's the adulterer's ideal of a cuckolded husband.'

'That's hardly fair, Marcus. After all, if Gaius took a shine to his wife, seduced her and then chose to drop her, what could he do about it, practically speaking? It was one of the dangers of the circles he moves in. She was the emperor's one-time sister-in-law, after all.'

'Yeah, well, maybe. But the result is that now he's survived at least two, maybe three conspiracies that he may well have been mixed up in, where he was close to the principals concerned, just because Gaius can't take him seriously. If he isn't genuine then that takes some managing.'

'Perhaps he is.'

'Perilla, there is no way. Certainly not this time. He had to be the one who set me up for that mugging on the Janiculan, for a start, because for one reason or another his pals at that dodgy confab in Longinus's villa are out of it. Which means he's involved in this thing up to his eyeballs, maybe even at the centre. And like I say his cover's perfect. What better position for a mover and shaker to be in than as the target's prime buffoon? No, Asiaticus is our man, all right. One of them, anyway.'

Bathyllus came in with the drinks, refilling my cup from the new half-jug. Perilla took her steaming honey-herb abomination and sipped.

'Very well,' she said. 'What about the other two? The ones Capito named, Clemens and the freedman secretary?'

'Yeah, now they're interesting.' I swallowed some of my own wine. 'Asiaticus has a personal axe to grind, sure, regarding his wife, but as far as I can see, Clemens and Callistus don't, quite the reverse, because it's thanks to Gaius that they're both at the top of their respective trees. If they want him gone – which they may well do – it's out of pure altruism.'

'Don't sneer, Marcus, it does happen sometimes. From what

you told me, Julius Graecinus had no personal axe to grind either.'

'True. And I wasn't sneering.' I frowned; Graecinus's wasn't a name I wanted to be reminded of. I like my villains to be villains, and he just didn't qualify, or if he did the price the poor bastard had paid was too high for me to stomach. 'Fair enough. Altruism it is. For the time being, anyway. Mind you, Lentulus didn't know much about Callistus apart from the fact that he's good at his job and seems to be all that's saving Gaius from having to hock the silver and rent out the Treasury vaults as vacant office space.'

'Really?'

'More or less.' I took another swig of the Setinian. 'Apropos Callistus, though, I've come across one or two of those shit-hot-genius-with-numbers guys before. Their brains work a different way, they live in a world of their own, and they've got different priorities. Maybe seeing treason and assassination as a viable means of solving the niggling problem of a minus figure at the bottom of his monthly balance sheet makes perfect sense to him. Or maybe he has other reasons. Gaius did say he was ambitious.'

'Ambitious in what direction?'

I shrugged. 'Pass, lady. I've never even met the man. It's all hearsay.'

'How about Clemens? Altruism again, yes?'

'Yeah. At least, like I said, no other reason that's obvious, which is why he didn't end up chopped along with the others before the festival or at best moved to where he couldn't do any harm. Gaius admitted himself that having a Commander of Praetorians on the team would be a pretty big plus for any conspiracy, yet he didn't take the thing any further. And Gaius is no fool.'

'Then perhaps he's innocent after all.'

'Maybe he is. Still, like Callistus, he's got strong professional reasons for wanting Gaius out of the picture that happen to fit with his personal inclinations.'

'Namely?'

I told her what Lentulus had told me about Jamnia, the business of the statue, and the potential Jewish problem. Not that I needed to go into too much detail: Perilla had been with me in Alexandria and seen for herself how a cultural head-to-head could end up. By the time I'd finished she was staring at me wide-eyed.

'But, Marcus, that's dreadful!' she said. 'The emperor can't be serious!'

'Yeah, well, as far as putting his statue up in the Jerusalem Temple's concerned, that side of it's been shelved for now. But you know Gaius. Tell him he can't do something because of the possible consequences and he'll go ahead and do it anyway, just to show who's boss. And the Jews are just as bad. They don't give an inch either. Throw in the Greeks and their keep-poking-and-watch-the-bastards-jump attitude, and with Gaius running things it's a disaster waiting to happen.'

'And you think Clemens means to stop it? By killing the emperor?'

'That's the idea. Certainly as a motive for treason it makes sense. The guy's sympathies first and foremost are with the Jews, sure, that'd weigh pretty heavily, but it wouldn't be the only factor. According to Lentulus he's a professional soldier. Just to sit on his hands and watch while Gaius put the whole of the east at risk militarily wouldn't be an option. For someone who thinks in straight lines, in terms of doing, assassination would be the obvious answer.' I took another swallow of wine. 'Besides, there's a valid link between him and Capito. Gaius said they didn't know each other, that there was no connection. But it turns out that Capito was the emperor's rep in Jamnia when the whole thing started.'

'Why should that be significant?'

I shrugged. 'Search me, lady. Maybe it's just coincidence; these things happen. But certainly the link is there. Maybe when Capito was recalled to Rome Clemens went round to see him, spoke his mind a bit too freely, even went a bit OTT where criticising Gaius's response went. That can happen too.'

She was twisting a lock of hair. 'One thing you haven't considered, dear.'

'Hmm?'

'Who they're doing it for. I mean, you can't just have a conspiracy to topple an emperor in a vacuum. If they want to get rid of Gaius then surely they'd have to have someone to put in his place. Someone valid, I mean.'

'Yeah.' I was frowning. 'Actually, I was coming to that.

Lentulus mentioned a name at the end of the conversation. Just pulled it out of the air apropos of nothing, then dropped the subject like a hot brick.'

'What name was that?'

'Vinicianus. Annius Vinicianus.'

'Ah.'

'You know him?'

'I know of him, certainly. We may even have met once or twice at literary get-togethers. He's Marcus Vinicius's nephew.'

Right; I should've guessed from the name, or at least that there was some sort of family connection. Marcus Vinicius was the closest we – or rather Perilla – had to a VIP acquaintance: ex-consul, political high-flier, one of the imperial set, married to Gaius's youngest sister Livilla, and the star member of Perilla's poetry-klatsch circle. We'd met a couple of years back, at the time of the Macro business, when Perilla engineered an invite for me to a reading at his house, and I'd been very favourably impressed. Not a bad guy, Marcus Vinicius. For an imperial.

'Is that so, now?' I said.

'You can't mean Vinicianus, though. As a replacement for Gaius, that is. Oh, he's certainly well liked and respected, from what I hear, but I wouldn't've thought he was emperor material, even in his own estimation.'

'Actually, I was thinking of Vinicius himself.'

Perilla stared at me. 'You're not serious!'

'Why not? He's got the political mileage and the street cred, easy. He's proved a dozen times over that he can handle responsibility. He's level-headed, popular with the senate and the army. He's even married to Gaius's sister. What more could you want?'

'Marcus, be sensible! We've been through all this before. Two years ago. Vinicius is no traitor, he hasn't got it in him to be: you suspected him then, and you admitted you were wrong. You can't go back on that now.'

'Sure I can, lady, because this time we're in a completely different ball game. And I never said Vinicius was a traitor, one of the conspirators. If Lentulus had wanted to finger Vinicius per se, he'd've done it, not faff around being cryptic.'

'What, then? And why should Cornelius Lentulus know anything about the plot?'

I grinned. 'Perilla, never underestimate Lentulus, right? What he hears and what he admits to hearing, let alone acts on, are two different things, which is why the crafty bugger's survived with all his wollocks attached through sixty-odd years of politicking, three emperors, the gods know how many conspiracies and more senatorial intrigue and back-stabbing than you can shake a stick at. Plus he's got a brain like a razor. Which means that, no, I haven't a fucking clue how he knows about the plot, but I'll bet you a dozen new mantles against a used corn plaster that he does. OK?'

She ducked her head. 'Very well, Marcus. And there's no need to swear, thank you. Even so, I'd like an answer to my other question, please. If you aren't saying that Marcus Vinicius is involved in the plot, then what are you saying?'

'Look. The situations two years ago and now are completely different, right? Two years back Gaius was doing OK; the guy wasn't perfect, but no one had any real legitimate grouses. That conspiracy – Lepidus and the rest – was just about power and greed. Yes?'

'Fair enough. So?'

'So this one isn't, or not completely so. You said it yourself: sometimes there's a place for altruism where motive's concerned. Two out of the three guys we've got earmarked as conspirators here have no personal grudge against Gaius, quite the contrary: Callistus is his freedman, with all the obligations that entails, and the guy's been promoted according to his merit rather than his social standing, while Clemens is holding down one of the top military jobs in the empire. Not bad for a no-namer from Arpinum.'

'Cicero was from Arpinum, dear, and look how far he went. Plus the fact that one of Clemens's predecessors was Aelius Sejanus. Another no-namer as far as family was concerned.'

'Don't quibble. You know what I mean. Although yeah, Cicero's relevant as well, as it happens. Didn't he have the idea of forming a sort of alliance of the orders, a party above party?'

'Marcus, that is very good! Sometimes you surprise me. How on earth did you know that?'

'Bugger off, lady. What I'm saying is that that's exactly what we've got. Asiaticus, Callistus, Clemens: senate, imperial admin, military. And my bet is that they're not the only representatives in their class. The three main divisions of the state, all wanting rid of Gaius for the good of Rome.'

'The good of Rome. Where have we heard that phrase before?'

'Yeah, well, maybe this time it's genuine. The man's becoming a luxury that the empire can't afford.'

She sat up. 'Marcus, whose side are you on here? I thought you wanted to *stop* the emperor from being assassinated.'

'Yeah, well, I do, if I can. Murder's murder, whatever the excuse. But the point is that this time at least there *is* an excuse, and a valid one. Oh, sure, Vinicius may not be in on the conspiracy himself, but six gets you ten his nephew is. Maybe for the best of reasons, but nonetheless. And if it succeeds – *when* it succeeds – my guess is that he'll fling his uncle's cap into the ring.'

'Vinicius would never be a party to that sort of arrangement! How many times do I have to tell you, dear? *The man is not political!*'

'He wouldn't have to be. And he needn't even know about the existence of the conspiracy in advance; in fact it might be safer if he didn't. By the time the knowledge became relevant, Gaius would be dead, Rome would be short one emperor, and there'd be no one else on offer to take on the job. Plus the invitation would be official; as a senator, Vinicianus could put his uncle's name forward to the senate himself, and I'll bet he's already sounded out some of his colleagues on the benches. Which probably explains why Lentulus knows.' I topped my cup up from the jug. 'The broad-striper brigade would fall over themselves to vote Vinicius in.'

Perilla sighed. 'I'm sorry, dear,' she said. 'Yes, I do hear what you're saying, and yes, it does make sense, but I still can't see Marcus Vinicius agreeing, not even out of altruism. He's very old-fashioned in many ways, very much the traditionalist. A bit like you, really.'

'Hah!'

'I mean it. And it's a compliment. Vinicius has principles, and he keeps to them. Gaius would be dead as a result of treason, and whether he'd known beforehand that he was a factor in the plot or not, that would matter to him. He'd never agree to become emperor under those circumstances. Not even for the genuine good of Rome.'

'You're very sure about that, lady?'

'Yes, I am, as it happens.'

Bugger. I frowned, and let it go. Me, well, I had my serious doubts about her reading of Vinicius. Oh, sure, I was ready to grant from my own knowledge of the guy that he wasn't the conspiring type and didn't seem to have an ambitious bone in his body, but timing and circumstances were all-important here; like I said, he'd be the perfect man for the job, and modesty aside he'd recognize that. A strong sense of duty, plus the pressure that would no doubt be put on him by his broad-striper colleagues, would do the rest.

'OK,' I said. 'That still doesn't solve the problem of Gaius's replacement. If not Vinicius then who?'

'What about Claudius?'

I stared at her. '*What?*'

'Why not? He's Gaius's uncle, and the only remaining male of the direct-line imperial family.'

'Why *not*? Jupiter, Perilla, where do you start? He's Gemellus over again, or as good as. The guy's a mental defective, he's never held political office barring a grace-and-favour suffect consulship when Gaius came to power, never served in the military, never even been given the smallest bit of real responsibility. You can practically count the times he's even appeared in public on the fingers of one hand. And this at, what, age fifty or thereabouts? The senate would never ratify him as emperor, not in a million years. And that's what the conspirators would need, because with Gaius dead and no one being groomed for crown prince, it'd be the senate choosing the emperor.'

'Claudius is *not* a mental defective. He limps and stammers badly; he twitches, yes, of course he does, but those are physical disabilities, not mental ones. There's nothing wrong with his brain, quite the contrary.'

'Yeah?'

'Yes. I've met him, at Vinicius's, several times, and if you have the patience to wait until he gets the words out and ignore the twitching, you realize that he is a very intelligent man indeed. If he's been kept under wraps all his life then it's not through any fault of his own but because he offends the imperial family's sensibilities.'

Well, I wasn't going to argue. Still, if Claudius was our

conspirators' emperor of choice – and remember we were talking altruism and the good of Rome here – then I'd eat my sandals.

Bathyllus buttled in. 'Excuse me, sir. Madam,' he said. 'I've given instructions for the furnace to be stoked. I thought that having been out in today's inclement weather you might like a hot bath before dinner. Meton says that will be a little earlier than usual.'

'Good idea, little guy,' I said. 'Very thoughtful of you.'

'Thank you, sir.'

He left, and I cocked an eye at Perilla. 'You noticed our new hyper-conscientious major-domo, lady?' I said.

She was grinning. 'Don't complain, dear,' she said. 'Make the most of it while it lasts. It has something to do with the emperor's dinner invitation, I think.'

Yeah. Which was for the next day as ever was. Whoopee, I could barely contain my excitement. Still, it mightn't be too deadly; we'd probably just be two out of at least fifty or so, and we could leave as soon as it was polite.

I took a last swallow of wine and got up to change for our pre-dinner steam.

TWENTY-SIX

Next day, we turned up prompt at the palace in our best bib and tucker – by litter, of course, despite the fact that it was a dry evening, since if I'd even hinted about thinking of walking and meeting her there, Perilla would've handed me my head. As it was, she'd made sure our litter slobs were given a decent scrub-up and polish before they started, and they pulled up at the gate gleaming like thoroughbreds. I nodded to the two very large Praetorians on guard, gave my name and the invitation to the door slave on duty, and we were escorted through.

I'd been inside the palace before, naturally, more often than I'd've liked, but this bit was new to me, obviously one of the function suites and decorated to impress. Which it did, in spades: top-grade mosaic flooring with tesserae so small you could practically have used them for signet-ring inlays, cedar wall panelling, bronzes that could've belonged to Postuma's pal Alexander – and probably had. And above was a ceiling featuring every god and goddess in the pantheon, scattering their benevolence down on the favoured mortals beneath. All lit by more gilt candelabra than you could shake a considerable stick at. Gaius's oil bill alone must've been eye-watering.

How the other half live, right enough.

'Close your mouth, lady,' I murmured as we cleared the threshold and went into the room itself. 'You're gaping.'

'Nonsense, dear.'

I'd been right about the numbers; the place was crowded. So; not a cosy, intimate, snuggle-up-to-your-couch-partner dinner party, then. Even though I'd neither expected nor wanted that, my heart sank: me, I hate these stand-up affairs, where you have to make polite conversation stuck with a plate in one hand and a wine cup in the other. Although to be fair this'd be just the drinks-and-nibbles stage, and we'd be eating elsewhere, probably in the room beyond the set of folding doors in the far wall.

'Drink, sir?' said a slave with a wine tray. I took a cup of wine.

'You got anything soft for the lady, pal?' I said.

'Of course, sir. Barley water and honey?'

I shuddered. 'Yeah, that'll do fine.'

'I'll have one of the other boys bring it over.'

'Great.' I took a sip of the wine. Not Caecuban, which was fair enough. It was a reasonable Falernian, though; not as good as Lentulus's, but getting there. I couldn't complain that Gaius was saving a few of his precious pennies by serving his guests mass-produced Spanish plonk.

Perilla had drifted over to a sort of lectern.

'There's a seating plan here with names,' she said. 'How very well organized.'

'Yeah, well, it was hardly likely to be a free-for-all scrimmage, was it?' I said, joining her. 'So where are we?'

She pointed. 'On the right at the back. Not with anyone I know, unfortunately, but—'

'Rufia Perilla! Now this is a pleasant surprise!'

A dapper, middle-aged guy in the group to our immediate left had turned round, smiling, and I recognized Marcus Vinicius.

Perilla smiled back. 'Good evening, Vinicius,' she said. 'I was just wondering if there was anyone we knew here. Lovely to see you.'

'Completely mutual, my dear, I assure you. You're a life-saver. Join us, please.' He stepped aside, opening a space in the group. 'Oh, and, ah, Corvinus, isn't it? Valerius Corvinus?'

'That's right, sir,' I said.

'Oh, tush, tush! No *sirs*, if you don't mind, I doubt if I could give you ten years. You're in a better state than you were the last time we met, aren't you?' He chuckled and turned to the other two men in the group; one of them I didn't recognize, but the second, I realized with a shock, was Gaius's Uncle Claudius. 'The last time I saw Corvinus he'd just had an argument with a runaway cart and turned up at my door looking like an arena cat's leavings. Not completely an accident, Perilla told me later. Quite the sleuth, our Valerius Corvinus. Mind you, thinking back on that evening, I might've gone for the cart myself in preference to . . . who was it doing the reading again, Perilla?'

'Annaeus Seneca.'

'Ah, yes, rot his guts. The would-be poet. Livilla's protégé. Frightful tick, currently, I think, living on beets in Lusitania or wherever the hell Caesar exiled him to, and serve him right. Oh, but I'm sorry, Corvinus, I should make the introductions. Tiberius Claudius you probably know already, him being a relative of yours now.'

I nodded at the guy. Despite the fact that I'd been at his wedding, it'd been along with a couple of hundred other people, so this was the first time I'd really seen him close up. He didn't look all that bad, certainly not the disaster I'd been half-expecting: well turned out, neatly shaved and barbered, longish, thinish face with regular features that reminded me of old Tiberius's. Which, I suppose, was fair enough, since his father Drusus had been the Wart's brother.

'C-C-Corvinus,' he said. 'P-pleased to meet you.'

Pleasant-enough voice, too, if you ignored the stutter.

'Likewise,' I said.

'And my nephew, Annius Vinicianus.'

Hey! I turned to face the other man. Not all that younger than Vinicius himself, for all he was a nephew; I'd put him at about my age. Clean-cut, impeccably dressed in a snow-white broad-striper mantle, fit looking, radiating confidence. And with cold

grey eyes that were looking at me in not exactly a hostile way
but the next thing to it. Speculative, certainly.

'Corvinus.' He put out his hand, and we shook.

A slave came up with a tray. 'The barley water, sir,' he said.

'Oh, that'll be for me,' Perilla said. She took the cup. 'Thank
you. The emperor hasn't arrived yet?'

'No. He likes to make an entrance,' Vinicius said. 'Imperial
prerogative. So, Rufia Perilla, what are you doing slumming it
here with us poor devils?'

'Hardly slumming it.' A waiter with a tray of candied nuts
came up. I noticed that Claudius took a handful. Liked his food,
obviously, did Gaius's uncle. 'Why should you say that?'

'My dear lady, when you've been to as many bashes like this
as I have, you'll use the term too. Where've they put you, by the
way?'

'Hmm?'

'Which table?'

'Oh. One of the ones at the back.'

'Dear me, we can do better than that! We're two short where
we are, as it happens. No Shadow, either; Caesar doesn't approve
of them.' Shadows are the odds and sods drafted in at the last
minute to fill up any unoccupied places in the dinner party's basic
unit of nine. Me, I tended to agree with Gaius: you choose the
people you want to eat with for themselves, not just to make up
the numbers. And the professional Shadows – they do exist, for
a wonder – try so hard to be the life and soul that they're a pain
in the arse. 'Old Latiaris's gout is playing up again, so he and
his wife have had to call off. You're more than welcome to move
over to us, my dear. Unless you know the people on the other
couches where you are, of course, in which case you'll probably
want to stay.'

'No, actually, we don't,' Perilla said. 'And yes, thank you,
we'd be delighted.'

'Then that's settled. Claudius? Lucius? You've no objections,
do you?'

'None at all.' Vinicianus was looking at me as he said it, the
grey eyes still cold and level. 'I'd be delighted to get to know
Valerius Corvinus better.'

'Fine. Perilla, you're on the other side of me from Claudius,
on the bottom couch. Three writers together, if I can include

myself in that category. It should make for quite an interesting evening, for a change.'

'Tiberius Claudius writes?' I said, startled.

Perilla nudged me hard in the ribs just as Claudius said blandly: 'He d-does indeed, C-Corvinus. S-Surprising as it may seem. He also r-reads quite well. S-Speaking, I'll grant you, does p-pose a p-problem, although he can m-manage it quite s-successfully on his own behalf. G-Given sufficient time.'

Ouch. I felt myself redden.

Vinicius chuckled. 'A bit of advice, Corvinus, if you'll forgive me,' he said. 'Don't judge a book by its wrappings. And Claudius, go easy on the poor man. He doesn't know you as well as we do.'

'Uh . . . yeah,' I said. 'Yeah, I'm sorry. My apologies.'

'N-None n-necessary. F-forget it, p-please.'

'Tiberius Claudius is a very distinguished linguist and historian, Marcus.' Perilla gave me a tight smile, and her tone of voice was straight off a glacier. Shit; we were in real trouble here, or would be later, I could tell. 'His work on the Etruscans is groundbreaking.'

'W-Well, I w-wouldn't go so far as—'

'Nonsense, my dear chap!' Vinicius clapped him on the shoulder. 'Groundbreaking is exactly right. You and Perilla can both tell me what you're working on at present and I'll bore you by reciprocating.' There was a stir by the door behind us. 'Ah. That's Caesar and Caesonia arriving now. About time, I'm starving.'

I looked round. Gods. Yeah, well, I supposed that being emperor and the fact that he was footing the no doubt whopping bill for the evening excused the guy from conforming to the usual dress code; mind you, a get-up that would've been seriously OTT at the Great King's court in Parthia was taking things a bit too far, I thought. Caesonia, dolled up to the nines as she was and hung with enough jewellery to fit out a couple of shops in the Saepta, was drab in comparison.

His make-up was a bit overstated, too. *Trowels* came to mind. Not exactly one of your shy, self-effacing characters, our Gaius.

'Marcus,' Perilla murmured. 'You're staring. No one else is. Stop it.'

'Uh . . . right. Right.' I shifted my eyes to where slaves were folding back the doors at the end of the room.

'Well, I think we can go in now,' Vinicius said. 'Over to the left near the front, Corvinus. The ladies will be there ahead of us, I expect.'

Near the front was understating things; we turned out to be almost slap bang next to the top table itself, where Gaius and Caesonia were lying. I didn't recognize any of the other seven at it, but the impeccably mantled ramrod-stiff guy and matching frozen-faced matron on the lowest couch must've been the new year's suffect consul and spouse. Frozen-faced, because from the looks of things their table-mates for the evening were Gaius's flavour-of-the-month pals and gals, one of whom had the muscle-bound look of a professional gladiator. She wasn't one of the pals, either.

Well, it was all part of life's rich tapestry.

Vinicius had lain down in the host's place at the top end of our bottom couch. The three wives were already there, together on the couch opposite; at least, I recognized Livilla and Messalina, and the third, on Livilla's far side at the couch's end, had to be Vinicianus's.

'You're next to me, Perilla.' Vinicius patted the place to his left, where the principal guest usually lay. 'No, I insist. I told you.' Livilla shot him a look that was pure venom, but he either missed it or chose to ignore it. Not the happiest or best-matched of couples, Vinicius and Gaius's sister. I noticed she'd put on even more weight than she'd been carrying the last time I'd seen her; Messalina and Vinicianus's wife were going to be pretty pushed for space here. 'Claudius on my other side, Vinicianus beyond Perilla, if you will, Lucius, my boy, and then Corvinus. Can't have husband and wife together, can we?' Hell; that put me next to Messalina reclining at the near end of the top couch. Relative or not, I'd've preferred to steer well clear of that lady. 'Oh, and I'm sorry. Corvinus and Perilla, I should've introduced you to Vinicianus's wife, Fulvia Procula.' We nodded to each other. 'Now. I think that should do us. Let's get on with it, shall we?'

We reclined. Messalina gave me a sunny smile and what was almost a wink. She was a looker, sure, always had been, and even now in her mid-twenties and two husbands down the road with her slim figure, soft features and clear skin, she could've passed for ten years younger, easy; minimum of make-up and jewellery, although I noticed that she was wearing a ring with a ruby in it the size of a quail's egg that must've cost Claudius an arm and a leg.

'Why, Cousin Corvinus,' she said. 'What a surprise.'

'Yeah. Yeah, it is.' I kept my voice neutral.

'A pleasant one, of course.' She laughed and held her hands out to the slave coming round with the perfumed water. 'And Perilla's looking extremely well. For her age.'

Uh-huh. I glanced sideways, but fortunately the lady was already in deep conversation with Vinicius, as was Livilla with Procula. It looked like Messalina, Vinicianus and me were going to form a threesome. At least for the moment. I held my own hands over the basin while the jug slave poured.

'So, Corvinus,' Vinicianus said. 'What's this sleuthing business my uncle mentioned? It sounds fascinating.'

The slave behind the one with the water jug dried my hands with a napkin. Including the guy holding the basin, that made three of them. Obviously hand-washing duty was pretty labour-intensive: there was certainly no shortage of bought help around.

'Oh, it's nothing much,' I said.

'That's not what I've heard.' Messalina held up her cup without looking at the wine slave who was following behind the hand-rinse guys. He poured. 'Quite the little busy bee, so I'm told.'

I held up my own cup. The slave filled it.

'Thanks, pal,' I said. 'Yeah, well, it keeps me off the streets and reasonably sober.' It didn't do either of those things, mind, but at a dinner party you're not under oath.

'Are you working on anything at the moment?' Vinicianus said, lifting his cup for the slave.

His tone was polite interest, no more. Uh-huh. Well, if that was how he wanted to play it, it was absolutely fine with me.

'Actually, I am,' I said. I sipped the wine and blinked as the taste registered. Shit, that was Caecuban! Real imperial Caecuban, from Gaius's own cellar. By tagging along with Vinicius we'd obviously moved up a considerable notch on the drinks scale. 'A guy by the name of Naevius Surdinus, murdered on his estate a couple of months back. You know him?'

'I'd have recognized the face, yes, and I've certainly heard his name. But no, I didn't know him, not personally.' On the open side of the table, the slaves were laying out the starters. 'How dreadful. Do you have any idea who killed him?'

'I'm getting there,' I said easily. 'The actual perp, yes, because he was seen. A freedman with a distinctive scar or a birthmark on his left cheek.' I took another swallow of wine. Beautiful! 'You don't happen to know who or whose that might be, do you?'

'No, I'm afraid I don't. Why on earth should I?'

I shrugged. 'No reason. I've just got into the habit of asking people, that's all.' Interesting; very interesting. I'd been watching closely, and his eyelids had definitely flickered. The bastard was lying.

'I had a freedman once,' Messalina said, reaching for an olive. 'Or rather Daddy did. He'd always been a bit strange as a slave. Talked to himself, you know? Muttered. Anyway, when he freed him Daddy set him up in a hardware shop. One day for no reason at all he picked up a vine-pruner's knife from the bench and killed a customer with it. Slit his throat from ear to ear. The man had only come in for a set of door hinges.' She smiled. 'You can't trust the poor dears – slaves and freedmen, I mean. They're quite unreliable. Something to do with the breeding, I expect. Oh, lovely, we've got these little cheese and fig things again.'

'I had a curious slave myself, actually.' Vinicianus took a stuffed vine leaf from the dish next to him, put it on his plate and dissected it with his knife, frowning as he inspected the contents. 'Curious in both senses of the word. The man was always poking, couldn't leave anything alone. We had a stork's nest on the roof one year, and he decided he'd go up and have a look at the eggs. Only he stepped on a loose tile, lost his balance, fell off the roof and broke his neck.'

He raised his eyes and looked straight at me.

Messalina laughed. 'That's *exactly* what I mean,' she said. 'Sometimes they are *so* silly, and then they're their own worst enemies. Don't you agree, Corvinus?'

'Yeah. Yeah, I do.' I reached for the pickled cheese balls.

No doubt about it. I'd been warned.

There was a movement to my left, behind Messalina. I looked over. A Praetorian tribune in dress uniform, helmet under his arm, was approaching Gaius's table. He stopped and saluted.

'Oh, hell,' Vinicianus muttered.

I glanced back at him. 'What's going on?' I said. 'Trouble?'

'No. Nothing like that. Just the evening watchword.'

'Watchword?'

His face was set. 'For the palace guard. It changes every night, and the emperor gives it. Nothing to do with us. Eat your dinner, Corvinus.'

And he turned back to his plate. I'd noticed, though, that a lot of the other guests seemed to be taking a great interest in what was happening. There were a few suppressed giggles.

Gaius was in deep conversation with the man next to him; a pantomime artist, by the look of him, with hair frizzed out in golden spangles. The Praetorian didn't move. He stood at the salute, ramrod straight, waiting: not a young guy like Sextus Papinius or his brother Lucius had been, but a balding veteran, fifty if he was a day.

Finally, Gaius looked up.

'Ah, Chaerea, it's you,' he said. 'You'll be wanting tonight's word, will you?'

'Yes, Caesar.' Although the words were barked out in strict military fashion, the voice didn't match; it was high, almost feminine in pitch.

'Right. Right. Let's see now.' Gaius frowned. 'What was it yesterday? Not a single word; a phrase. On the tip of my tongue. Come on, man! Remind me!'

There was a perceptible pause. Then the tribune said stiffly: '"Give us a hug", Caesar.'

The spangly haired guy next to Gaius choked on his wine and had to have his back pounded. All of the people occupying the nearby couches had been watching what was going on, and most of them, men and women, were laughing openly now, as if it were part of the evening's entertainment. Which, in a way, I supposed it was. Certainly Gaius was showing all the signs of playing to the gallery here, and his sycophantic dinner pals were obviously eager to show their appreciation.

'Tribune, now *really*!' he said. '*Not* in front of all these people, please! Control yourself!' The man still didn't move, or answer; his arm was still up at the salute. Finally, Gaius tutted, rose from his couch and pulled the arm down. 'Chaerea, darling, you are absolutely no fun whatsoever!' he snapped. 'Do you know that, you bum-face?' He waited, but there was no answer. 'All right, have it your own way. You'll like this. The watchword for tonight is "Chubby-chops". Oh, and you have to do this as well.' He leaned forwards and planted a smacker of a kiss on each cheek. The room – at least the part of it where people were close enough to see – erupted. 'Now bugger off, sunshine, I'm busy.'

The tribune saluted smartly, turned and marched off. I had a good view of the man's face as he left, and it radiated pure frustrated hatred.

Gods!

I turned back to Vinicianus, who had been arranging a selection of nibbles on his plate with deliberate care. 'That happen every night?' I said.

'So I believe. With that particular tribune, at least.' His voice and face were expressionless. 'Caesar does like his little joke.'

'Who was the tribune?'

'A Cassius Chaerea.'

'*Cassius* Chaerea?'

That got me a slow look. 'That's what I said, yes.'

'He any relation to Cassius Longinus? The Asian governor?'

'Not that I know of. A distant cousin, perhaps, but nothing direct.'

'He is a bit of a bum-face, isn't he?' Messalina giggled, and looked up from her own selection of starters. 'And that voice! I'm not surprised the emperor makes fun of him.'

Vinicianus ignored her. 'He was wounded in the groin, Corvinus,' he said. 'While he was serving with Germanicus on his Rhine campaign.' Shit. Veteran was right. And Germanicus . . . just mention his name to any soldier any time in the twenty-odd years since the overrated bastard's death – Praetorian or legionary, officer or grunt, it didn't matter who – and he'd go all dewy-eyed; having served on the Rhine with Germanicus was equivalent to deputizing for Ganymede in bringing Jupiter his morning cup of nectar. Military street-cred just didn't get any higher.

No wonder being given a watchword like 'Chubby-chops' had had the guy spitting nails. And if the emperor's treatment of Cassius Chaerea was at all typical, then the chances of a strong Praetorian involvement in a possible assassination plot had just taken a substantial hike.

The 'Cassius' was interesting, too, right?

'Marcus, petal! You came! How delightful!'

Hell; I looked over my shoulder. Gaius was standing behind the couch, although 'standing' was a bit of an exaggeration: the emperor was pissed as a newt and swaying. Handling it well, on the whole, though, apart from the goggle-eyed stare and the slight slur.

'Ah . . . yeah. Yes, Caesar,' I said.

'And lying beside the most beautiful woman in the room, too. My Caesonia excepted, of course. How on earth did you manage to wangle that, you crafty bugger?' He reached down and patted Messalina's bottom. She smiled up at him and arched her back like a cat. 'Look at her! Couldn't you just eat her up, the little minx? Wasted on a poor old stick like Claudius. Isn't she, Uncle?'

Claudius was already holding his cup up for more wine to the slave behind him; he obviously liked his booze, too. He turned back round.

'Hmm? Oh. Yes. Yes, if you s-say so, C-Caesar,' he said equably.

'I do s-say so. I kn-know so, and I s-speak from experience.' Gaius ran the back of his index finger slowly up Messalina's spine and tweaked the stray lock of hair at the nape of her neck. 'Don't I, darling? You're a lucky sod, Claudius, you randy old bugger. Far luckier than you deserve.'

'Th-thank you, Caesar. I'm e-extremely aware of that.'

Gaius gave the bottom another pat and smiled. 'Oh, I *am* glad,' he said. 'I would just *hate* for talent like this to go unappreciated. And she does have the most *marvellous* tits. Well, boys and girls, enjoy. Livilla, try not to eat too much, my dear, or the next time you go sea-bathing at Baiae you may find yourself harpooned.'

He lurched back to his own table.

'Yes, well,' Vinicius said after a long pause. 'There you are, then.'

He reached for the bowl of pickled radishes.

We settled down to eat.

It was a good four hours later that we finally climbed into the litter, thoroughly bloated and gently pickled. At least, I was, although as far as food's concerned Perilla can shift it when she likes.

'Urp.'

'Yes, well, dear,' she said icily as the litter louts took the unaccustomed strain, 'you've only yourself to blame. Three helpings of flamingo was just a tad excessive, wouldn't you say?'

'That wasn't the flamingo, that was the radishes. You can tell.'

'Marcus, please!'

I grinned and settled back against the cushions. Actually, our evening out hadn't been all that bad in the end, if you made allowances for the earlier part. The food had been pretty good, well up to Meton's standard, which is saying something. And a generous supply of imperial Caecuban makes up for a hell of a lot of shortcomings elsewhere.

'Your pal Tiberius Claudius was a bit of a revelation,' I said.

'Really? How so?'

'I reckon I've misjudged him. You're right, he is smart.'

'I kept telling you that, but you wouldn't listen.'

'No, not just book-smart. That's nothing. He's a survivor, like Asiaticus.' I frowned; hadn't Lentulus said that Asiaticus was a Claudian client and a personal friend of Claudius himself? 'You saw how he reacted, or didn't react, rather, when Gaius was feeling up Messalina? And six gets you ten it hadn't stopped there. He's had her, when and how serious the affair was I don't know, but that's practically a cert.'

'Obviously he has. She's very beautiful, completely unprincipled, and she's been one of his intimate circle for years, long before Claudius came on the scene. It'd be surprising if he hadn't.'

I shifted on the cushions. 'Yeah, but that's not all,' I said. 'I was watching what's-his-name, Chaerea's face when he marched out. The guy was fit to be tied. No one could've missed that; Gaius certainly couldn't. Which of course is why the sick bastard does it. Needles people, winds them up, knowing that they can't do a thing about it.'

'Marcus, it's late and I'm tired. Will you either shut up or get to the point, please?'

'The point is that Claudius wasn't like that. You saw for yourself. He shrugged the whole thing off. He didn't even look or sound interested, from start to finish.'

'Maybe he wasn't. Livilla has affairs, Vinicius knows that. Like the one with that greasy smarmer Seneca. He ignores them for the puerile nonsense they are, and quite rightly so. The marriage was one of convenience; it isn't as if they have any liking for each other, let alone affection, so why should he bother?'

'Maybe because Vinicius is a survivor too. He's certainly survived.'

Perilla stifled a yawn. 'Marcus . . .'

'Yeah, OK, lady. But all I'm saying is that unless Claudius genuinely doesn't have any feelings for his wife, not even at the basic sexual level, then he's a bloody good actor, and it's probably what's keeping him alive. And Gaius swallowed it whole. That's his weakness, not taking people he despises seriously. He's doing it with Claudius, he's done and is probably still doing it with Valerius Asiaticus, and he is sure as hell doing it with Chaerea. That's playing with fire, especially with everything else that's going on. Me, I reckon that if the egotistical bastard isn't very careful it'll kill him.'

She was quiet for a long time. I wondered if she'd dozed off, but when we happened to pass a door with a lit torch outside it and I looked at her, her eyes were open and she was watching me closely.

'So what can you do?' she said softly.

I shrugged. 'Not a lot. Just what I've been doing all along, really. Dig, see what comes up. Rattle a few cages, see if anything jumps. And hope to hell that somewhere along the line before the stupid bugger gets himself chopped I find something concrete that I can take to him without risking him telling his guard to cut my throat or ordering me to slit my wrists. Even if he would regret it ten minutes later.'

'It's dangerous, dear. You know that, don't you?'

There wasn't any answer to that. Not one I hadn't given her already, anyway, and she could've supplied it herself.

I was glad I'd met Vinicianus, mind; he'd been a real possible for a conspirator, virtually a cert. But if I was going to rattle anyone's cage it would have to be the guy's who'd come across so far as the weakest link. Which meant Sextus Papinius's brother and fellow tribune, Lucius. We'd have a crack at him tomorrow.

Like Perilla had said, it was late. I closed my eyes, concentrated on the swaying of the litter, and let myself drift into a doze.

TWENTY-SEVEN

I was over at the house on Patricius Incline by the fourth hour the next day. This time the gate slave was awake, and he remembered me.

'You'll be wanting to see the young master, no doubt, sir,' he said. 'Master Lucius.'

'Yeah, that's right,' I said. 'He at home?'

'That he is, sir, but there's another gentleman with him at present, and if you don't mind I'll make sure that he's not occupied first. If you'd care to wait a moment?'

'Who's the—?' I began, but the guy was gone, disappearing through the garden gate.

He took his time coming back; in fact I'd been kicking my heels for a good five minutes before he reappeared.

'I'm sorry for the wait, sir,' he said. 'You're to go in. The gentlemen are in the atrium. You know the way?'

'Yeah,' I said. 'Yeah, sure.'

I went through the garden, into the house and through the lobby to the atrium. The couch where young Sextus's body had lain was still there, but the man sitting on it I recognized from the time at Longinus's place. So, Valerius Asiaticus himself, right? This was going to prove even more interesting than I'd expected.

Papinius was sitting next to him, in his tribune's uniform minus the hardware, and he was scowling. There was a folding stool – probably the same one Papinius had been using when I'd visited the house before – set about four feet in front of them, dead centre.

The whole thing felt staged, set for a trial. Or maybe 'inquisition' would be a better term.

'Well, well.' Asiaticus was smiling, or at least his mouth was. 'Valerius Corvinus, as I live and breathe. How very nice to see you again. Please do come in and have a seat.'

I moved forwards and glanced down at the stool. 'No thanks,' I said. 'I'll stay where I am.'

'As you like.'

'I thought the guy on the gate had brought the message that I wanted to see Lucius Papinius.'

Papinius raised his head, but he said nothing. He still had the deep scowl on his face, and he was looking at me with something very close to hatred.

'And you are seeing him,' Asiaticus said. 'The only difference is that you're seeing me as well. I thought you might be pleased about that.'

'Oh? How so?'

'Because you think we're both conspiring against the emperor.'

Shit; the gloves were off here and no mistake!

'Are you?' I said.

Asiaticus laughed. 'Oh, now, Corvinus!' he said. 'You know Caesar doesn't believe that! It's been thoroughly gone into by better men than you, and the possibility has been dismissed for the nonsense it is. You're not thinking of accusing us to him again yourself, are you? Because trust me, that would be very, very silly.'

'Yeah, I know that, pal,' I said equably. 'The thought never entered my head.'

The smile slipped a bit. 'Then why are you here?'

'I told you that the last time I saw you. Or at least I told Cassius Longinus in your hearing. I'm investigating the death of Naevius Surdinus. At his niece's request. She wasn't satisfied – and quite rightly so – that the job was properly finished. I'm finishing it now, that's all.'

I'd fazed him, which was all to the good. Always nice to see one of those cocksure bastards have to go in for a bit of drastic retrenching.

'What have I to do with Surdinus?' he said. 'I hardly knew the man.'

'But I said,' I was bland, 'I came to talk to the tribune here. I didn't even know you'd be visiting. Still, now you mention it, I think you had some connection with him, at least. Maybe quite a lot.'

'Such as what?'

'The day after I called in at your pal Longinus's, somebody arranged for me to be attacked. For reasons that we won't go into, it must've been one of the four of you, and for more reasons ditto it had to be you.'

'That's complete nonsense!' But his eyelids had flickered. 'I

told you, beyond a nodding acquaintance I had no connection
with Naevius Surdinus whatsoever. Why the hell would I want
to kill him?'

'Because I think he . . . posed a danger.'

'Oh? What sort of danger?'

Shit; I was sweating here myself, now. The answer, of course
– if the theory held, precise whys and wherefores aside – was
to the members of the inner conspiracy, of which, if he'd been
the guy behind Surdinus's death, *ipso facto* Asiaticus was one,
if not the actual guiding force. Exactly the area I was pussyfooting around. From the smug way the guy was looking at me,
he knew it too. This was a challenge.

Like he'd said, I didn't have enough in the bank for a direct
accusation. I folded.

'I'm not completely sure of that yet,' I said.

'Fine. Fine.' He was smiling again. 'Well, you just keep it that
way, will you, Corvinus? It might be safer.'

'Incidentally,' I said, 'where's Anicius Cerialis at present?'

The smile faltered. 'What?'

'Mind your own fucking business,' Papinius ground out. Silent
or not up to now, he hadn't taken his eyes off me throughout the
whole conversation.

I turned to him. 'It was an innocent-enough question, pal,' I
said mildly. 'This is his house, after all.'

'He's in Capua,' Asiaticus said. 'Negotiating the sale of some
property he owns there. Why do you ask?'

I shrugged. 'Just curious,' I said. 'It just struck me that he
wouldn't be exactly flavour of the month here, that's all.'

'Why shouldn't he be?'

'Well, you know best about that. But me, if I'd found out that
he was responsible for blowing the whistle on some of my friends,
even though they were . . . misguided' – I chose the word carefully
– 'then I'd be pretty miffed with him. Particularly if they'd ended
up tortured to death. I'm thinking primarily of Julius Graecinus.
He was a good mate of yours, wasn't he?'

'Yes, he was,' Asiaticus said stiffly. 'But, as you say, he was
misguided enough to conspire against the emperor. I'm afraid he
deserved all he got. And I certainly don't hold Cerialis's loyalty
against him.'

I glanced at Papinius. He was clenching and unclenching his

fists. Yeah, well, pal, I thought, if you don't then someone else does, in spades. I remembered the last time I'd been in this room, with Papinius's brother lying dead on the couch and Papinius himself getting stewed and gritting his teeth while he went through the motions of covering up for the guy's murderers. That'd been an instance of loyalty as well, although in the elder Papinius's case it'd been a conflict of loyalties. Which was why I'd come here in the first place. If it hadn't been for the accident of Asiaticus being here, I might've had a chance of turning him. As it was, he'd clearly been told to keep his mouth firmly closed and toe the party line.

Ah, well. You win some, you lose some. And there might be another opportunity later.

'While we're on the subject of your mates,' I said easily, 'I was at a dinner party yesterday evening with a couple more of them. At the palace. We sat together, as it happens.'

'Really. How splendid for you.'

'Yeah. Tiberius Claudius and Annius Vinicianus.'

Was that another flicker? 'Claudius, I know very well,' he said. 'We've been close friends for years, and of course I owe what political career I once had to the good graces of his mother, the Lady Antonia. But Vinicianus . . . no, you've misunderstood, Corvinus. I certainly know the gentleman, and we've sat together at dinner parties at the palace ourselves, but I wouldn't count him a positive friend. Only an acquaintance.'

'Uh-huh. These, uh, dinners at the palace. Your wife'd be there, wouldn't she? The emperor's erstwhile sister-in-law?'

'Yes, of course.' He'd coloured slightly. 'What has that got to do with anything?'

'Not a lot. I'd just heard that the emperor was sweet on her for a while, that's all.'

I thought Asiaticus was going to hit me. Even Papinius looked startled.

'My marital circumstances, Corvinus,' he said through gritted teeth, 'are no bloody concern of yours. Now if your only remaining business is to waste everyone's time by making snide remarks, I'd suggest that you leave.'

I glanced at Papinius, but he was still obviously obeying instructions and keeping out of things. Well, under the circumstances there wasn't much more I could do in any case.

'Fine, pal,' I said. 'We didn't get round to the subject of

Arrecinus Clemens, mind. Your boss, Papinius, the joint Prefect of Praetorians. Not that it matters much, I've got enough to be going on with at present.' Both of them were staring at me now. Papinius's mouth was slightly open. 'Me, I'd like to see this thing wrapped up by the start of the Palatine Games, but we'll just have to keep our fingers crossed, right?'

'*What did you say?*' Asiaticus whispered. His face had gone grey.

I gave him a sunny smile. 'Just some nonsense of Naevia Postuma's,' I said. 'You know she talks to Alexander? *The* Alexander, I mean. Well, seemingly she – or he, rather – thinks it's some sort of key date. Nonsense, like I say, but I'd rather keep the old girl happy.' I turned. 'Well, thanks for all your help, gentlemen. It's been most . . . illuminating.'

I left. I could feel their eyes boring into my back all the way to the front door. Cages duly rattled, with a vengeance.

I just hoped I hadn't shaken the bars too hard, that was all.

'Marcus, you absolute *fool!*' Perilla snapped when I told her how the interview had gone. 'You've put yourself in terrible danger!'

'Yeah, well, maybe I did get a bit carried away, but—'

'Don't you realize? If you're right, which you probably are, those men are on the verge of staging a *coup d'état*. They can't take risks, and they are *not* going to balk at killing anyone they even suspect might prevent them succeeding!' She was sitting up on her couch and glaring at me. 'You bloody, *bloody* idiot!'

'Perilla, look, there're only seven days to go to the Games. If that's when it's going to happen—'

'You can*not* help the emperor by getting yourself killed. And frankly I can't see why you should even risk it. You admit he's a monster, or rapidly becoming one, and that Rome would be better off without him.'

'True, but—'

'Holy Mother Juno, you don't even *like* the man! You haven't even got that excuse!'

I sighed. 'Perilla, we've been through this already. I told you: liking or whatever has nothing to do with it. Murder is murder, and treason's treason. Gaius is the emperor, and he's a human being.' I held my hand up as she opened her mouth. 'OK. The jury's out on that last one, I admit, but still. I can't just sit back twiddling my thumbs and let it happen. Not when there's a chance I can stop it.'

'Very well. Take your chances. Go to him and tell him what you know. At least then it'll be out of your hands, and it may well save your life.'

'Don't be melodramatic.'

'I am not being melodramatic, Marcus! I'm being . . . *bloody* . . . realistic!'

Jupiter! I took a deep breath and tried to speak calmly.

'I can't do that,' I said. 'I keep telling you, I don't actually *know* anything. Not for absolute sure. That's the problem.'

'Very well. Tell him what you *think* you know. It's better than nothing, and as you say you're running out of time.'

Fair point. More than fair: I couldn't spend the next seven days faffing around in the hope that something would magically pop up, only to have Gaius murdered at the end of them. I sighed again.

'Yeah. Maybe you're right,' I said. 'I'll go round to the palace first thing tomorrow morning. You happy now?'

She sniffed. 'Not especially. In fact, not at all, really, but I suppose it's the best I can expect under the circumstances. So. What have we got? What's the theory, at least?'

'That there's a conspiracy to assassinate Gaius during the Palatine Games. That the earlier conspiracy was a blind, constructed by the conspirators to distract Gaius's and his man Felix's attention from the real one a couple of months later and have them drop their guard. That . . .' I stopped. 'Shit!'

'What is it?'

'They'd need an *agent provocateur*. Someone party to the real conspiracy but involved – on the surface of things, anyway – with the fake one. And someone who, when the time came, would blow the whistle to Gaius and have the whole boiling rolled up.'

'Valerius Asiaticus. Yes, we know.'

'Uh-uh.' I shook my head. 'Not him. Oh, sure, he's involved in the real conspiracy up to his neck, no arguments. But if he had been the whistle-blower, either Felix or Gaius himself would've told me in so many words. Besides, Gaius obviously despises the man.'

'Very well, then. Who?'

'Anicius Cerialis.'

'*What?* Marcus, that is just silly! Cerialis was an *agent provocateur*, certainly, but he was working for . . .' She stopped, and her eyes widened as her brain caught up. 'Oh.'

'Yeah,' I said. 'Right. It had to be him. He was playing it three ways. The dupes in the first conspiracy – Graecinus and so on – thought he was with them right up until he sold them down the river to Gaius, which was how Gaius – or Felix, anyway – thought he'd arranged things. Only Cerialis wasn't working for Gaius either; he was working for his pals in the real conspiracy, or acting on their instructions, anyway. My bet is that that's why Surdinus died. Whether or not he was one of the dupes I don't know; he may've been, because like a lot of them he was a starry-eyed idealist at heart. In any case, he found out somehow – or suspected, at least – that Cerialis was playing it two ways. Knowing he was working for Gaius would've been bad enough, but my guess is that he'd cut the corner and discovered he was with Asiaticus and his mates.'

'Why so?'

'Lady, we've been through this before, remember? Because if Surdinus had only discovered he was a double, Gaius – Felix, whoever – could've cut his losses and rolled the conspiracy up there and then. Like he did when I shoved my oar in. Inconvenient and scrappy, sure, and it'd offend Felix's passion for neatness, but not the end of the world, because most if not all of the conspirators were known names already. Only if Surdinus were to tell Gaius that Cerialis was hobnobbing with someone outside the net, and that person was involved in the real conspiracy—'

'It might well be blown in its turn.' Panic attack forgotten; the lady was looking quite excited. Thrill of the chase; it happened every time. 'Cerialis couldn't take that risk. Marcus, that is *brilliant!*'

'Yeah, well . . .'

'So who have we got on the revised real-conspirator list?'

I ticked them off. 'Definites – at least, definite as far as I'm concerned: Cerialis himself; Valerius Asiaticus; Annius Vinicianus; Arrecinus Clemens. Plus Lucius Papinius, because the bets are that when the time comes, as one of the emperor's guard, he'd be the actual assassin – him and enough of his like-minded and seriously armed mates to do the job properly. As Praetorian commander, Clemens could arrange that because he'd be able to fix the duty rosters. Distinct possibles: Cassius Chaerea – another candidate for the sharp end – and the freedman-secretary guy, Julius Callistus. Oh, sure, there'll be others, there must be, but they'll do for a start.'

'What about the emperor's replacement? You still believe it would be Marcus Vinicius?'

Yeah, I'd been thinking a lot about that. I rubbed my chin.

'Sure,' I said. 'Vinicius is still the best bet. Not that I think he's directly involved, mind; I'm with you on that. But his nephew definitely is, and like I say, with Gaius safely dead and Vinicius himself with his arm halfway up his back, he could get the appointment through the senate easy. Even so, after last night I'd take out a small side bet on Tiberius Claudius.'

'*What?*'

I grinned. 'Yeah, I know. But like you said, he's no fool in himself. Far from it. And he's the last surviving male Julio-Claudian. If Vinicius were to refuse, which he might well do because he obviously has a lot of time for him personally, Claudius would be in with at least a chance. Besides, he'd have Asiaticus fighting his corner.'

'Messalina would be pleased.'

'Over the moon, lady. She'd give her eye-teeth to play Livia to Claudius's Augustus. Even so, I reckon she'd have her work cut out. I take it back; that guy is no puppet material, he has a mind of his own. It's just that so far he hasn't been given the chance to use it.'

'Marcus, you don't think . . .' She stopped again, and shook her head. 'No, of course not. It's silly. He wouldn't.'

'Wouldn't what?'

'Get himself involved with the conspiracy. Consciously and actively, I mean.'

'It's possible. I can't say. How well do you know him yourself?'

'Hardly at all, really. Certainly nowhere near as well as I know Vinicius.'

'There you are, then. We'll just have to mark it down as . . .' I looked round. 'Yeah, Bathyllus, what is it?'

The little guy had tooled in on my blind side.

'A visitor, sir,' he said. 'A freedman by the name of Leonidas. He says that you know him.'

I frowned; who the hell was Leonidas? Then I remembered, and sat up sharply.

Naevius Surdinus's estate manager.

Oh, gods. Please, please; just this once!

'Wheel him in, Bathyllus,' I said. 'Spit-spot.'

'Yes, sir.' He went out, leaving Perilla and me looking at each other in what your Alexandrian bodice-ripper would term 'wild surmise'. It might be; we'd just have to keep our fingers crossed . . .

Bathyllus came in with the little Sicilian in tow. Leonidas was beaming from ear to ear.

'I thought that you'd like to know, sir,' he said. 'I've managed to trace our freedman friend. The one with the birthmark?'

Joy in the morning! 'Yeah, yeah, right,' I said.

'I put it out that I was looking for him as soon as you left, but to tell you the truth I'd given up hope. The news only came this morning. His name's Valerius Sosibius and he has a—'

'*Valerius* Sosibius? You're sure?'

'Yes, sir. Quite a coincidence, isn't it? I knew he couldn't be one of yours because . . . well, still, there you are.'

Shit! If this Sosibius was a freedman of Asiaticus's – and he'd have to be, with that name – then we'd got the bastard cold. And if we'd got Asiaticus then we'd got the lot of them, because if I could lay physical hands on Surdinus's actual killer then I'd have something concrete to take to Gaius after all. Once he was in the bag and talking – which he would do, trust Felix for that – the rest would follow . . .

Score one for the freedman-cum-slave grapevine. Thank you, Jupiter! Thank you, thank you, thank you!

I punched the air. '*Yesss!*'

Leonidas was looking a bit bemused. So, for that matter, was Perilla.

'Marcus, dear,' she murmured.

Oh, yeah, right; *pas devant les domestiques*, or whatever the hell the correct Greek was. Let's have a little Roman *gravitas* here. I lowered my arm quickly and cleared my throat. 'I'm sorry, pal,' I said. 'Forgot myself for a moment. Carry on. You were saying?'

'He has a shop in the Subura, sir. On Safety Incline. He's a bookseller and copyist.'

'He is a *what*?'

'A bookseller and copyist, sir. He copies and sells books.'

'Yeah, I got that bit.' Gods! A homicidal bookseller! Now *there* was a first for you! At least he hadn't beaten Surdinus to death with a first edition of Cato's *Farming is Fun*. 'Now you're absolutely one hundred per cent cast-iron sure about all this, are you?'

'Oh, yes, sir. My informant was a slave in Rubellius Rufus's household. The old gentleman often uses Sosibius's services, and Caeso – that's the slave, sir – is in and out of the shop regularly. There's no mistake, certainly about the birthmark. At least I hope there isn't.'

'Fantastic.' I took out my purse and emptied out the contents – five gold pieces and a dozen bits of silver – into his waiting palms. 'Pass half that on to Caeso, will you?'

'Of course, sir. I don't know him personally – the news came to me at third or fourth hand – but I'll see he gets it.' He was beaming again. 'Even so, like I told you: myself, I'd've done it for nothing. Naevius Surdinus was a good master.'

'You're welcome, pal,' I said. 'You deserve it, both of you. Oh, one more thing. The big guy who saw the freedman originally. What was his name again?'

'Cilix, sir.'

'Right. Cilix. I'll need him with me to make a formal identification. You think you can get him to come over here tomorrow morning? Say the third hour?'

'Of course. I'm sure that won't be a problem.'

'Fine. And thanks again, Leonidas.'

He left.

'Well, lady,' I said when he'd gone, 'it looks like we're home and dry after all. I'll go over to the Subura tomorrow with Cilix, check this guy out. If he's the one we want, I reckon I can go straight to Gaius. That sound fair?'

'I suppose so, dear. But I'd rather you left things alone.'

'Yeah, well, we can't always have our druthers, can we?'

'As long as you're careful.'

'I'll be walking on eggs, I promise you.' I would, too.

We might be inside Alexander's deadline after all.

TWENTY-EIGHT

Cilix turned up the next morning bang on time. Not that I would've recognized the guy, because they'd hosed him down, given him a new tunic, a shave and haircut, and a final wax and polish before sending him over, with the result that he was a gleaming picture of pristine cleanliness and sartorial elegance.

Raring to go, too. He stood there – loomed, rather – at the foot of our steps, grinning like a six-foot-six yard-across-the-shoulders schoolboy being taken out for a birthday treat. Which I supposed wasn't all that far from the reality: as far as domestics go, which isn't all that far to begin with, garden slaves are at the bottom of the pecking order and their social life is zilch. The fact that they spend a large slice of their time interacting with manure in one way or another doesn't help matters, either.

'You ready for this, Cilix?' I said.

'Yes, sir.'

'OK. *Modus operandi.*' He blinked. 'Uh . . . the way we're going to do things, right?'

'Oh. Yeah. Got you, sir.'

'The guy – Sosibius – doesn't know me. Or at least I'm hoping he doesn't. And he didn't see you either, right?'

'Yeah. 'Cos I was crouched down in the bushes taking a—'

'Fine. Fine. So we go in as ordinary customers; at least I do. You tag along behind, and – this is really, *really* important, right? – with your mouth tightly zipped. Eyes only, OK? Get a good look at the bastard while I'm talking to him, but say nothing until we're back outside. Got it?'

'Yeah. Got it.'

'Great. Well done. So off we go.'

Off we went.

The Subura's like a rabbit warren, one of the oldest and poorest parts of the city with streets even narrower and messier than they usually are in Rome, zig-zagging between tenements that're in such bad nick that you have to keep one eye on the road and the other leery for falling tiles. Other things, too, deliberately thrown, or poured, rather: no sanitation in a tenement, the top floor's a long way from even the most basic comfort area, and the locals don't bother too much about the courtesy warning. Not the ones doing the pouring, anyway, although the poor buggers on the receiving end of things can get pretty vocal.

Safety Incline, Leonidas had said – a misnomer, if ever there was one, because this time of year it was slippery as hell with a mixture of the previous night's rain and the variously compounded organic element that covered the one-in-four pavement and made walking a tricky business. If you were lucky enough to get to use the pavement for walking on, that was. Half the Subura seemed to have decided to go either up or down Safety Incline that morning, and Suburan bag-ladies don't take prisoners: we spent most of the time with one foot in the central gutter while a large sample of the local matriarchy barged past us on both sides loaded down with bagfuls of assorted root vegetables and dried pulses for the family's dinner. If it hadn't been for Cilix's bulk diverting the stream, as it were, they wouldn't've bothered about the *both sides* aspect of things much, either.

We found the bookshop about three-quarters of the way down the Incline, sandwiched between a cobbler's and a second-hand clothes merchant's.

'OK, Cilix,' I said. 'Remember, I talk, you just look, OK? Whether it's him or not, you wait until we're outside again. Clear?'

'Yeah. No problem.'

I crossed my fingers and went in, with Cilix following.

It was like any copyist's shop you'd find anywhere in Rome. Most of them, of course, are in the more salubrious districts, especially near the Palatine with its Pollio Library, but there are a few properties in both the Subura and on the Sacred Way that've kept to their original purpose through a dozen generations of owners while the buildings around them have slid steadily downmarket. This one looked like it'd been built in with the Suburan bricks; no doubt when the Gauls had occupied the city four hundred years back, Brennus or one of his more bibliophilic mates had dropped by to pick up Plato's latest before getting down to a hard day's pillage, arson and rape.

The two copyists sitting at the tables under the window, making use of what daylight had made it between the tenements, ignored us completely, without even a cursory glance. In the body of the shop behind a counter laden with book-rolls was a guy in a freedman's cap. Definitely not Sosibius, I could see that for myself, even though his left cheek wasn't in full sight: he was eighty if he was a day, and he looked like he'd have serious problems crossing the room, let alone climbing up several builder's ladders and along a dodgy parapet.

Fuck; things did *not* look good!

'Yes, sir,' he said. 'Can I help you?'

He sounded nervous as hell; strange. Unless of course the quaver in his voice and the slight twitch were just age and infirmity. Which, given that he looked less than a fingernail's breadth from an urn, was pretty possible.

'Uh . . . I'm sorry, pal,' I said. 'Maybe I've come to the wrong place. I was looking for a Valerius Sosibius.'

'Oh, no. He's here, sir. If you'll wait I'll get him for you.'

He shuffled off through a curtain at the far end of the shop, and I could hear a murmur of voices. I turned round and rested my backside against the counter. The copyists were still bent over their work, and did not give so much as a sideways glance. That was strange, too: me, if I'd been stuck in a place like this, scribbling away in semi-darkness day in day out, I'd've been grateful for any break in the routine . . .

Something smelled, and it wasn't Cilix. Things were definitely wrong here. Very, very wrong.

'I think we'll leave,' I said to the big guy. 'Quickly and quietly.'

Which was when the curtain parted again and the three Praetorians emerged. I made a move towards the door, but one of the buggers was there first. He was about the size of the blunt side of the Capitol, and he had a drawn sword in his hand. Not much mileage there, then. And his mates who'd taken up position either side of me were even bigger.

Shit.

The curtain moved and Lucius Papinius came out. He was holding a sword as well. I swallowed. Shit, shit, shit! Fuck, fuck, fuck!

'You.' With his free hand he pointed at Cilix, then jerked the thumb sideways. 'Out.'

The Praetorian by the door stepped aside. Cilix gave me a single apologetic look, ducked under the lintel, and disappeared into the street. The copyists hunched down even lower and scribbled away like their lives depended on it. Which maybe they did.

Speaking of which . . .

'You were warned, Corvinus,' Papinius said. 'I am *really* going to enjoy this. Hold him, lads.'

Fuck.

The two Praetorians either side of me grabbed my arms, pinning them to my sides and lifting me slightly off the ground. Papinius moved towards me and I lashed out with my right foot, but he stepped back and the kick never landed.

Bugger, bugger, *bugger*!

He drew back the sword for a thrust, hesitated, then turned it sideways. The pommel and guard, together with his fist holding it, slammed into my face and the world exploded in a burst of pain as I heard and felt my nose break. Then I was down on the ground, hugging myself for protection as three pairs of hobnailed military boots began kicking the hell out of me. I felt one of my ribs go, then one of the boots connected with the side of my head and everything went mercifully black.

I woke up in bed at home, with Perilla looking down at me. At first I was just relieved not to be dead after all. Then the pain started, and I changed my mind: the first and second joints of the little finger on my left hand felt OK, but everything else was bloody agony.

'Marcus? You're awake?' Perilla asked anxiously. She'd been crying, I could see that.

'Yeah. More or less.' I must've whispered it, because she bent down and put her ear a couple of inches from my mouth. Speaking wasn't easy; my mouth felt like it was full of rocks, and my nose kept getting in the way. If that makes sense. 'Unfortunately.'

'Thank Juno! Don't try to move.'

I grinned, or tried to; my facial muscles weren't up to grinning at present. 'You kidding, lady?'

She stood up and glanced behind her. 'Sarpedon?' she said. 'He's woken up at last.'

Turning my head wasn't an option at present, particularly

turning it to the right, because that side of it felt like one of those big medicine balls the more sedate punters chuck around when they're exercising after a bath. Sarpedon. Right. My father's old freedman, the family doctor, and had been ever since I'd come down with my first dose of nappy-rash.

His face replaced Perilla's. Not an improvement, because the guy had the features of a well-bred octogenarian camel.

'How are you feeling, Valerius Corvinus?' he said.

Bloody stupid question; and with the amount the bastard charged for home visits, even to family, I'd've expected something just a little more searching and clinical.

'I've been better,' I said, then repeated it when he put his ear where Perilla's had been. He grunted, took my pulse and pushed up one of my eyelids.

'Any double vision?' he said.

'You mean there aren't two of you?'

'Very droll, sir.' Not a smile, but then Valerius Sarpedon never had been much of a lad for jokes. 'The good news is that you'll almost certainly live.'

'Ah . . . only *almost* certainly?'

'I would say so, yes. I can't be absolutely sure at this point, of course, but it seems very likely.'

Joy in the morning. Nothing like a bit of positive encouragement from your doctor, is there? I did a bit of subjective body analysis on my own account: head and face, as I've said, pretty much a disaster area, ditto for the chest and ribs – from the tight feel of things there, I was bandaged neck to waist – various assorted aches, pains and bruises on my arms and legs. Short of killing me, Papinius and his heavy-footed pals had done a pretty thorough job. Apart from my nose and ribs, nothing broken, though. At least, that was what it felt like.

So why *hadn't* they killed me? I wasn't complaining, mind – or I wouldn't be, when everything settled down to a dull ache – but still; it was a puzzle.

Apropos of which . . .

'How did I get here?' I said; at least my mouth was working a bit better now, and I could manage a bit more than a geriatric mumble. Plus I seemed, miraculously, to have kept all my teeth intact, although my lips were split to hell.

'The slave – Cilix, wasn't it? – brought you back in a hired litter. Once the, ah, perpetrators had safely gone.' Sarpedon frowned. 'It's none of my business, of course, but . . . Praetorians?'

'Yeah,' I said. 'And you're right, pal. It is none of your business. Believe me, it's better that way.' I frowned; my brain had just caught up with something. '"At last"?'

'I'm sorry, sir?'

'Perilla said that I'd woken up "at last". How long have I been out?'

'Ah. This is the fifth day. Late evening.'

I stared at him. 'I've been unconscious for *five days*?'

'Not as such. However, you were running a high fever for most of the time. I wouldn't imagine that you'd have any memory of the period between the attack and now. Or am I wrong?'

'No, you're absolutely . . .' I stopped as the implications kicked in. Five days. Shit! 'Hang on. So this is nine days before the kalends, right? The twenty-fourth; the first day of the Palatine Games?' I tried to struggle to my feet, and my head and most of the rest of me exploded with agony. '*Fuck!*'

Sarpedon's hands were pressing against my shoulders, forcing me back down on to the bed.

'Sir! Please!' he said. 'You *must* lie absolutely still! You are in no condition to—'

'Fuck that!' I snapped. 'I have to warn the emperor! He's—'

'Gaius was killed this afternoon, Marcus.' Perilla's voice came from behind Sarpedon's back.

I stopped struggling.

'What?'

'A few hours ago, in the temporary theatre on the Palatine. I don't know the details, of course, but it's quite definite.'

Oh, shit. Oh, gods. I felt sick; in fact, I found myself heaving. Sarpedon was just in time with the bowl beside the bed. Not that the result was too impressive.

He held out a napkin and wiped my lips.

'The emperor's dead?' I said.

'Yes.' Perilla's voice was toneless.

'So who's in charge now?'

'I don't know. Or at least I'm not sure; no one is. The rumour is that the Praetorians – the ones involved in the plot – have taken Claudius off to the camp outside the city, but that's all it is, a rumour. They may have killed him, or perhaps he's being held as some kind of hostage. I don't think anyone really knows what's happening.'

Jupiter Best and Greatest! I felt empty, gutted. Gaius might've been a total head case, latterly anyway, but he had been the legitimate emperor. When the Wart had died, at least we'd all known where we were, whether we liked it or not – presumably, too, when old Augustus went, although at fourteen I'd been too young and too interested in chasing girls to pay much attention to politics. There'd been nothing like this since old Julius got himself chopped, and that was eighty-odd years back.

If I'd only got to the guy in time! Oh, sure, the business with Sosibius had been a set-up, I knew that now: the bastard probably didn't exist, at least under that name. But still, there'd been those five days . . .

'Hey, Perilla,' I said.

'Yes, Marcus?' She was still out of vision. I turned my head, ignoring the pain. The lady was standing by the bedroom door.

'Why didn't you send a message to the emperor?' I said quietly. 'You could've done; you'd plenty of time. I was out of it, sure, but he might've listened. Especially under the circumstances.'

She didn't answer for a good half-minute. Then she said: 'Because I decided not to.'

'You *what*? Why?'

'For four reasons. First, because those men didn't kill you; they could have done, and it would have been by far the most sensible thing to do, but nevertheless they didn't. I'm very grateful not to be left a widow. Second, because Gaius was a psychopathic monster, and liable to get worse. The world is far better off without him.'

'Yeah, granted, but—'

'Third, if you're right, and I see no reason why you shouldn't be, the new emperor – and I agree, there must be one – will be either Marcus Vinicius or Tiberius Claudius. I know, like, and respect both of them, and with either in charge, Rome will be a much safer place.'

'OK. That's three reasons. What about the fourth?'

'The fourth, Marcus, is that it was my decision to make, and I made it. I decided for me, not for you, because I thought you were wrong.'

I closed my eyes briefly. You live with someone for twenty

years, you think you know them, and they can still surprise you. Not all the surprises are pleasant ones, either.

She could be a tough lady, Rufia Perilla, when she liked.

'Yeah, well,' I said. 'It's done. Finished business. We'll just have to see what happens next, that's all.'

We would indeed.

TWENTY-NINE

Me, personally, I hate lying around in bed, but having the shit kicked out of you by a set of beefy Praetorians who're determined to make a proper job of it doesn't leave you with all that many options. On the other hand, three days of healthful, nourishing barley gruel for breakfast, lunch and dinner and a total ban on wine – which was what that sadistic bastard Sarpedon had prescribed – was no joke either. When the expected summons came from the palace, boredom and alcohol deprivation had me practically climbing the wall.

Mind you, three days of enforced thumb-twiddling at least meant that I'd filled in the missing bits of the puzzle. Not that it'd been all that difficult, given we and the rest of Rome now knew that Claudius was running the empire. Total absence of flying pigs or not, unless of course there had been and the augurs were just too bloody embarrassed to let on.

There was my hindsight-driven rereading of Surdinus's letter, too, which put the lid on things. For what it was worth at this stage, because I wasn't stupid enough to go pointing accusing fingers, was I?

So it was the palace, and in a litter sent specially for the purpose; a goodwill gesture on their part, probably, rather than to make sure I came, because after all where could I have run to, barring Parthia? I gave Perilla what I hoped was a see-you-later kiss, eased my still-aching and seriously strapped-up body on to the cushioned chair, and off we went.

The Praetorian at the gate detached to lead me into the Presence finally stopped outside a lavishly panelled door. He knocked, waited a moment, and then opened it, stepping aside.

'In you go, sir,' he said.

The same room I'd been in with Gaius, the one above the torture chamber. Probably some sort of imperial inner sanctum reserved for cosy, off-the-record get-togethers which, I suspected, was what this was. I went in, and the door closed behind me.

'Hi, Messalina,' I said. 'Hi, Felix. How's it going?'

The little guy reclining on the right-hand couch was beaming. 'Oh, very well done, sir!' he said. 'Not a smidgeon of surprise. I told the mistress here you'd've worked it all out, but she didn't believe me.'

Messalina, stretched out demurely on the other couch, gave me a butter-wouldn't-t-melt smile, but said nothing.

'Yeah, well, as far as the lady's concerned I'm kicking myself, pal,' I said. 'Surdinus practically told us in his letter that she was involved. He was never at her wedding, so why would he say he was and that we'd talked, except to bring her name in? And if he and my father weren't neighbours on Vatican Hill then he and hers definitely were, because that's where Barbatus had his villa. You . . . well, there must've been a reason why the emperor' – I glanced at Messalina, who was still smiling at me like a cream-fed cat – 'the *ex*-emperor wasn't taking the real conspirators seriously. He wasn't a fool, Gaius, whatever else he might've been. Just a bit too trusting where his so-called friends and allies were concerned.'

If I'd meant to embarrass the bastard – which I did – then I was disappointed. He shrugged. 'True, sir. But then he had to go, because he really was becoming impossible. Putting far too many backs up, both for his own good and the good of Rome.'

'The good of Rome, eh? Uh-huh. I'd been wondering when we'd get to that bit.' This was my first day out of bed, and I was beginning to feel pretty woozy. I reached for a chair and sat down. 'So you murdered the guy out of pure patriotic altruism, right? You and the lady here?'

'Oh, we weren't alone, Corvinus,' Messalina said. 'Far from it, as you well know. And your answer is, of course not. Or not where I'm concerned, at least.' Her smile broadened. 'Altruism's all right in its way, and very useful in other people, but between ourselves it really is just the teensiest bit silly, isn't it?'

'So you get to play Livia to Claudius's Augustus?' I said.

She giggled. 'Claudius is no Augustus, darling,' she said. 'Not by a long chalk. But yes, of course. That's the plan. It's always been the plan, right from the start. Why do you think I married him? And believe me, cousin, that was how it was. *I* married *him*, not the other way round, whatever he chooses to think.'

'Does he know? That you were involved in the conspiracy?'

'Claudius? My goodness me, no!' Another giggle. 'He never even knew it existed, the poor lamb. And in case you're thinking of telling him yourself, I really wouldn't advise it. You're only alive in the first place because Felix here is a complete softie. Do *not* push your luck.'

'Yeah, I was wondering about that,' I said. 'Taking a bit of a risk there, weren't you, Felix?'

'Oh, not really, sir.' Felix smiled. 'Or if so then it was a carefully calculated one. Papinius was given strict instructions to draw the line at killing you but put you seriously out of action, and we did have men watching your house to make sure that no message was sent to the emperor. Besides, if you'll forgive the liberty, I've always thought of you as a friend and colleague, and as I told both my former employer and my present one, you are far more interesting alive than dead. Dead without good reason, that is, naturally.'

'Naturally.'

'Fortunately, both of them were willing to indulge me. Against, I may say, their better judgment.'

'Yeah, right.' Jupiter! Still, gratitude where it was due. 'Thanks.'

'Don't mention it, sir.'

'In fact, don't mention any of it, Corvinus.' Messalina gave me another silky smile. 'That is really, *really* important. Remember that minds can be changed, and that not mentioning things is all that's currently keeping you alive.'

'Lady, I have absolutely no intention whatsoever of talking about this to anyone, ever,' I said. I meant it, too; after all, who would I tell? And with Gaius dead, why should I bother? Finished business was right.

'There's a clever boy.' But I could see that both she and Felix had relaxed slightly. 'Now. That being understood, and in exchange, Felix here says that you'll have questions that you'll want answered.' She sat back against the cushions and folded her hands in her lap like a prim schoolgirl. 'Carry on, I really don't mind. Anything you like, ask away.'

'OK. The most basic one first. Why kill Surdinus?'

'Oh, you surely don't need us for that, sir,' Felix said.

I shrugged. 'Maybe not. Your pal Cerialis made the mistake of trying to recruit him, right? For the fake conspiracy, along with the other airhead idealists. Surdinus was having none of it, but he drew the line at peaching to Gaius, because as a good Stoic he'd no time for tyrants, and it'd mean that friends of his like Graecinus who were involved were likely to get chopped. That should've been the end of it, only he saw something he shouldn't have seen, or heard something he shouldn't have heard, that suggested the whole thing was a set-up and his friends were for the chop in any case. Yes?'

'Not quite, Corvinus.' Messalina smiled. 'Surdinus was a loyal member of our group of expendables practically from the start. But your second guess is absolutely right. What he chanced upon – under compromising circumstances – was a meeting between Cerialis and Sosibius.'

'Sosibius? He exists, then? But . . .' I caught myself as the penny dropped. Bugger! 'He's a freedman of yours, right?'

'Well done, sir,' Felix said. 'Better late than never. And you can't complain that I didn't play a fair game. If you assumed that his given family name came from Asiaticus rather than from the mistress, that was your mistake.'

Hell; I'd forgotten about the devious little bugger's liking for setting puzzles. And I'd hardly call this business a game of any sort. Still, he was right by his lights; if I'd connected Sosibius with Valerius Asiaticus rather than Valeria Messalina then it was my own stupid fault.

'Sosibius was my father's secretary originally,' Messalina was saying, 'which explained why Surdinus knew him, because Surdinus and Daddy were close friends. He's frighteningly clever, the dear, and he always had a soft spot for me, so when I married my first I took him with me and gave him his freedom. Daddy was long dead by then, of course, and when Surdinus walked in on Sosibius's confab with Cerialis, he couldn't've clapped eyes on him for donkey's years. Pure bad luck, really. It was just a pity that the man had such a good memory for faces, and of course there *was* the birthmark.'

'Would it have mattered all that much?' I said. 'That Surdinus had recognized him? After all, there might've been a perfectly innocent explanation.'

'We couldn't take the risk. Surdinus was obviously suspicious, or beginning to be, and he was a clever man. If the others had begun to suspect Cerialis it would've put the whole thing in jeopardy. Besides, when the conspiracy was blown, Sosibius's name and identity were bound to come out, and even with Felix here looking after our interests that would have been far too dangerous. So of course I had Sosibius kill him.'

Spoken without a smidgeon of emotion; a feather of cold touched the back of my neck.

'OK,' I said. 'That brings me to my only other question. Herennius Capito. Was he part of the real conspiracy?'

'Oh, yes. Not one of the inner circle, fortunately as it turned out, but it was a shame he had to die. That was completely your fault, by the way.'

'Me?'

'Ordinary damage limitation, sir,' Felix said. 'According to the original plan, of course, when the decoy conspirators were rounded up I would have ensured, as I did in Asiaticus's case, that he was quite safe. In the event, since you'd made the connection yourself and made it official, as it were, I had to go through the motions.'

'Meaning torture?' I said.

'It's not something I take pleasure in, Valerius Corvinus,' he said severely. 'Unlike the former emperor. However, under the circumstances it was necessary, to a certain degree. Going through the motions, as I said. Unfortunately, Gaius chose to be present and direct matters himself.'

'So Capito folded?' Not that I blamed the guy. And if he knew – as he would – that he had something major to sell, then he probably thought he was in with a chance.

'Yes. Luckily, as the mistress has told you, the information he had was limited. He knew about Julius Callistus, naturally, because as his superior in the imperial fiscal department, Callistus had recruited him. He also, probably through the Papinii, knew about Clemens, the Praetorian commander. He did not, fortunately, know that I was involved, or things might have become embarrassing. That was a *very* closely kept secret, for reasons that you'll readily understand.'

'Yeah. Right. So what about this Caesonia business? Was she involved after all?'

'*Caesonia?*' Messalina sniffed. 'Don't be silly, Corvinus!'

Felix ducked his head. 'Actually, there we were lucky,' he said. 'At that point in the proceedings Capito was – well, you saw Graecinus, you'll understand the condition he was in. He was very indistinct and scarcely capable of more than a mumble. Fortunately all Gaius could make out from where he was standing was the word "wife".'

'Uh-huh.' I looked at Messalina; she was frowning. Shit; *lucky* was putting it mildly! I'd been so, so close; if Gaius had caught that bit the whole boiling would probably have gone down the tubes right at the start, without any extra help from me. 'So what the poor bastard said was "Claudius's wife", right? Only you passed it on to Gaius as "the emperor's wife", or "your wife", or whatever.'

'Yes, sir.'

'Pretty quick thinking.'

'Thinking, fast or otherwise, is my job. And as I said, we were lucky. You know Caesonia yourself, and how the emperor felt about her. He wouldn't entertain the thought that she was involved in a conspiracy against him for one second, and naturally that cast doubt on the rest of Capito's evidence. Sufficient doubt to allow me to persuade him that both Callistus and Arrecinus Clemens were innocent.'

'And just to make sure there wouldn't be any more embarrassing revelations, you pulled the guy's plug for him, yes?'

That got me a long stare. Finally, Felix said: 'Valerius Corvinus, let us come to an understanding here. First of all, the fact that Capito knew about the mistress's involvement came as a huge shock, and was hugely dangerous; *how* he knew, I had and have absolutely no idea, but because Gaius had taken a special interest in the man and would want to be present on subsequent occasions, I could not risk a repetition, nor could I be sure that our erstwhile colleague did not have other names to hand that might have persuaded the emperor to change his mind. Secondly, which may perhaps weigh rather more with you, Capito would have died in any case, eventually, and after undergoing terrible agony. In the event, when Gaius had gone I put him out of his misery as quickly and as painlessly as I could manage.' He hesitated. 'Also relevant is the fact that, as the mistress told you, he was only there in the first place because of your interference. Accordingly, I would be grateful if you would remember that and cut out the fucking self-righteousness. *Sir!*'

Yeah. Fair point. More than fair. Plus, I don't think I'd ever, ever heard Felix swear, or step outside the bounds of master-servant correctness. I nodded.

'My apologies, pal, I'm sorry,' I said. 'Forget that I said it, right?'

'Duly forgotten, sir.'

'So.' I looked at Messalina. 'What happens now?'

'As far as you're concerned? Absolutely nothing.' She stretched luxuriantly. 'We have a bargain, and so long as you keep to it, you're perfectly safe. Besides, we are cousins, after all.'

'Fair enough.' I stood up, trying not to wince too much as my bandaged ribs kicked in.

'You won't mind if Claudius and I don't invite you to the palace for dinner all that often, will you? I don't want you to be *too* tempted.'

'Believe me, that is not a problem, lady,' I said. 'None whatsoever.'

'That's good.' Another smile. 'I'd hate you to feel that you were being slighted.'

'Yeah, well, I'll try to bear up.'

She giggled. 'A pity, really. You'd be much more fun than most of Claudius's po-faced friends. Still, needs must, I suppose.'

'You're not too upset with me, I hope, sir?' Felix said. 'Or disappointed? After all, it was for the best. And I did keep you alive.'

True. Between Gaius and Messalina, not to mention Cerialis's hit-men over on the Janiculan, this time round by rights I should've been for the urn half-a-dozen times over. Besides, in the ten years I'd known him I'd developed a sneaking admiration for the devious sod.

'No, no hard feelings, pal,' I said. 'I'll see you around.'

I left.

Well, that was that, then, I thought as I hobbled out the gate and into the waiting litter. You win some, you lose some. This one I'd definitely lost, although maybe – Messalina apart – Rome had come out ahead. We'd just have to see what kind of a job Claudius made of things. Personally, I was pretty optimistic: at least, like I said, despite surface impressions and popular opinion, the guy was no idiot. Plus, whatever she believed to the contrary, Messalina was no Livia, either; I'd had enough to do with that brilliant, cold-minded bitch to be certain of that. Valeria Messalina wasn't even in the same league. So one of these days the lady was going to overreach herself, and it'd serve her right . . .

There was only one box I hadn't ticked, and it wasn't one that Felix could help with, nor could anyone, for that matter: Naevia Postuma's firm conviction, backed up by the changes he'd made to his will regarding Perilla's – and my – bequest, that her uncle knew he was going to be murdered. Or, at least, was going to die very, very shortly. Oh, sure, he may have guessed that he was a marked man, but that didn't quite explain things.

Me . . . well, ever since my conversation with the Wart just before Sejanus was chopped, I've kept an open mind where the casting of horoscopes is concerned. And if Tiberius knew, thanks to the astrologer Thrasyllus, exactly when he was going to cash his chips in and who his successor would be, then I couldn't see any problem in Naevius Surdinus having got his information in the same way. Weird, sure, but if it ticked the box when no other explanation did then weird I could take. The same went for Postuma's Alexander; whether you liked it or not – and, as I say, personally I didn't have a problem there – he'd been absolutely spot on about the assassination. Plus, from what I knew of the bastard in life, he and Gaius would've been bosom buddies and kindred souls. Given the fact that he did still exist on some sort of astral plane, his wanting to shove his ectoplasmic oar in made perfect sense.

So we'd just have to shrug and move on, wouldn't we?

Maybe, at present, though, not all that far, or all that fast. Renatius's wine shop wasn't much out of our way, or if it was then what the hell: I hadn't had a proper cup of wine for days, and I reckoned that I was owed one. The future could look after itself for the next couple of hours.

I pulled aside the curtain and gave the litter guys their new orders.

AUTHOR'S NOTE

The story is set between November and January AD 40/41. As I've done with all the political Corvinus books, I've kept (I hope!) more or less strictly to the historical facts as far as I know them, even where these are a little surprising. Herennius Capito's evidence under torture and Gaius's discounting of it were as I've given them, as was the emperor's rather strange response to his soothsayer's warning to 'beware of Cassius' by recalling Cassius Longinus from Asia while ignoring the much more immediate threat posed by Cassius Chaerea, who was one of his eventual assassins. Introducing a reason for the anomalies in the form of a trusted advisor who was actually part of the conspiracy himself made a great deal of sense. To me, at least.

I have, though, made two changes, both minor, both dictated by the demands of the plot. First of all, 'my' two conspiracies are closer together in time by at least two months than the real ones actually were. The upshot of the second, of course, was unalterable where the date was concerned – Gaius had to be assassinated on 24 January AD 41 – so I left it alone; the first conspiracy was unmasked at some time in the autumn or very early winter the previous year.

The second change had to do with the fate of Sextus Papinius; 'my' Papinius died just before the first conspiracy came to light, while the historical one was arrested and executed with the other conspirators. I don't feel too guilty about this; if the young man died slightly sooner than he would have done, death from a broken neck is far cleaner than death by torture would have been.

Oh – and one more slight departure from the historical facts, again for plot reasons. In January 41, the real Messalina would have been heavily pregnant with Claudius's son Britannicus, who was born in February of that year; accordingly she is very unlikely to have been present at a public dinner party, and certainly not in the sylph-like condition I ascribe to her. Readers well up on their history will just have to forgive me.

Unlike the entire Surdinus ménage and the murder itself, my conspirators are real enough, albeit drastically trimmed in number to avoid over-complexity of plot; however, the connection between the two conspiracies, and, of course, their different nature and Messalina's involvement in them, are complete inventions of my own – although all three factors can, I think, be defended as at least possible. Interestingly enough – although I decided not to include the fact in the body of the text – the day after the assassination, 25 January, was Messalina's birthday; a gift for a dedicated conspiracy-theorist like me. Being elevated at a stroke from her position as the wife of a second-rate imperial to that of the empire's First Lady would have been quite a birthday present, particularly given the historical Messalina's character, and I really can't help feeling that the timing of Gaius's death was deliberate on someone's part.

Regarding the lady herself. It may have surprised fans of Robert Graves's *I, Claudius* – of which I'm very much one – that 'my' version of Messalina is about ten years older and had been married before, but this is probably so: her father, Valerius Barbatus, was dead by AD 20, and at the age of more than twenty-one it is more than likely that she had had a husband previous to Claudius – although who he was, and whether she was a widow or a divorcee, isn't known, at least as far as I'm aware. When I've referred to him or the marriage in the text I've left things deliberately vague.

As for the assassination. 'My' Gaius, of course, dies offstage, but you may be interested in how Suetonius (writing, admittedly, eighty years after the event) describes things:

> On 24 January at about the seventh hour [i.e. early afternoon], his stomach still being slightly out of sorts as the result of a heavy meal the previous day, Gaius was in two minds about leaving his seat in the theatre to take a lunch break; however, his friends persuaded him to go out with them. In the covered walkway which they had to pass through, he met a group of boys, sons of distinguished families, who had been brought over from Asia to stage a theatrical performance and who were currently rehearsing. He stopped to watch them and give them some encouragement, and if the leader of the troupe had not said that he was unwell,

would have liked to take them back into the theatre with him and have them perform straight away. From this point on, there are two versions of what happened. Some authorities have it that while Gaius was talking to the boys Chaerea came up behind him, and shouting 'Take that!' struck him on the neck with his sword, wounding him seriously; and then that the tribune Cornelius Sabinus, another of the conspirators, stabbed him face-on, in the chest. Others say that Sabinus told his NCOs (who were also in the plot) to disperse the crowd before asking Gaius – as was the military custom – for the watchword. When Gaius answered 'Jupiter', Chaerea shouted 'That's confirmed!' and on his turning round split his jawbone at a stroke. The emperor lay hugging himself on the ground and shouting 'I'm still alive!' but the other assassins finished him off, inflicting no fewer than thirty wounds, including sword thrusts to his genitals. For the word in everyone's mouth was 'Give it to him again!' At the first sign of trouble, his litter men ran to his aid, using their poles as weapons; they were closely followed by his German bodyguard, who not only killed a number of the assassins but also some of the senatorial bystanders.

(Suetonius, *Caligula* 58; my translation)

Two last, general things that I'm often asked about, so perhaps some explanation is called for: purple stripes and time of day/ dates. First, the stripes.

An ordinary male citizen would, on formal occasions, at least, wear a plain white toga (my 'mantle'); hence my use, for the Roman-in-the-street, of the term 'plain-mantle'. My broad-stripers are members of the senate, which was composed of magistrates who held, or had held, at least the rank of *quaestor* (junior finance officer). They wore togas with a broad purple stripe at the edge.

The second class of purple-stripers were the *equites* (knights) – my 'narrow-stripers', so named for obvious reasons. A good phrase to define them (which Michael Grant uses in his excellent translation of Tacitus) would be 'gentlemen outside the senate'. The knights were variously Rome's businessmen (senators were forbidden to engage in trade), imperial administrators (some important posts – e.g. Egyptian governor and commander of Praetorians – could only be held by an *eques*) and members of 'senatorial' families who for one reason or another had never held office: Corvinus would be one of these.

As to time of day and dates. The first is easy: the Roman day began at dawn and ended at sunset, and it was divided into twelve hours, as was the period sunset to dawn, where the hours were grouped into four 'Watches' of three hours each. This meant, of course, that the length of a Roman hour varied depending on the time of year, and it played merry hell with the calibration of any time-keeping device other than the sundial. Water-clocks (*clepsydrae*) were a particular headache.

Dates are more complicated, because the Romans didn't use our consecutive numbering system. Instead, calculation was based on three key points in any given month (probably, originally, market days): the Kalends, Nones and Ides (because the Greeks used a different system, the Latin expression 'on the Greek Kalends' meant the same as our 'never in a million years'). The Kalends were always on the first day of the month; the other two dates were normally on the fifth and thirteenth respectively, except that:

In March, July, October, May
The Nones are on the seventh, the Ides the fifteenth day

Which explains why Julius Caesar was murdered on the fifteenth, not the thirteenth of March.

Now, this is where it gets tricky, so take a deep breath before reading the next bit.

The Romans not only counted backwards from the next key date; they counted inclusively.

So 24 January would be – as I've given it in the text, rather tongue-in-cheek because I'm sure that mathematicians will jump on it as a mistake – nine (not eight) days before the Kalends of February.

Except when . . .

The system breaks down for the day immediately before a key date; so if it had existed, the Roman Hogmanay (New Year's Eve) would've been 'the day before the Kalends of January', while 30 December would be 'three days before the Kalends'.

No such thing as 'two days before', you see . . .

I trust that's all perfectly clear. You can now indulge in hours of innocent amusement working out the birthdays of your loved ones, pets and so on by Roman reckoning. Have fun.

I hope you enjoyed the book.

David Wishart

Lightning Source UK Ltd.
Milton Keynes UK
UKOW04f2128250215

246879UK00001B/6/P